Before Home Found Us

a novel by

Kendra Havlicek

inspired by true events

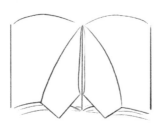

Veseli Publishing House
New Prague, Minnesota

for Grams

There is no greater agony than bearing an untold story inside you.

Maya Angelou

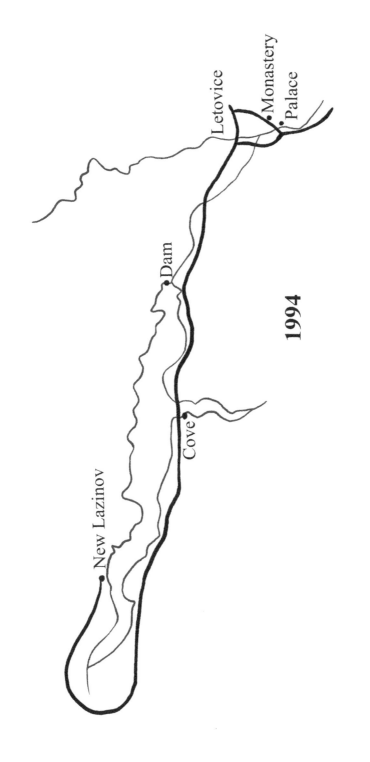

New Lazinov

Cove

Dam

1994

Letovice

Monastery

Palace

Prologue
July 5, 2012

The day's fever broke as dusk seeped into the night air like a tea brewing an earthly blend. It had been an eventful day; not only was the biggest city festival of the year in full motion, but it was also Kena's birthday. Kena was one of the young foreigners who had traveled over four-thousand miles to spend a week helping at the festival. The newly-turned seventeen-year-old may have been the only one not to doze off during the documentary film after the boisterous day. Maybe Kena had more energy than the rest seeing that she was still living up every second of her birthday, but no one could blame the tired audience after a week of rapidly-paced festival activities. Yet, it wasn't just an influx of energy from sweets and cake that kept Kena awake, but something captured the passionate teen as she listened to the documentary film of a war hero who had been long forgotten. The testimonies and accounts surrounding the hero held her gaze to the screen; that and the subtitles deciphering the unfamiliar language. As the evening grew longer, she lay in the front of the make-shift theater, which was a projector screen in the largest room. She propped up her head in the palms of her hands and supported the weight on her elbows. Stealthily, she slid her seat cushion under Katie's head, her dozing friend who stretched out on the floor next to her.

She stayed in that position until the film credits rolled over the screen and someone in the back awoke the overhead lights with a single switch. Kena casually got up from her spot on the floor and nudged Katie awake. Rubbing her eyes, Katie glanced around the room to see if anyone else noticed she had fallen asleep for the last half of the film. Noticing that most of the audience was also rubbing their eyes, Katie gave a big yawn and reached her arms toward the high ceiling. Kena grabbed the cushions from the floor and tossed them on the chairs before pulling her baseball cap back on her head, looping it through her long ponytail. Kena started following her sleepy friend out of the hall but remembered Katie had been wearing sunglasses when they came to watch the film. Katie was already swept up in the group exiting the room, still shuffling from grogginess that was infectious among much of the crowd. A contagious yawn was passed from the front of the exiting line to the back.

While the film had been interesting and insightful, the crowd had not been the most attentive audience for the late-night documentary. Even Kena felt worn down from the week, and the yawn caught in her breath too. She slipped out of line in an empty aisle of seats and waited for the crowd to pass before returning to the front of the room for Katie's almost-lost sunglasses under the seat. After locating the forgotten item under the chairs in the front row, Kena moved back down the center aisle with the sunglasses in hand to look for Katie; not that she would be needing them this evening seeing that the stars were already peeking through the black cover of night.

There were still a handful of people gathering their things and clearing out the room when Kena exited for the second time. As she walked toward the door, the foreign birthday girl noticed the film representative standing on the side of the aisle.

The gentleman had introduced the film at the start of the evening before the lights dimmed, and the crowd faded. He was not much taller than herself and wore a tweed overcoat with a white collared shirt, the top button unhooked. With his hands clasped behind his back, the grandfatherly man gave Kena a gentle smile. Kena stopped, not knowing how to thank the representative of the forgotten hero's association for coming to show the inspiring documentary. She stumbled over words, trying to choose the simplest in her native tongue for the elderly gentleman to understand. Language had created a barrier for her in this country all week, but the representative gave another quick grin and a nod of his head. Kena could only hope he understood; believing that at least smiles translate multilingually. Thinking nothing more of the limited, one-sided conversation with the gentleman, she continued on her way to join back with Katie in the main hall to deliver her lost item.

The quick pace of the festival lifestyle drew Kena into other evening activities and conversations. Being an extrovert at heart, the tiredness that had affected her moments earlier was overpowered by the delight of being with people. Katie also had a new wave of energy, the quick nap having refreshed her to carry on at the festival into the night hours. The girls bubbled in chatter with a small group of friends about the activities and upcoming festival events.

"I'm going to get some lemonade," Katie stated. "Do you want a glass, Kena?"

"No, thanks. I'll just wait here," replied Kena. Though the lemonade was a homemade festival specialty, Kena had already had her fill throughout the long, hot day.

Katie nodded in agreement. The other girls joined Katie's short quest to the next room that was set up as the festival cafe to get lemonades and continue in the conversation that Kena had a hard time understanding in a language still unfamiliar to her lips. As Kena waited for her friends' return, she glanced around at all the conversations in the acoustic hall. As multiple groups of people chatted, their conversations bounced along the walls and flooded the airy room with sounds of fellowship. A group of kids raced through the hall, giggling at the fun they were having past their bedtime. Kena's ears picked up some of the conversations spoken in her native tongue, but it was drowned over with the fullness of chatter in the room.

As she stood in the center of the large hall, the grand-fatherly representative silently approached her. His hair was carefully combed to the side of his head, the silver strands matching the starlight of the night, but it was his eyes that Kena noticed the most. His eyes simultaneously looked sympathetic and as though they held a secret. Kena smiled again at the representative, unsure what he wanted to say or whether he knew the words for her to understand. When he reached her, the gentleman she had only met moments before pulled her into a hug, kissed Kena on the cheek, and placed the golden-colored documentary DVD case into her hands. Kena looked up at the kind representative, unaware of what she had done to receive such a generous gift. With a whispered, cracked voice, the elderly gentleman said, "Keep this story alive." He squeezed her hand and left faster than he had arrived. Kena hugged the DVD under her chin, realizing that she had received a story of gold for her final birthday present.

August 6, 1972
— Niky

A home isn't always intended to resemble a building with walls, a roof, and glass windows. Birds make a home in a light-weight nest balanced on the branch of a tree. A spider finds refuge in a threaded web invisibly clinging two fence posts. Moles reside in a damp underground maze of tunnels, and a beaver will make his home in a rustic dam.

My home is Lazinov.

Historical accounts never seem to give this little village the credit of recording the name accurately throughout the dated documents of land trades among the dukes and lords of the ancient world. How anyone could have forgotten this place, I will never understand. The village was built on the banks of a valley where the earth ruffles like a vacuumed rug. Along the stretched valley, small houses and trees sprinkle the land. A meadow extends on the north side, and a gravel country road weaves through the hills around all the hobby farms. There's a river that splices the valley in two and splashes in little waterfalls over rocks and stones. Even though Lazinov is located within walking distance from the nearby city, it feels like the edge of the earth — a peaceful and secluded oasis for us inhabitants.

There are no more than fifty houses in my village, and the population this year is a bustling two-hundred and thirty-

seven. (That is already including Ms. Novak's baby due at the end of the year.)

My house is tucked into the hillsides, the soft earth cocoons around the foundation and back wall. It isn't a big house, but I have a room upstairs that I share with my little sister, Marie. The best part of the bedroom is the window which looks over the garden right into Patja's window. Patja has been my best friend since I was two years old, and our mothers sat us in the sandpit together while they hung the laundry on the lines between our houses. Sometimes, when I can't sleep at night and when Marie has already dozed off, I shine my flashlight into Patja's window, and we go out to listen to the crickets and find fireflies in the meadow. We know we shouldn't go out after curfew, but I never miss a chance to explore. I'm always very careful not to wake Mother or Dad, but I think Mother has an inkling of what I've been up to and is a worried mother hen running circles around the pen in anticipation for a fox to crawl through the wire fence. Truth is, I've never seen a fox in the henhouse before.

When Mother gave me this journal, she said, "Your mind is always running through adventures! Write some of it down." Maybe what she meant to say was, "You are always running! Sit down awhile." She says I'm like Dad — always exploring, climbing, and getting into trouble; though, I haven't seen Dad do anything like that since long before Marie was born. To me, he seems as reserved as the sun in February; always hiding behind fog and clouds.

Mother bought the journal at the little stationery store at the corner of the only intersection in Lazinov. ("Intersection" is *an ambitious word considering there are only three houses on the road if you continued straight instead of turning left to drive out of Lazinov.) For a village of fewer than three hundred people, it would seem more effective to have a small food market instead of the stationery store, but compassionate people like Mother keep the only shop in Lazinov afloat.*

I'm certain Mother expected me to sit at home and write about my adventures, but I simply seem to come alive in nature! So I have been balanced on this branch for nearly half an hour with the journal propped on my knees as the sunlight hits the helicoptering leaves overhead, making a kaleidoscope on the ink-stained paper. I don't mind the rough bark that scratches at my back because, from where I am perched just past the fence of Dvorak's farm, I can see nearly all of my beloved valley. Patja knows this is my favorite spot in all of Lazinov and will find me here.

After all, this is my home.

June 6, 1994
— Krista

Krista strained her neck to try to catch a glimpse of the stars through the window of the moving car, but the streetlights obstructed the pinpoints of light in the darkened sky.

"We're almost there," Krista's dad, Rick, whispered from the passenger seat to avoid waking his wife, who had fallen asleep hours ago next to Krista. Their driver, Jakub, a friend of Krista's parents, nodded in agreement. Jakub had chatted with Rick for the first hour of their journey in the car but had been pretty quiet for the rest of the trip, seeing as it was the middle of the night, and he would have normally been asleep at this hour. However, Rick and Krista were experiencing a full dose of jet lag.

Krista noticed her mom didn't seem to have a problem with the time difference. Doma had fallen asleep shortly after they started their drive from the airport. Krista glanced at the clock above the car dashboard. It was nearly two in the morning, but she was wide awake. They have been sitting in the car for almost three hours. Yet, without a flashlight to read her book or a hope to fall asleep, Krista succumbed to replaying the day's memories in her head to entertain herself.

Actually, she was still replaying yesterday's memories too. The jet lag and time difference mushed everything together. They had left for the airport quite early yesterday morning to allow for enough time to check in all their luggage. Instead of driving themselves, Rick had asked Mr. Everson if he could taxi the three of them to the airport. The Eversons are longtime friends of Krista's parents, and of course, Mr. Everson quickly agreed. Krista and Mr. Everson's youngest daughter, Ruthie, had been best friends since they were in the same pre-k Sunday School class. It was no surprise that Ruthie also came with her dad in the morning to bring her best friend to the airport. Krista thought about the events of yesterday for what seemed like the millionth time.

"Your suitcases are so big!" Ruthie commented as their dads loaded the oversized bags into the back of the pickup.

"Well, we will be gone all summer," Krista said between yawns. It was too early, but Ruthie was awake enough for the both of them.

"It sounds so exciting! You will be in Europe for the whole summer!" said Ruthie as she excitedly shook Krista's shoulders.

"I'll be in a small town visiting my sick grandmother who I have never met before," corrected Krista. "I don't think I will even be able to speak with her."

Ruthie's face scrunched as she pondered what her best friend meant. "Why?" she asked.

"I'm sure she doesn't know English, and my Czech isn't so good," Krista shrugged, accepting her fate. "My parents both learned English quite quickly after they arrived in America, and they only occasionally talked with me in Czech until about five years ago. That's when they started teaching me and Jack. I guess because, when the communist government left Czechoslovakia, Dad wanted us to know Czech so we could enjoy visits too. Jack picked up speaking faster because my parents still spoke Czech with him before I learned to talk, so he remembered some of it. I can understand the language okay now, but it's the speaking that still sometimes trips me up."

Krista often wondered why her parents hadn't encouraged learning their native tongue sooner, but believed they wanted more than anything to fit into their new American lifestyle. It must have been hard enough being young newlyweds in a new country with a new language and culture; then, becoming parents before they turned twenty brought them quickly into adult life. Krista had always admired her parents for their strength even though they've never told her much about their lives before they moved to America. She would sometimes ask Jack, but even though Jack was four years older, he knew about as little as she did. At one point, Krista got unreasonably upset as she supposed her parents were trying to hide their previous lives from her, but Jack consoled her. "What if they aren't hiding it from you, but protecting themselves? We know that their lives haven't been easy, so maybe Mom and Dad don't talk about the past because it hurts."

"Maybe I'll learn more about their past this summer," pondered Krista before Ruthie interjected her rabbit's trail of thoughts.

"Speaking of Jack, how did your brother transition into life at summer camp last week?" asked Ruthie.

"Ever since Jack started going to Camp Pinewood as a camper, he has dreamed about being a counselor someday. I know he will have a really fun summer there, but I am sad he won't be coming with us. Jack went with Dad to visit grandma four years ago right after the borders opened, so I guess my parents didn't feel they needed to push him to come with us this time."

"Well, I'll miss you at camp this summer. I don't know who I will share my bunkbed with!"

Rick leaped down from the bed of the truck, cupped his hands together, and blew into his airtight fist. A deep owl sound filled the morning stillness in the quiet neighborhood — his call that it was time to head out. Krista and Ruthie, who were sitting on the curb where the driveway meets the road, rose to their feet. Ruthie stretched up her arms and gave a satisfying moan. Krista reached down to grab her carry-on knapsack lying at her feet. The girls shuffled over to meet their parents, who were already waiting in the truck. They buckled up in the backseat, Krista snug in the middle between her mom and best friend. The engine purred, and the headlights awoke to beat the sunlight still trying to intersect the morning fog.

They arrived at the airport and unloaded the luggage just as the sun finally broke through the fading mist. Even though it was still very early on that summer morning, Krista recalled the liveliness once inside the airport doors. Krista and Ruthie had each grabbed onto the handle of Krista's suitcase, and they worked together to weave through the airport concourse until they arrived at the baggage check line.

"I wish we could see you off at the terminal," started Mr. Everson.

"It's okay, Pastor. We are just happy you could bring us so early on a Sunday morning to the airport." Rick stretched out his arm and gave Mr. Everson a firm handshake.

Mr. Everson pulled him into a one-arm hug saying, "I've still got plenty of time before the ten o'clock service. You take care now. Come back in one piece."

Doma held out two manilla envelopes to Mr. Everson. On the first was printed HOME INFORMATION. Inside the envelope was a hand-written note for Mrs. Everson about some basic housework. She had promised that Ruthie's two older brothers would mow the lawn and look after the house while Krista's family was away. At the bottom of the envelope was a lonely spare key to the house. In the same block-print handwriting on the second manilla envelope was written, JACK KOPECKY.

"Pastor, this has all of Jack's health care information and how to contact us. Thank you for letting us put your name as the person-to-contact if Jack needs anything at Camp Pinewood or in case of an emergency this summer," said Doma.

"I should be at the campsite many times this summer to check in on our youth students. Don't worry, I'll look out for Jack."

Krista saw her mom give a reassuring smile as she thanked Mr. Everson. At that moment, Ruthie wrapped her arms over Krista's shoulders. Krista thought it was only a hug until she felt a small added weight around her neck and glanced down to see Ruthie had successfully clasped a necklace that dangled just below her collarbone. She read the word printed on the half heart upside down, FRIENDS. When she looked up, she saw Ruthie pulling a chain out from under her shirt. In the center of the chain dangled the other half of the heart, BEST.

"Oh, Ruthie!" Krista exclaimed.

"Now, we will be a little bit together all summer," said Ruthie. She wrapped her arms around her friend, this time for a hug. "Send me emails this summer when you get access to a computer and take lots of pictures!"

"I promise." Krista wrapped her arms around Ruthie and held her tight. "I packed extra film for my Polaroid just for you!"

As the girls released their hug, their new necklaces became intertwined, and they laughed as they twisted the chains free again. Both girls apologized for the tangle at the same time and then giggled at how their necklaces seemed to know it needed the other half. They said one last goodbye before Krista grabbed the handle on her suitcase and followed after her parents like a little duckling.

"Stay safe!" Ruthie called after Krista. Krista turned and gave her a big wave and blew a kiss before turning to keep up with her parents through the airport lines.

When they arrived at the baggage counter, Doma took a luggage tag and, in big block letters, wrote KRISTYNA MARIE KOPECKA before tying it onto Krista's knapsack. They slowly weaved their way through groups and lines of people before arriving at their terminal. During the lengthy waiting ordeal, Rick made soft cattle sounds in Krista's ear that sent the young teen into a fit of giggles. Krista tried to muffle her laughs with a cough and then playfully glared at the only man responsible for the "dad joke." While youthfulness had blessed Rick in spirit, it had blessed his wife in appearance. Doma's thin face and tight waistline made onlookers wonder if she and Krista were sisters rather than a mother-daughter pair. Though Doma did have her children at a young age, she had also needed to mature rapidly due to circumstances that forced her into adulthood. Doma carried professionalism with her always, which helped in situations of ridiculous comments regarding her looks and age.

Such was the case with the desk clerk at the airport that morning. As the clerk had been looking over the passports of the three sojourners, he made one of those age-commenting mistakes.

"I would not have guessed you are her mother," the young man behind the desk said as he lifted the passports to study their faces next to the pictures in the little book. Not stopping there, he continued, "If I hadn't seen the date of birth on her passport, I wouldn't have believed you had a fourteen-year-old daughter. I may have pegged you as her sister, but definitely not her mother."

He slid the passports back across the desktop, and Doma slipped them into the zippered pouch of her purse before saying, "Then, you would certainly not believe I also have a son not much younger than you, who is wise enough not to comment a lady's age." With that, Doma motioned for Krista to follow, leaving Rick to gather the printed tickets from the embarrassed clerk.

Krista slouched in one of the chairs by the window and looked out in time to see a plane taxing to the runway. She suddenly became very excited about the new adventure that awaited, even though she had no idea what to expect. Rick left Krista and Doma at the terminal and returned ten minutes later, holding a small paper bag with a fresh bagel for Krista and a large coffee to share with his wife. It would be three months before Krista stepped on American soil again, and even though she knew she would miss out on all the summer activities with Ruthie, she was looking forward to seeing the homeland of her parents for the first time.

Krista's memory of the cross Atlantic flight was interrupted as her dad excitedly whispered, "Krista! You awake?"

"Uh-huh."

"We've made it! We're in Letovice."

Krista looked out the window to see a church steeple stretching up into the night sky and the outline of the disheveled palace Jack had mentioned before. She glued her nose to the window as Jakub drove them through the city square and turned down narrow roads until they arrived at their destination. Krista unbuckled her seatbelt as Rick gently woke up his wife in the seat behind him. The front door of the white home opened, and a woman who looked to be about the same age as Mrs. Everson appeared on the front step in her robe.

"Hello, Zofie!" Rick called in a whisper to Jakub's wife. After quick introductions, Zofie led the three tired travelers and her husband inside.

"We will get your luggage from the car in the morning," Jakub explained as he guided the group up the stairs to a room with three beds. Two of the beds were pushed together for Krista's parents.

"The place is just how I remember it," said Rick as he looked around the bedroom.

"Well, with the in-laws no longer on the main level, we decided to take their room, which allows you all to stay up here," Jakub explained, "but we're still using the kitchen and living room across the hall on this level while we slowly upgrade the appliances in the downstairs apartment."

The two chatted in their native tongue, and Krista followed along for the most part, but she was suddenly exhausted and plopped onto the single bed. Her dad noticed and politely wrapped up the conversation.

"Thank you for accommodating us," said Rick.

"It's our pleasure! Sleep as long as you need in the morning. Goodnight," Zofie replied. She gave Doma a quick squeeze and motioned for Jakub to close the door behind them.

Krista slid her knapsack off her back and let it fall onto the floor. Even before her head was cushioned by the feather pillow, her eyelids had closed like weights pulling her into a dream.

August 8, 1972
— Niky

Escaping from home to avoid chores should be registered as an Olympic sport. Mother had asked me to clean upstairs, which in her standards meant everything from washing the windowpanes to the floorboards, fluffing the duvet quilt, and putting away mine and Marie's laundry. When it comes to chores, I am the first to practice the art of procrastination. (However, Mother's standards of weekly chores are a little repetitive.) I was lying on my bed, glancing through a nature guide about rodents and reptiles when a pebble ricocheted off the window. I didn't hesitate as I slid from my bed — the nature guide tumbling from the edge of the mattress with a solid bellyflop. Flashlight signals are how Patja and I communicate at night and pebble throwing during the day (unless the window is already open, and then we just whistle or make some birdcall). Maybe it is a little cliche, but the system works for us. There is never a shortage of pebbles. I pulled open the window and leaned outside to see Patja, a story below, holding a bulging cloth sack impossibly hiding the shape of a soccer ball.

"Please don't tell me you actually wanted to spend today inside," Patja teased.

"Apparently, there is to be an inspection of every floorboard in Lazinov in a great conquest of approving the most righteous home and granting the housekeeper with the Sacred Seal for the Most Domestic," I smirked back.

"You are not one to participate in a silly competition of such matter." Sarcasm is a language Patja and I have perfected. Best friends just know. Patja continued, *"Let me challenge you in a competition to suit you better. Your previous record of escaping from your room on Cleaning Day is five minutes. I bet you can't do it in under five."*

"I'll do it in under four — and for my reward, I would like that plum scone I know you have in your pocket from your mother."

"How could you possibly know that?"

Best friends just know. Patja's mother always opens the kitchen windows when she does the morning baking, making it impossible not to smell the scones this morning. As for the plums, I knew Mr. Pokorny had brought a basket over to our neighbor friends yesterday. He had given us more than enough from his fruit tree last week. After storing plums for winter and making jam, cake, and eating heaps of plums on breakfast oatmeal, there isn't much left but to pass it off to a neighbor.

"Alright. I will make that deal." Patja's eyes narrowed before declaring, *"Go!"*

I leaped into action, grabbing the feather quilt by the corner and throwing it over the windowsill to fluff the feathers in the daylight. I splashed some water on the floor from my cup I left on the nightstand and used my pajama shirt to slide the makeshift mop across the floorboards. Using the damp shirt, I wiped the windows and fanned the nature guide over the glass to dry it in this summer humidity. Obviously, there are some streaks that I am sure Mother will notice, but she will just sigh saying, "at least Niky tried," as always. Taking the hamper of clothes, I emptied the bin into the bottom of the wardrobe behind mine and Marie's winter boots. (I will sort them later, of course.) I draped the wet pajama shirt on the back corner of the wardrobe where Mother wouldn't see it. I lunged for my backpack under my bed, tossed in my journal, the nature guide, and shoved in a pair of old shoes. I leaned out the window to hear Patja call, "Two minutes!"

"Catch!" I commanded as I threw my backpack out the window into Patja's grasp.

Now, the hard part — getting past Mother. I clung to the banister as I glided down the stairs, making sure to skip the third step from the bottom as the creak gives away any intruder — or, in this case, escapee. Marie hasn't figured this out yet and is always curious how Mother knows the second she has snuck from her room to the kitchen to steal scones and biscuits. Since Marie is my little sister, I have an obligation to look out for her and help her, but if I told Marie, I know she would blab to Mother, who would tell Dad to fix the step and there would be a new security system in place before I could even say a word. (Such as the loose banister that banged against the staircase at the slightest touch — that was last summer until Marie tried sliding down the banister as in one of her fairytales and nearly toppled over the other side! Dad fixed the banister that afternoon. My parents don't loosen floorboards or banisters to create this barricade system; somehow, it just seems to happen. This old house creates an obstacle course in itself.)

With the staircase behind me, there was one final challenge. To reach the front door, I would have to walk past Mother and Marie in the kitchen, but going out the side door is risky because the door is overdue for oil and squeaks louder than a cat in an alley quarrel. (Yet another of the house's innovative security.) I weighed the options momentarily when, suddenly, the kitchen door swung open with Marie chanting, "I'll be right back, Mother!" as she galloped toward the bathroom. In that moment of shock in the hallway, I dove into the living room — also Mother and Dad's bedroom. I was running out of time and options, but even in the chaos of the escape, there was one final idea. I quietly pulled open the window in the living room and slipped out onto the sloped earth surrounding our little home. Reaching up, I coaxed the window closed again (I'll remember to lock it from the inside when I get back home) and raced around the bushes, nearly colliding with Patja.

"Time!" I heaved.

Patja said nothing, only stood holding out the scone. Best friends just know. I victoriously took a mammoth bite out of the scone and then shoved the rest back into Patja's hand, knowing my best friend would have shared it with me even if I had lost the bet. However, losing to Patja has never been my style.

June 7, 1994
— Krista

Krista awoke to the strong smell of coffee. For a moment, she forgot where she was but quickly regained her senses as she looked across the room to see her mom sitting in a rocking chair.

"Good morning, sleepyhead," Doma sang.

Krista groaned and flopped her head back on her pillow. "I have a headache."

"It's the jet lag. Your body is trying to catch up to the new time," her mom reasoned. "Here, come take a sip of my coffee."

"Really?"

"Just a sip."

Krista, still in her travel sweatpants and one of Jack's tattered baseball shirts, swung her legs over her bed. Her bare feet met the cool wooden floor. She wrapped the duvet over her head and shoulders, and like a monk going to morning prayer, she shuffled to where her mom was extending the cup of coffee. Krista reached out with both hands and grasped the hot mug, her makeshift robe falling around her ankles. She closed her eyes and held the mug under her nose before letting her lips touch the edge. She then tipped the mug to reach what her mom had purposefully left at the bottom for her. The coffee was strong, but there was enough milk and sugar to take away the bitterness. She let the taste linger in her mou.. moment before the creamy, rich liquid glided down her throat. Krista placed the empty mug on the side table near the rocking chair and retrieved the duvet puddled around her feet.

"I didn't know this room had a balcony!" Krista exclaimed after glancing around the room. It had been so late and dark when they arrived in the middle of the night that she had hardly noticed anything in the room other than her bed.

"A pretty good view too," said Doma.

Krista pulled open the door to the balcony and walked to the edge guarded by a wooden railing. The first thing she saw was the palace ruins on the hill in the distance, a lookout tower slightly lower on the hill was almost completely hidden by overgrown trees. Still, a structure of that size was hard to miss. There was a valley separating Krista's balcony from the palace, but the tree branches and garden sheds parted as if Moses had commanded them to give the balcony a direct view of the palace. On the street below, a young mother was pushing a stroller as a toddler tried to keep up on a tricycle. Krista noticed there was only one more house at the end of the road before it turned and weaved up the hill into the forest. She pivoted to rejoin her mom back in the room only to find that Doma was standing in the doorway, also looking at the view. However, Doma's expression didn't imitate the calm morning. She seemed to look through Krista, her eyes glassed and her mouth as straight as the edge of a ruler. The wrinkles above her eyebrows became more defined for only a moment and then relaxed into her forehead again.

"Mom?" Krista's voice hesitated.

Her mom's expression was quickly replaced as her glassed eyes focused on Krista rather than the horizon.

"Oh. Sorry, Krista!" Doma said. "I suppose I am also affected by the jet-lag; sometimes, it still just feels like I'm dreaming."

It was at that moment Krista realized it was her mom's first time back in Czech since she had left her homeland nineteen years ago. Krista's mouth gaped slightly as she wanted to ask her mom more about the former life she only knew snippets about. Before she had the chance to ask, the door clicked open and, with four long strides, her dad joined them on the balcony.

"Beautiful day!" said Rick as he bit into a roll covered with strawberry jam. "You ladies can grab some breakfast in the kitchen, and then, we will figure out our plan for today." He rested his arm over his wife's shoulder and kissed her forehead before heading back through the room and across the hall to get another roll with fresh strawberry jam.

Doma looked at Krista. "Shall we?" Doma asked and tipped her head in the direction of the door. The two followed after Rick across the hall into the bright kitchen. They were greeted by a round table that held a basket of rolls and a buffet of jams. At the table, Rick sat between Jakub, a sticky puddle of jam dripping from his roll onto his plate, and Zofie, who wore a bandana over her short, bronze hair, though it didn't completely cover the greying roots.

"Are you ready for a refill on that coffee? I heard you Americans drink it by the liter in the morning." Zofie stood up from the table and wrapped her thick arms around Doma's slender frame.

"I sure missed you," Doma laughed.

Though Krista isn't a little girl anymore, she felt like a shy toddler in the presence of the woman she had only briefly met the night before, and instinctively Krista stood slightly behind her mom. Jack had told Krista about Jakub and Zofie when he and Dad visited four years earlier, but with the new environment came a wave of timidness.

"I suppose we didn't formally meet last night. You must be Kristyna." Zofie reached out her hand. "I'm Zofie. Make yourself at home since you'll be here for the next three months."

Krista grasped Zofie's handshake, aware of Zofie's rough hands, but equally aware of the gentleness in her eyes. Krista's momentary case of shyness fled nearly as quickly as it arrived.

"Everyone calls me Krista," she smiled.

"Well then, Krista, are you hungry? Help yourself to some rolls and my homemade jam. We've got strawberry, apricot, blueberry, apple, and plum."

"So many choices!" Doma chimed in.

"We've got a plum tree out back and a small patch of strawberries in the garden. The blueberries we collected in the forest. We got the apricots and apples from the trees at my in-laws' hobby farm," explained Zofie.

Krista dragged a chair out from under the table and sat onto the sturdy seat. She shoveled out spoonfuls of fresh strawberry jam and evenly layered it on the roll.

"I think I'll like it here," thought Krista as her teeth sunk into the fresh roll. Looking over at her parents, who were sitting and chatting with Zofie and Jakub, her thoughts

continued, *"It looks like they like it here too. After all, they did grow up here. Why haven't we all visited Letovice sooner?"*

August 9, 1972
— Niky

If Mother had known I'd be using this journal to record my escaping adventures, maybe she would have considered giving me a lecture instead of blank pages to encourage my endeavors. I laugh at the irony in that she thought writing would keep me still, whereas I find myself absorbed in wondering what next crazy adventure will flow from the tip of my pen.

Yesterday afternoon was perfect. After running through the bushes so Mother wouldn't see our escape from the yard, Patja and I made our way to the center of the village where the brook divides our valley, the gap in the valley only held together by one wooden bridge. We waded through the river as the water rose nearly to our knees and cooled our feet on the slippery, wet stones. Years of practice has taught me how to balance atop of the smooth rocks and shuffle my feet along the bottom of the brook to move with the current. The little village itself can be a blessing and a curse in that all the neighbors know me and Patja.

I'll explain...

1. Nearly everyone will give us a snack or water while we are out playing in the village: blessing.

2. *Nearly everyone will ask for help in their garden or with chores if they see us outside: curse.*

3. *Lazinov is one big backyard, and we can go anywhere: blessing.*

4. *All the mothers and grandmothers watch over the backyards like hunting hawks and will quickly phone home if something is awry: curse.*

5. *Lazinov is practically one extended family. We all know each other's business and give advice: blessing.*

6. *Most times, I don't want unsolicited advice: curse.*

The advantage of the sticky summer day was that no one was outside. Patja and I were free from the watchful eyes of the backyard grandmothers, free from acts of service to our fellow neighbors, and free from any wagging fingers telling us we should be home helping our mothers. It was just two best friends doing what we always do.

Of course, I beat Patja in a sprint to our climbing tree. I always win the sprints, but Patja will eternally be better at long distance. We always start at the last fencepost of the Dvorak farm and race the sloped incline to the best climbing tree overlooking the valley. I remember Patja winning the sprint only once in those years, all because I tripped over a molehill that erupted from the earth like a mini-volcano. I didn't see it as I was running (obviously, or I would have avoided it). Patja was gaining on me when, suddenly, I was flat on the ground tasting the dirt on my lips. Tasting dirt was the least of my troubles; it was tasting defeat that created the pit in my stomach. Unlike the legendary Zdenek Miler, who created the iconic Little Mole cartoon, I was less than inspired to create a new fairytale about the blind, furry creature that caused my misfortune. Rather, I wanted to stomp the impeding mound of dirt back into the ground with the satisfaction similar to popping a zit from my skin — but I composed myself, stood up, brushed the dirt from my hands, and congratulated Patja on the win (and promised it would only happen that once, and I would never again be left behind as Patja sprinted on).

We played soccer in the heat yesterday until Patja's thin hair was all matted with sweat. So, I laid in the shade under the tree while Patja used a twig to aimlessly carve trenches in the dirt. We stayed like that for a while before Patja said, "What do you think they will talk about at the town meeting tomorrow?"

"Huh?" I sat up, resting my weight on my elbows.

"You know, the meeting for adults in Lazinov tomorrow night."

"No one told me."

"I don't know what it is about, but my dad said every homeowner in Lazinov must be present."

"That could be anything." I twirled my finger around a blade of grass and gave it a satisfying tug to examine the thread-like roots.

"This time it sounds important, Nik."

"It's always important."

"I guess we will know after tomorrow." Patja flicked a stone and watched it summersault in the grass.

Marie was the first to notice me come through the side door when I arrived home because she was sitting at the top of the staircase, cradling a baby doll. Mother noticed second; the sound of the squeaking door imitating an alley cat gave me away.

"I thought you were upstairs," Mother interrogated.

"I just needed some fresh air." I glanced at the top of the stairs in time to see Marie roll her eyes and rest her chin in the cup of her hand. Well, the nine-year-old wasn't fooled, but she wouldn't dare tattle to Mother.

"I see," said Mother, her lips pursed together. Her gaze changed to look at Marie, who just shrugged. "Chores?" Mother questioned.

"Done," I replied.

Mother remained focused on Marie for confirmation. Marie peeked her head into the bedroom and gave Mother a thumbs-up.

"Both of you, wash up before Dad gets home," Mother said defeatedly.

Marie still had flour sticking to her forehead from helping Mother in the kitchen. She left the baby doll on the top step and followed me into the bathroom.

When I looked in the mirror, I noticed I had a layer of dust covering my cheeks and my backpack was still slung over my shoulder. Mother definitely knew I bailed today. I splashed my face and then scrubbed Marie's before bringing my backpack to my room. I pulled the duvet from the window ledge back onto the bed and then made my way to the wardrobe to sort out the clothes. I had been so absorbed in my thoughts that I *hadn't noticed Marie followed me back up to the bedroom. She didn't say anything, only started pulling some of her dresses and t-shirts to hang in the wardrobe. I stood frozen with two unmatched socks in my hands. When Marie learned to walk, she followed me everywhere. Dad said I had a second shadow. I guess I just realized then, in front of the wardrobe, that the shadowing never stopped.*

"Thank you," I whispered to Marie.

Marie grinned and gave me a wink.

So I didn't mind babysitting Marie while Mother and Dad are at the town meeting tonight. I owe it to Marie, at least. We watched the regular evening cartoons before Marie got on her pajamas and brushed her teeth. For as long as I can remember, the black-and-white evening cartoon program has aired each night at a quarter to seven with a ten-minute bedtime fairytale. While Little Mole had always been my favorite as a child, after the collision with the molehill on the race with Patja, it always seemed the cartoon was mocking my misfortune. Mother and Dad said the meeting could go late, but it's almost nine o'clock. Marie has been asleep for an hour, so I've been writing from the light of my flashlight while lying on my bed. Mother will make sure we are asleep once they arrive home, but there is time. I'll read the nature guide until then. After all, the third stair from the bottom gives me plenty of warning to switch off the flashlight.

June 12, 1994
— Krista

Over the course of the first few days in the country of her heritage, Krista had successfully tried all of Zofie's jam options. She had decided the sweet strawberry jam was her favorite, with the tart apricot coming in a close second. Some mornings she couldn't decide which to put on the roll, so she layered the two jams and created a strawberry-apricot blend.

Krista spent most of the first week either following her parents on short outings into the city or shadowing Zofie in the backyard. Normally, she would not be so thrilled to follow adults around for the whole week, but the time difference had taken longer for her to get accustomed too, thus she moved through the day as a duckling chasing after its mother. Some days, Krista groggily tried to stay awake, but she found that she was becoming more acquainted with the soft grass under the plum tree as she frequently napped sprawled out on an old rug. On occasion, she joined her parents on their daily walk to the nursing home to visit her grandmother. Her dad explained that his mother had always struggled with a weaker immune system, making it difficult to care for herself when Rick's father passed away a few years back.

Additionally, Grandmother's memory wasn't as sharp when remembering details. With no other family on this side of the ocean, Rick's mother had been administrated into the nursing home. The staff explained she has often been fatigued and resting from the slightest cold or allergies, though when she is awake, she fills her time reading over the letters Rick had sent regularly from America over the past four years. Pictures taped to the wall around her bed showed Jack and Krista's birthdays, among other family events. Each picture was labeled "grandchildren Jack and Kristyna," so as not to give her memory the option to let the names slip away.

Krista didn't mind visiting the nursing home and embraced finally meeting her grandmother. However, it wasn't answering her grandmother's questions about school and hobbies that kept her interest in these visitations, but rather the nursing home building itself. It had been an old monastery built on the sloped hill leading up to the palace. It now housed a good portion of the city's elderly population. Krista found herself elated as she explored the halls adorned with art, occasionally seeing the monk who still resided in the building. The tall, airy halls circle a courtyard where the patients of the nursing home sit in their wheelchairs and watch birds at the feeders. Naturally, the old monastery building included a chapel at the end of the lowest level for the residents to attend weekly mass and never leave the building.

After a few visits to the nursing home, there was not much more to explore, and Krista's language ability wasn't yet at a comfortable level where she could engage in extended conversations with her grandmother. She succumbed to simply nodding or shaking her head when the questions were directed towards her. While Krista understood the language from the past five years of practice, she was used to talking solely with her dad and Jack. Krista sometimes found the words were still stiff and unfamiliar for her tongue, and she was embarrassed at her preliminary grammar mistakes. Zofie encouraged her to try stringing together as many words as she could and was confident Krista would be more comfortable speaking the language quickly. Krista, however, wasn't so convinced.

Even in a new place that was unlike home, Krista had found a sense of regularity in the days as the week blended together. This day was a repetition of the previous days as she layered strawberry jam on her roll for breakfast, helped Zofie wash the breakfast dishes, grabbed the book from her bed, and laid out the old rug in the backyard under the plum tree. It was late morning, but the chill in the air caused the hair on her arms to rise. She pulled the rug out from under the shade of the short tree and let the morning sun warm her. She flipped open her book, and five chapters later, the shade had returned, dimming the pages. After dog-earring the corner of the page, she rolled over on the rug with the intent to move it to the sunshine again. As she flipped over, Krista realized it wasn't the shadow of the plum tree that had followed her, but her dad stood over her.

"Zofie kicked me out of the kitchen because I kept pulling uncooked dumplings out of the pot." Rick let his bottom lip protrude as if mimicking a child, then plopped down next to Krista on the rug.

Krista laughed, "That's why mom bakes bread when you are gone all day at work! She was tired of cutting loaves with huge holes in the middle from where you dug out the dough."

"But that's the best part!"

"It will be cooked soon, Dad, then we can eat lunch."

Rick gave a dramatic sigh and slumped his shoulders. "Why cook it and ruin it?"

The window from the kitchen opened above, and Zofie shouted, "Lunch is on the table!"

Krista grabbed her book and quickly rolled the rug before following her dad into the house. She took her place at the table between her parents, sliding her book under her seat.

Zofie poured juice into the tall glasses and said to Doma, "Go ahead and start serving out the food. I've still got a couple more dumplings to put on the stove."

"I'll help!" chimed Rick and started to stand up from the table.

"You will not!" exclaimed Zofie as she grabbed a wooden spoon and held it defensively as a young child imagining it was a sword. "Now, you sit and eat this wonderfully *cooked* food." Then, to herself, she mumbled, "I spend an hour cooking, and he wants to eat everything raw. Humph!"

Rick looked at Doma and winked. His wife stifled a laugh. She had given up the cooked food "fight" years ago and now leaves a ball of dough next to the bread-maker for her ravenous husband.

Krista mopped up the rest of the gravy on her plate with the final piece of her dumpling and started to lean back in her chair. Before her shoulders met the backrest on the seat, Zofie cleared Krista's plate and brought it to rinse off in the sink. Krista admired her hospitality. A few minutes later, Zofie came back to the table with mugs of coffee for the adults and a plate of biscuits. Krista took the pitcher of milk, filled her cup, and dunked a chocolate biscuit into the thick, white liquid. She watched the milk drip off the biscuit as she pulled it out and slid it all into her mouth. Soon, the milk was tainted with chocolate, and cookie crumbs partially dissolved at the base of the cup.

Krista had been at the house long enough to know that the adults would be seated for a while with their afternoon coffee, so she quickly finished the chocolate milk cocktail and slipped out of the dining room to her bedroom. Shuffling through her knapsack, she found her notepad and a pencil. She tossed her feather pillow onto the floor and flopped onto it to write a letter to Ruthie. She told Ruthie all about the flight, spending time with Zofie and Jakub, meeting her grandmother, and walking through the city with her parents. Three and a half pages later, she was signing her name at the bottom when her dad came into the room.

"Do you want to come visit Grandmother today?" Rick asked. "We can stop for ice-cream on the way," he added.

Krista folded the papers and slipped them into an envelope. "Can we stop at the post office too?" she asked.

"Sure."

Krista pushed herself up from her position on the floor, tossing the pillow onto the bed and dumping the rest of the contents of her knapsack over the comforter. She placed the letter for Ruthie and her book back in the bag. As she reached for the Polaroid camera, she said, "I'll be out in two minutes, Dad."

Krista stepped out onto the balcony and snapped a picture of the palace in the distance. It was Jack's old camera that she came into possession of when he got a new film camera for camp a month before they went their separate ways. She waited for the picture to slowly appear, being careful to only touch the edges of the frame as it developed. Krista pulled the envelope back out of the knapsack, slipped the fresh picture inside, and wrote Ruthie's address on the front. She realized she didn't know Jakub and Zofie's address and made a mental note to ask her dad when they arrived at the post office. She tossed the envelope and the Polaroid camera into the knapsack and quickly slid on her sandals before joining Rick outside.

"I was trying to hurry, but it looks like I still beat Mom," Krista laughed.

Rick pulled the gate open. "Actually, Mom is a bit tired, so it is just us going today."

"Oh."

"We can still stop at the post office and for ice-cream — and since Mom isn't coming, we can get two scoops instead of just one!" Krista's dad gave her a playful nudge.

Krista slung her knapsack over her shoulder. "Alright, you've convinced me!"

The two made their way down the sloped road to the railroad tracks. There was a train crossing, but with all the trains running through this part of the country, neither Krista nor Rick were surprised to be waiting as the locomotive passed. They rounded the corner past the soccer field, noticing what looked like two children's teams warming-up before a match, and then continued on the short trek to the city square. Rick walked into the first corner building as they approached the city center. Krista followed up the three steps and noticed they had entered the post office. She relied on her dad to communicate with the lady at the desk. Rick quickly scratched Zofie and Jakub's address on the top left corner with a dying pen that had been left on the counter. He licked the tip of the pen to get the blue ink to flow more consistently. The postwoman layered the right corner in stamps and then tossed it in a bin on the desk. Krista pinched the half-heart necklace still clasped around her neck, wishing she could see Ruthie's face when she opened her mailbox.

"I think Mom is working on a letter to Jack," Rick stated as they exited the post office.

"We've been without Jack all week; it has started to feel normal." Krista shook her head with disappointment in herself for not writing a letter to her big brother sooner. "Do you think Mom will have space in the envelope if I write to Jack too?" She imagined her mom's loopy cursive handwriting filling line after line to cover a stack of pages. While Krista's hand started cramping after the three pages to Ruthie, she had seen her mom write letters that looked more like bulging pamphlets.

"It gets better than that. Mom has an email address for Camp Pinewood and already wrote with the director to see if we can write Jack via email! The director said he would print out the emails for Jack. Jakub has an old computer, but it works to access emails and type, so you can write Jack an email whenever."

"That's really neat! Maybe I can ask Ruthie for Mr. Everson's email, and we can do the same thing. We just started typing in Technology Class in school last year with a scarf over our fingers so we couldn't see the letters, but I'm not so fast."

"I think Jack would also enjoy getting a letter in your handwriting, but there are certainly more options to communicate these days."

Krista mulled over a question that came to her and said, "Did you write letters to your parents when you and Mom moved to America?"

The question went unanswered. Whether it was deliberate, Krista couldn't tell, for at the same time the question was asked, her dad called to a man across the street.

"Karel! Hey, Karel!"

The man turned and gave a big wave calling to Krista's father by his full name, a name he never introduced himself as, although Krista had heard it regularly from her grandmother and hosts over the past week. Karel glanced down the street and grabbed the hand of the young girl next to him, practically dragging her as he ran to meet Rick. The two grown men excitedly shook hands, and with his free hand, Rick clapped Karel on the back. The men talked quickly, but eventually, Krista caught what they were saying.

"My sister said you would be back in town!" said Karel.

"Yeah, we've just been getting accustomed to everything. She is a great hostess, that sister of yours," Rick responded.

"Zofie never changes! I can't get the kids to leave her place with the way she fills them up on sweet jam and biscuits."

Rick laughed, "That's exactly what she's doing to my Krista." He put his hand on Krista's shoulder, bringing her into the conversation.

"Krista, this is Karel, Zofie's little brother. Your mom and I went to school with him."

Krista extended her arm and shook Karel's hand. She noticed he had a strong grip, just like Zofie's. "It's nice to meet you, Krista," he smiled. Dropping his arm around the young girl next to him, he said, "This is my daughter, Magdalena." Magdalena's doe eyes and long eyelashes contrasted with the pigtails that burst crookedly from each side of her head. Krista immediately noticed that one of the pigtails drooped slightly lower than the other, and she wondered if it was the handiwork of Karel or Magdalena herself. Krista gave Magdalena a smile, which seemed to catapult Magdalena's monologue, leaving Krista scrambling to understand each word.

"Almost everyone calls me Madla, so you can call me that too if you want. Only my little brother called me Madi when he was first learning to speak. He is eight years old now; I'm three years older than him, but he still sometimes calls me Madi just for fun. He is playing soccer today, so we are going to the soccer field now to watch him. We brought him there earlier for warm-up, but then we came back into town for Daddy to stop at the bank, which is why we are arriving late. Do you want to come watch the soccer match with us?"

Madla's eyebrows arched high into her forehead as she waited for Krista to answer. Krista, unsure how to respond to the chatter-some eleven-year-old girl, glanced questionably to her dad.

"We were on our way to visit Krista's grandmother, but it would be okay if Krista went with you to the soccer match," said Rick.

"Great! Let's go. They've probably already started playing." Madla grabbed Krista's hand and started pulling her back in the direction she had just come from.

Karel caught Madla's other hand and, like a leash on a dog, refrained her from pulling Krista along further. "Let's ask Krista what she would like, don't you think, Madla?" he coaxed.

Krista looked at her dad, who nodded giving her confirmation that she could go.

"It's maybe better than going back to the nursing home. I've already explored all the hallways," thought Krista.

She focused her gaze on Madla and said, "Okay."

Rick passed Krista a few coins, saying she could buy a treat at the soccer game rather than the ice-cream they had planned for today. He didn't need to remind her when to be home; Rick was confident Karel would make sure his daughter made it safely to Zofie's house. Madla grabbed Krista's hand again, and they moved swiftly around the corner en route to the soccer field.

"Wow! This will be so fun. Normally, I just sit and watch alone with Daddy and sometimes Uncle Jakub while Kai plays soccer. That's my brother's name, Kai. It's short for Karel. He is named after Daddy, so we had to give Kai a nickname so he won't get confused if someone is talking to him or to Daddy. Do you like watching soccer?" Madla chattered.

Krista shrugged her shoulders as she thought, *"Madla sure makes friends quickly."*

"I think soccer is more fun to play than to watch, but the boys in my class only pass the ball to each other. So, if you don't watch soccer, do you watch any sport?"

"Baseball," Krista remembered all the hours at Jack's little league competitions and then at the high school matches. She enjoyed cheering on her brother and his teammates and suddenly craved a pack of salted peanuts and a root beer.

Madla brought her wandering thoughts back to reality. "Oh! That's an American sport. I don't know anyone who plays baseball here. You don't talk very much. Are you shy?"

"I'm not shy. I just can't make the words I want to say come out of my mouth faster than you ask the next question," Krista chastised herself. She responded to Madla's question by simply shaking her head.

Madla began talking about a time once when she was shy, which from what Krista could tell, lasted a whole three minutes at the start of preschool and never relapsed.

"Was this really a good idea?" thought Krista.

"How old are you anyway?" Madla inquired.

"Fourteen." Numbers were easy enough.

"My birthday's next month; I'll be twelve then. I asked my parents if I could have a new bicycle for my birthday because I keep growing, and my knees are almost hitting the handlebars on the one I have now," Madla continued talking about the style and color of the bike she dreamed of riding, all the while Krista racked her brain, trying to form one sentence that wouldn't come out sounding like Yoda.

"You sure don't talk much," Madla finally stated.

"Even if I wanted to talk, she doesn't give me much of a chance to jump in," thought Krista. She tried the language, "I don't speak much Czech, but I can understand well. English is easier." The syllables were too forced, and the sentence hung as if it was just said by a toddler with a lisp rather than a fourteen-year-old. Krista looked at the sidewalk, believing Madla will erupt in laughter at any moment.

"I think it is amazing that you understand so well even though you've never been here before!" Madla's response surprised Krista. She looked up.

"How did you learn Czech?" Madla continued.

"My dad and my brother practiced with me."

"That's impressive! You learned a lot by only talking with two people. Doesn't your mom practice with you too?"

"Mom likes English better."

Madla nodded, "Aunt Zofie tries to talk in English with me when I visit her house, but she says it is like trying to teach her pet turtle to speak."

"Zofie has no turtle."

"Not anymore! Last summer, I took the turtle outside in the garden and got distracted by climbing the plum tree. When I remembered the turtle, we couldn't find him anywhere. It had run away! I think it is rather silly to imagine a turtle running away, but they can be quite fast, you know," Madla laughed at her own story.

Krista joined in with the laughter, "It is very funny."

Krista was surprised by how much fun she had at the soccer field. She and Madla didn't watch the match the whole time but made trips to the snack counter and challenged each other to races behind the benches of onlookers. After a week of missing Ruthie, Krista was thankful to have a friend. Madla was three years younger and very chatter-some, though with Krista still hesitant to speak, it was only fitting to have a new friend who did enough talking for the both of them.

August 10, 1972
— Niky

I never heard Mother and Dad come home last night, but I'm sure they didn't stay out after curfew. They'd never do anything to draw government attention on themselves. I have no idea about their political views, but they would never knowingly disobey the communist rules — especially curfew. That's why this is so difficult now. I feel like I'm all alone in the fight to save my home, my village Lazinov!

I woke up this morning to the usual clanging of the bell, faithfully rung by Mrs. Kobzova every morning, midday, and evening — or to rally the fire brigade or to signify a death in the village. (Which in the case of today, "death" would have also been relevant.) I found that my flashlight was switched off and on my nightstand. The nature guide was tucked neatly on the shelf. I'm sure now that Mother had come in after I had fallen asleep. (Thankfully, I had put the journal in my backpack under my bed last night!) I slid on my slippers and went to the kitchen to find Mother and Dad in their normal spot on the bench by the window drinking tea. Dad was reading the newspaper, and Mother, holding a pencil, was making modifications to a recipe in her cookbook. Nothing seemed out of place. Everything was normal — too normal.

"How was the meeting last night?" I asked. I am way too curious for my own good, but how am I supposed to go about my day knowing nearly the whole village was present at this meeting?

"There was a lot to discuss," said Dad.

"About?" I pried.

"There are going to be some changes in Lazinov," he continued.

"What kind of changes?"

Dad sighed and lowered his newspaper. "The government has decided Lazinov is the perfect location for a water energy source because of the creek and river that join on the south side of the valley."

Mother chimed in, "It is good that we can use our own resources for energy. It shows we are an independent country."

I glanced from Mother to Dad, trying to read their facial expressions, but they were stoic statues. I'm no electrician, but this wasn't adding up. "It's just a small, lonely river. They can't expect to get that much energy from it, can they?"

"They're building a dam," Dad stated nonchalantly as he turned the page of the newspaper.

I must have looked confused because then Mother drew an imaginary long, wavy line on the table with the eraser on her pencil saying, "Okay, Niky, imagine this is the river." Then, she took the cookbook and chopped the tail off the imaginary brook. "They will build a dam here, and the water will pool so that a steady flow of water through the dam can be used for energy."

Suddenly, it started adding up.

"They're going to make an ugly pond from our little river just for energy?!" my voice grew.

"Listen, Bug..."

I hate when Mother calls me Bug. That's what you call babies. All mothers and grandmothers say the baby is as "cute as a bug," and now nearly every little child in the country has been called Bug. But I'm not little. I'll be fifteen next month. That's too old to be called Bug, but Mother still returns to the childish pet-name when she's codling — it's all I heard last summer for a week when I got the stomach flu.

I clenched my teeth together.

"Listen, Bug, they're going to flood the valley."

My head spun as Mother's words echoed in my head, "Flood the valley."

I didn't know whether to put my fist through the wall or sit on the floor and wail like a helpless baby. All the stomach flu symptoms came back: headache, nausea, and shortness of breath. Dad said something about moving some of the homes in Lazinov to a higher location that would overlook the new lake, but it felt as if he was talking to me underwater. Underwater like everything in this beautiful valley will be.

I needed to get out. I don't know if I swam or walked to the front door, but I know once I finally pulled it open, I was running. I sprinted down into the sloping valley. About halfway down the street, I realized I had been running in my slippers, but they flung off my feet into the ditch. Even barefooted, I was faster than ever before. Of course, I didn't want to continue down the roads looking like a gypsy as I ran barefoot with my hair untamed and still in the clothes I had slept in. All the while I could feel the heat from my face, which must have been redder than a ripe strawberry, and my jaw was beginning to hurt from clenching my teeth.

I swerved off the road and cut straight through Dvorak's field. I pulled myself over the wooden fence and kept sprinting through the pasture. I was so upset that I had forgotten about the ram who thinks he's a Spanish bull. Either he was on the other side of the pasture, or I ran fast enough through the pasture over the next fence that the old ram didn't even notice. (However, I'm surprised my reddened face didn't pull the ram into a wild chase.)

I've heard people say this experience is called "tunnel vision," not noticing anything around you, just moving toward your goal. But I didn't have a goal, or so I thought. After pulling myself over the next fence and tumbling over to the other side, I leaned up against the wooden barricade to catch my breath. I'm still just a sprinter, after all. As I looked up, I could see where my subconscious had brought me. Just up the slope, a short sprint away, was my climbing tree. By then, I didn't have the energy to full-out sprint anymore, so I half-sprinted, half-crawled up the slope until, finally, I had my arms wrapped around the tree trunk. I just stood there and hugged the tree. I'm not one to cry. I've gone through many injuries and set-backs without ever shedding a tear, but this was simply too much. My eyes puddled, and then rivers burned down my hot, sweaty cheeks. I cupped my hands over my eyes, and the tears flooded into my palms and seeped through my fingers. How fitting that I mourned Lazinov with a dam of my own tears.

I'm not used to crying, so just a couple of minutes was more than long enough before my tear ducts ran dry. I believe I have cried more from chopping onions for Mother's goulash, so I just sat at the foot of the tree and leaned up against the sturdy trunk. I didn't have the energy to climb up the branches. I have always climbed up those branches to get a better view of the valley; considering the circumstances, it just didn't seem fair to peer over the land knowing its fate, so I sat with my eyes closed and my hair sticking to the base of my neck.

For a long time, I just sat thinking about nothing. After a while, I began thinking about each corner of my beloved village and all the memories I have here. Though some may argue that my life experience is currently rather limited, I'm confident my extended knowledge of the details of Lazinov would make even the oldest villager embarrassed.

I know no one stole little Katerina Novak's sled last winter, but she left it out under a snowbank that melted as spring approached and the wood got all warped and musty. I found the sled across the valley in a ditch partially covered with wilted dandelions. It looked like a sad memorial for the little wooden sled. I don't know how Katerina dragged that dilapidated slab of wood there through the spring mud to hide it from her parents, but that five-year-old is ambitious.

I know Mrs. Kopecka has the best pastries on Thursday because she uses the rest of her sugar and jam before going to the market for her weekly Friday shopping trip.

I know there is a dent on the lower right side of the Pokorny's trash bin. I also know there is an almost invisible matching indent on the left side of the truck when Filip Pokorny decided he would take his dad's truck on the weekend he was gone fishing to see his girlfriend in Letovice. I watched the whole scenario from my perch in the tree one Saturday afternoon. The garbage can sounded like an orchestra cymbal as it banged against the truck and then flopped onto the street. Filip jumped out of the driver's seat with his hands on his head as if he was surrendering to the enemy. When he noticed no one else around, he quickly pulled the trash bin back to the curb, hopped in the truck, and whizzed off to Letovice. He figured out how to repair the dent to be hardly noticed, but I could still see the shadowed outline. I kept his secret for months until I realized I was about to fail mathematics before the school year ended, so I walked straight up to Filip and said, "I need you to tutor me in math."

"Why would I do that?"

I wouldn't call it blackmail exactly because he also had a secret of mine — if Mother ever found out I was failing math, I would have less freedom than a condemned prisoner, who are at least granted visitation rights. A strange friendship formed as we both carried vital secrets, but I passed math that year.

I know the best wild blueberries in all of Lazinov grow in a grove up the east hill. When I didn't want to risk going home for lunch and get roped into helping Mother, I'd fill my belly with handful after handful of blueberries. My lips and fingers dyed a blueish-purple from the sticky, little berries, which is difficult to hide from my suspecting mother. The first time, she thought I was terribly ill, complaining of a stomachache and displaying frightening blue lips. She called Doc Daniel, who was a doctor before the last ten years of retirement. He asked me to open my mouth so he could look down my throat. After finding the tip of my tongue also blue, he pried open my hands revealing my spotted fingertips. Mother was embarrassed and hasn't been fooled since.

I know a storm is coming when I see Mr. Halas bring his rocking chair out onto his front doorstep. He can always sense when a storm is coming over the valley and watches the lightning display as if it were a firework production.

I know the Svoboda twins always get on the bus with Viktor first followed by Vojta because Viktor likes to sit by the window, and Vojta likes to stretch his legs into the bus aisle between stops. They always sit together to and from school, and most people can't tell them apart, but I know who is who — after they get on the bus, at least.

My head was spinning with all the thoughts of Lazinov, and in a desperate state of trying to forget the horrible morning, I laid down on the grass and fell asleep. I'm not sure how long I slept, but it was lunchtime when I woke up. The midday bell was my alarm. I guessed Mother had sent Patja to look for me because next to me in the grass was my backpack. I sat up and reached over to pull the backpack into my lap. At the top of the bag was a sandwich smushed under a bottle of water. Under the sandwich were my sneakers, tied together by the laces.

Mother must have realized I ran out without my shoes and sent them with Patja. There was even a pair of socks rolled into one of the shoes. At the bottom of my backpack was my journal. I'm grateful I had thought to put it in the backpack under my bed last night. Maybe Patja or Mother had grabbed the backpack without knowing the journal was at the bottom of the bag. I pulled out the journal and saw it was tied closed with a pink ribbon that held a pen nestled up against the binding. I was puzzled. Neither Patja nor Mother would have tied the pen on with a pink ribbon. They wouldn't have dared to touch the journal even if they knew it was in the backpack. Then, I understood it was neither Mother nor Patja who had come to my rescue with the care package. One name came from my lips as soft as a puff air — Marie.

June 18, 1994
— Krista

The sun had just started peeking through the drapes when Krista's eyelids bounced open. Saturday morning. She had been waiting all week for today. After arriving back at Zofie and Jakub's house last Sunday, Krista couldn't stop ravishing about her new friend, Madla. Zofie was thrilled her niece had found a friend who would listen for as much as she chatters and was equally pleased Krista found a friend closer to her age. Zofie had become very fond of Krista in the week she had already been at their house but knew the fourteen-year-old would get bored if she spent the rest of the summer in the backyard with the adults. That evening after the soccer game,

Krista asked, "Do you think you could call Karel and see if Madla can come over tomorrow?"

"I am sure Madla would take any excuse to skip school," laughed Zofie.

"School? It's June."

"That's right. Our kids go to school through June."

"They only have two months of summer?"

"Right again! Didn't your parents tell you about when they went to school here?"

"They don't tell me much about when they were here at all."

Zofie's large, dark eyes swept over Krista with compassion. "I understand. Still, Madla needs to focus on school this month. She's in enough trouble with the teacher during the year for talking in class. I'm not sure how the teacher will grade her final exams after the year she's had."

"Oh," Krista sighed and tapped her toes together.

"Maybe I can call Karel and see if Madla has a free weekend. It might motivate her to study more during the week rather than leaving all her projects to finish on Sunday night." Zofie lifted the phone off the receiver and dialed the number she knew by heart. Krista heard Karel on the other end and an excited Madla piping up in the background promising her dad she would study during the week.

Saturday finally arrived. Zofie's prophetic wisdom rang true as Krista had undoubtedly gotten stir-crazy the past couple of days at the house. Every now and then, she ventured into the city, but without a friend to share the time with, she spent most of the day simply shuffling between tasks at the house. She had finished reading her book days ago, reluctant to start the next one and criticizing her decision to only pack two novels. All that didn't matter now because she was finally meeting with Madla again today.

Krista tossed back the covers and slipped into a pair of jeans. She quietly opened the wardrobe to avoid waking her parents as she rummaged through her pile of t-shirts. She landed on a faded brown shirt with a little cabin sketch on the pocket. In small printed letters under the pocket, it read "Camp Pinewood." Krista pulled the t-shirt over her head, remembering when she and Ruthie bought the matching shirts last summer at camp. She had reminded Ruthie to get a new shirt for her this summer at Pinewood since she was missing camp for the first time in six years. She wondered who would share a bunk bed with Ruthie this year and if she had remembered to pack a flashlight. Krista thought of Ruthie waking her up in the middle of the night, saying she needed to go to the bathroom and that Krista had to go with her because Ruthie didn't have a flashlight. Krista had always assumed it was because her best friend forgot to pack a flashlight, but as they got older, Krista learned Ruthie was afraid to walk outside at night, even if it was just across the trail to the restroom.

Krista reached up to her neck and pinched the half-heart necklace as she momentarily thought again of her best friend. She almost wished she could be back home with Ruthie at camp, but her excitement to spend the day with Madla quickly brought her back to the present.

Krista slipped from the bedroom and quietly closed the door behind her. She walked into the kitchen and found Zofie sitting at the table with a cup of coffee and a magazine.

"Someone's up early," Zofie's voice rasped from the early morning conversation.

"Yeah, I guess I'm excited to see Madla and to actually do something today, no offense."

"None taken. I assumed you would get a little edgy being stuck in this place after a while."

"That's for sure."

Glancing at Krista's outfit, Zofie said, "You'll need to change clothes before you go. It is supposed to be the hottest day yet. Put on a pair of shorts. Actually, bring your swimsuit. I'll bet Karel brings you to the lake today."

"The lake?"

"It's actually a reservoir, but it's quite large and a good place to go for a swim on a hot day like today."

Krista shrugged. She was familiar with lakes growing up in the Midwestern United States. She always enjoyed lake activities at camp and riding Mr. Everson's motorboat on fishing outings, but Krista had never visited a dam before.

A couple of hours later, Krista had eaten breakfast, helped Zofie wash the dishes, and read the first chapter of her second novel before Karel pulled into the short driveway. Madla and Kai jumped out of the car. They had only been sitting for the five-minute journey to their aunt and uncle's house but were ready to free their legs. Madla swung open the front door, knowing her aunt would have unlocked it for their arrival. With Kai close at her heels, she bounded into the kitchen calling, "Aunt Zofie!" Nearly colliding with her uncle, Madla skirted around him while Kai leaped onto Jakub's leg, begging for a ride. Madla found Zofie in the kitchen and started, "Hi, Aunt Zofie! Is Krista ready? I need to tell her to bring a swimsuit because Daddy said we can go swimming today. It is already getting really warm outside, and it isn't even lunchtime yet! I packed us some sandwiches for lunch, and I made one for Krista too, so you don't need to worry about packing her lunch. Aunt Zofie, you wouldn't believe it, I already finished all my homework for this weekend! I did everything after school yesterday because I wanted to go with Krista today. Isn't that great?"

It must have been a rhetorical question because, before Zofie could answer, Madla was already skipping through the hall looking for Krista. Karel came into the kitchen next followed by Jakub, who was limping from the eight-year-old weight that clung to his foot. Karel rested his elbows on the counter, and Zofie slid a full mug of coffee next to him.

"For me?" he asked.

"You, dear little brother, will need much caffeine to keep up with those kids today," Zofie consoled.

"Where's my coffee?" asked Jakub.

"I'll make another for you. Just wait for the water to boil," Zofie said.

"You mean that was *my* coffee?" Jakub teasingly glared at his brother-in-law, whose lips already curved around the steaming cup.

"Oh, I'm sorry, would *you* like to take these children all day?" Zofie sarcastically asked her husband as she waved her arms around, indicating the zig-zagging children.

"Enjoy that cup, my friend. It sounds like it comes with a death sentence," Jakub said to Karel.

"Nah, the kids will be fine when they are outside, running around and swimming. They shouldn't be a problem at all," Karel smiled.

"You have youth on your side as well," Jakub stated as he ran his hand over his balding head.

"And you have a ball and chains," said Karel.

"Excuse me!" Zofie whipped around, nearly spilling the container of sugar in her hand, ready to meet her insulter.

Karel simply pointed at Kai, who still clung to Jakub's leg like a weight. "Relax, Zofie!"

Jakub gave a deep belly laugh as Rick and Doma strolled into the kitchen. "What's all the racket?" asked Rick.

"Ball and chains joke," Karel said between laughs pointing at Kai, who still clung to his uncle's leg.

"Oh! That's a good one!" Rick laughed along.

Zofie rolled her eyes and put her arm around Doma. "What will we do with the three of them? Looks like us women have to stick together."

The adults were just about finished with their morning coffee when Krista, Madla, and Kai approached the table.

"Can we please go now?" Madla tugged her dad's sleeve.

"Please, Daddy," Kai pleaded along with his sister.

Karel took one last gulp of his coffee before he pushed himself up from the table and said, "Better get into the car; the vehicle will be departing shortly." He winked at the kids, and the three of them started moving toward the front door.

"Krista, hold up," Rick called. "Help Karel with Madla and Kai today; you're the oldest."

Krista nodded in agreement, "It'll be easy, Dad; they're my friends."

"Do you have everything you need?" Doma asked.

"Yep!" Looking in her bag, she made a verbal checklist, "Swimsuit, towel, and sunscreen."

"You're going to the pool?" asked Doma.

"The lake," replied Krista. "Or I guess Zofie said it's a reservoir."

Doma nearly dropped her mug of coffee. "The dam?" Doma's judging gaze fell upon Karel.

"Is that okay, Mom?" Krista asked, suddenly aware that she had forgotten to ask her parents for permission.

"That's alright, Krista, just be careful. The water is deep and drops off quickly," Rick answered for both himself and his wife. Then, he smiled, "And make sure to have lots of fun!" He blew her a kiss as Krista leaned over to give her mom a quick hug goodbye.

"Yes, have fun," Doma sighed, her shoulders slouched forward. She gave Krista a small peck on her cheek and sent her on her way.

"It's hot back here," Kai called up to the front seat.

Karel grabbed the lever on his left side and began rolling down his window, motioning for Krista to do the same on the passenger side.

"Better?" he called back.

The kids' answers were lost in the sound of the wind rushing through the car. Krista's hair whipped around in a tiny tornado attached to her head. She pulled the scrunchy from around her wrist and was able to grab most of her hair into a ponytail. She rested her arm on the window ledge and let the aerodynamics wave her hand up and down. They drove on a winding road around short but steep, rocky cliffs that were covered with tall trees, their roots clinging to the edges of stones.

The forest abruptly ended and, before her, Krista looked across a body of water that sparkled as if a kindergartener had spilled a layer of glitter over the water. It was a tint of blue so deep and bold that it reminded her of the blue jeans she had taken off earlier that morning. A line of trees reappeared, partially blocking the view of the water until it suddenly felt as if they were flying over the lake. Krista's eyes scanned over the bridge down the long drop to the water below. Not far from the end of the bridge, Karel turned into a dirt parking lot that overlooked a rocky shoreline. Madla and Kai jumped out of the car as their dad pulled up the parking brake, their towels unfolding and flying behind them like kites ready to be launched above the water. Krista sat taking in the beauty of the landscape; the little ruffles of hills that hosted small clusters of homes on the horizon, the land beyond the lake alternating fields and forests, and the sapphire ripples on the water that reminded her nothing of the murky, algae-filled lakes she had grown familiar within the American Midwest. The passenger door creaked open, and Karel peered over the doorframe.

"You ready?" he asked.

"You bet!" Krista exclaimed as she catapulted the seatbelt from the clasp.

She walked down the sloped path to the shore with Karel, careful not to slip on the loose gravel that rolled to the base of the path. At the water's edge, Krista watched the little waves lap hungrily at the rocks along the shore. She stepped on the heels of her shoes and launched them off her feet. Krista cautiously moved over the rocks with her bare feet until she stood before the water's edge. As the rippling tide rolled up over the pebbles again, it hugged the base of Krista's feet for a moment before retreating. Krista took a breath as if breathing in from a straw and curled her toes under her feet.

"Oh!" she exclaimed, taking a step back before the next wave reached her toes. "I don't know if we will be doing much swimming today. That water is frigid!"

Madla and Kai looked at Krista with wondering eyes; Kai cocked his head to the right like a curious puppy. Suddenly aware that she had been speaking in English, Krista repeated in Czech, "It's cold water. We won't go swimming today."

"We just have to get used to it," said Kai as he pulled off his sandals and stepped ankle-deep into the water. "See?"

Madla stood by her brother. "It's so hot today and the best way to cool off is to make sure your head and feet are cool too! That's why we have on caps." She pointed to the sunhat atop her head and a cap that was beginning to be too small for Kai's head. Then she added, "Even little kids know this. What do you do when it is hot in America?"

"We turn on the AC and eat *Freezies*," Krista recalled, feeling like a naive foreigner.

"What are *Freezies*?" asked Kai.

"It's flavored ice that you eat." She motioned how the ice is squeezed from the plastic wrapping like a game of charades.

"You eat the ice? It isn't good for your stomach, and the ice makes your teeth tingle," Kai reprimanded.

Krista had never met a child who had a problem with *Freezies* but shrugged it off, thinking Kai had never tried it before. She made a mental note to ask Zofie to freeze some juice in a small container for Kai to try.

"It must be like ice-cream," suggested Madla. "I've had something similar once with crushed ice. It was blueberry flavored. My tongue turned blue after I drank the whole thing, and my head hurt from the cold!"

"Daddy said you should drink it slower," Kai scolded.

Madla huffed and rolled her eyes at Kai's comment. She knew she wasn't a patient person, but then again, neither was Kai.

"Come on. Let's walk along the shore a while," Madla changed the subject.

Krista took a breath before joining the other two in the ankle-deep water. They walked a short way over the rocky beach before Karel called to them to come back. The kids turned and, like they were on a tightrope rather than walking on grass, stretched their arms out and followed each other in a line back to where Karel lounged near the water's edge.

"It'll get warmer outside soon, and then maybe you would prefer swimming more than just walking in the water, but until then, I think I will sit right here and watch those sailboats." Karel pointed across the reservoir where two men were getting onto their sailboats and slowly moving with the wind deeper onto the water's surface. Kai scrambled up next to his dad, declaring, "Yeah, I think I will watch those sailboats, too."

Karel reached over to his son, straightened Kai's cap, and smiled back at the girls, "Well, ladies?"

"Can I show Krista all the canoes and rowboats around the bend?" Madla pointed in the direction she knew the boats were stored.

"Sure," Karel replied. Then, looking at Kai, he said loud enough for the girls to hear, "I don't know why they want to look at rowboats sitting on the shore when we are watching sailboats moving on the water!"

"Girls are strange," nodded Kai in agreement.

Madla looked at Krista and explained, "They're just teasing."

Krista smiled. She knew the act all too well from her dad and brother. Madla led the way as she and Krista continued to wade through the water in the direction of the boats.

"Sometimes, I get tired of entertaining Kai, so I'm really glad you're here now. Why are you visiting Czech anyway?" Madla abruptly began. "It doesn't make sense why you would visit Letovice. It's such a small city. I'd think you would have more fun in Prague. There are many more things to do there."

"My dad grew up in Letovice."

"Oh, right! He said he was classmates with my dad, so are you visiting because your parents always wanted to show you where they grew up?"

"Not exactly. We came to see my grandmother. She is sick." Krista was beginning to feel more confident in her language skills. She was comfortable speaking with Madla, though there wasn't much yet to say in the conversation.

"Oh, so your parents didn't tell you much about when they grew up here?"

Krista shook her head.

"Maybe you can ask your grandmother to tell you more. Grandmothers and grandfathers like sharing stories," Madla smiled at her brilliant idea.

"Grandmother is often tired. Maybe her memory isn't good now." Krista was pleased with herself for putting all the words together, even if it did still sound a bit choppy as she stumbled over words.

Madla's moment of brilliance was replaced with a downcast face, but it didn't last long as another lightbulb appeared to have lit. "Hey! What are your parents' names again? Maybe my dad has told me stories about them. After all, they went to school together."

Krista grinned, "Great idea! My dad is Rick, and my mom is Doma."

"My dad never mentioned Rick before, but remember he called your dad by his full name when they met on the street last week, so he must have only started using the name Rick when he moved to America. And 'Doma' isn't a name. It's a word."

"What?"

"The word 'doma' translates to 'home,'" Madla took pride in being about the translate one Czech word in the whole conversation to English. "It just means 'home,' it's not a name," Madla stated again.

"I know it means 'home,' but it is also short for Dominika."

"Nope, not in Czech. It isn't a nickname at all. It's just a word."

"Why would my mom be called 'house'?"

"Home."

"Huh?"

"Not 'house'; 'home'. It is two different words, you see? Either way, Daddy never talked about them in his stories."

"And my last name? Kopecka," Krista tried.

Madla's head shook, "Daddy doesn't use last names in his stories."

"It doesn't matter. Mom never told me her..." Krista didn't know how to say "maiden name" in Czech. "Her name before," she used instead. Whenever Krista had asked her mom about her maiden name, Doma simply said she left it behind when she married Rick, and that's all there was to it.

The girls rounded the corner, and Krista saw the bridge they had crossed earlier high above the water level. She considered why her mom would be called a simple word in her native language rather than a traditional name. *"Maybe it was a childhood nickname that just stuck,"* thought Krista, *"or maybe a friend in America simply started calling her Doma for short because it was easier."* Krista rattled over the ideas in her head, promising herself to ask her mom when she got back to Zofie's house.

Krista followed Madla under the bridge to a narrower section of the lake. Lying upon the bank of the right shore were over a dozen rowboats and a handful of canoes. All had been pulled onto the sloped bank and flipped over to prevent rain from pooling inside. With each rowboat a different size and painted an array of colors, the shore resembled a jumbled rainbow. Krista noticed the paint stripping from the bases of many of the little boats, and some she wouldn't put her faith in on the water. Madla ran up the shore to the rowboats and canoes, climbing over some and peering under others. It was a playground for the energetic eleven-year-old. Krista ran to catch up, and together, they weaved around the mismatched, wooden boats. At one point, they peeked under a canoe at the same time from opposite sides. Madla rolled onto her back giggling, while Krista crawled atop the canoe and looked down at Madla in the grass. Krista pulled her legs over the canoe and straddled it.

"You look like you're riding a horse!" laughed Madla. She pulled herself onto the canoe behind Krista. With one arm, she held onto Krista's waist and, with the other, shot her fist forward as if pointing a flag declaring, "Onward!"

"Where exactly?"

"The princess has been taken captive, and we, the knights, must prove our loyalty to the king! We must save the princess!"

"Aha! Well, the journey is bad." Krista played along as she leaned left and right, and then finally leaned back.

"This horse has lost control! Bail!" screeched Madla as she pulled Krista over the side of the canoe, sliding to the grass.

"We make horrible knights," Krista stuttered between laughs.

Still overcome with the case of the giggles, Madla clutched her ribcage and sat up. As she looked down at the shore, she noticed an elderly fisherman sitting near the edge of the water. He wasn't looking at his fishing line; rather, he seemed pleased to be watching the girls in their excitement. Holding onto his fishing pole with one hand, he gave Madla a small wave with the other.

"Hello!" she called down to the fisherman. "I hope we have not scared away your catch with our laughter."

"On the contrary. I believe the fish are curious about what could be making such a joyous noise because, as you can tell, it looks like I have a bite." The fisherman tilted his head toward the line that now bobbed in the water. He gave it a sharp yank and started reeling in his catch, but the fish hadn't completely hooked and quickly freed himself giving a defiant splash. "Ah, well. Next time, ol' friend," the fisherman called to the trout. He reeled in the rest of his line and gave it a satisfying cast back out over the water.

Krista watched the old fisherman for a moment, wondering if they should go back to Karel and Kai and leave this man to fish in peace. Her unspoken question was answered as the fisherman said, "Well, it is good that I have some company before the next fish bites."

Krista and Madla inched closer, intrigued by the elderly gentleman they had stumbled across. Krista rested her elbows on one of the flipped rowboats while Madla climbed up and sat with her feet dangling over the edge.

The fisherman moved his eyes between the girls. "Are you two sisters? Cousins, perhaps?"

Krista looked at Madla. Madla's eyes were like two melted Hershey Kisses, and her dark hair waved over her shoulders, creating thick puddles of hair whenever she laid down. Krista had looked in the mirror enough to know her hazel-green eyes looked almost muddy at times. Her hair was a lighter brown that often flew around her face in wisps before it frizzed into little curls that mimicked a messy robin's nest. For this reason, she kept her hair chopped just above her shoulders. Besides that, the start of summer had already brought a delicate tan that covered Madla's face. It made Krista wonder how Madla could get so much color while still sitting in a classroom for most of the week. The summer sun didn't bring a tan for Krista's porcelain skin, only some faded freckles lined the bridge of her nose and curled beneath her eyes.

"No, we're friends," answered Madla.

"Ah! I thought you might be related. You remind me of two siblings," replied the fisherman.

Krista's eyebrows scrunched together. "We do?"

"Yep, there were two kids who grew up in my village. They also had some fun adventures and spent more time splashing through the water than some of the farmers' ducks."

Madla's eyes glowed as she looked at Krista. "I always wanted a sister!" Then, to the fisherman, Madla babbled, "My name's Madla, and this is Krista. I just have a little brother.

Krista only has a brother too, so I guess, this summer, we are like sisters to each other."

"That's a gift," responded the fisherman. Then he added, "I'm Dave. Most people around here call me Fisherman Dave."

"Are you always fishing?" asked Madla.

"I didn't get the nickname just by chance. I come here as often as I can. I live nearby, so it is easy to get to. There isn't much for an old man to do around here other than sit and fish."

Madla piped in, "My dad told me a story about the fish in this lake once."

"A fish story! You have captured a fisherman's heart already," beamed Fisherman Dave as he patted his chest.

Madla started, "My dad said the fish in this lake are quite clever, much more clever than the fish in other lakes. That's probably why your fish got away, Mister Fisherman Dave because these fish are smart. Daddy said the fish in this lake saw all the homes in the village next to the shore and decided that they also wanted nice homes with walls, and doors, and windows, so the fish worked together and pulled bricks that had fallen into the water to build homes on the floor of the lake! My dad says that when the water level is low enough, you can see the tops of their houses just peeking above the waves."

Fisherman Dave gave a satisfied chuckle, "Well, Madla! That is quite a legend your dad has told you, and a good legend it is, but I have another story that may change your mind a bit."

"Oh! Tell us, please!" the girls begged.

Fisherman Dave started, "A long time ago, but really not that long ago, this lake wasn't here. It was a very deep valley with two rivers that joined at the base of the hills. There was a little village by the river, and people lived there quite happily. One day, the villagers heard of a problem that there was too much water in their country and not enough place to keep the water. This meant that there weren't homes for all the fish. The villagers knew it was important to take care of the fish and their country, so they moved away from their village and built new homes. They gave their homes in the valley to the fish so they could have the nicest place to live. Some men came and flooded the valley by creating the dam, and the fish moved into the homes of the villagers." Fisherman Dave smiled at the girls, and looking at Madla, he continued, "So, like your dad said, when the water level is low, we can sometimes see the tops of the old, flooded houses in the lake. It is a reminder for us about the gift we gave the fish many years ago."

"Wow! That's neat. Who told you this legend?" asked Madla.

Fisherman Dave looked over the water. "No one told me this story. I was one of many who gave up my home for the fish."

August 11, 1972
— Niky

I spent all of today avoiding Mother and Dad. I stayed in my room until after they were done eating breakfast. Dad had left for work all day, so I only had to worry about Mother and Marie at home. I don't understand how this isn't harder for everyone.

When I got back yesterday, Mother and Dad were in the living room explaining to Marie the fate of Lazinov. When Dad explained we would need to move houses, and she would have more room in the new house and could go swimming in the new lake created by the dam, she was convinced flooding Lazinov was a splendid idea. I coughed from the doorway of the living room, letting my parents know I was there, and then sprang up the steps to my room and fell over my covers. Marie came into the room a short while later. I'm sure Mother and Dad had also mentioned my disdain for the small amenities of added bedroom space and an oversized swimming pool in my backyard. My sister didn't say anything to me until she switched off the lamp, then I heard a whispered "goodnight." It was impossible to sleep last night. I dreamed I was in my house as the water pooled over my feet and rose from my ankles to my neck. I woke in a sweat and fitfully tossed around in my bed until morning. How would I ever be able to close my eyes again after that?

Today during lunchtime, I complained of a stomachache and had soup in my room. I was impressed, I didn't even need to feign a stomachache as my belly gurgled and sloshed, likely still affected by all the sprinting and crying yesterday. Mother was concerned it could be the stomach flu again. Attendees from Scouts and Pioneer summer camps had come back early with symptoms of the contagious virus last week. Even though I did my camp credit earlier this summer, I didn't argue as

Mother ushered Marie out of the room in fear that she would soon fall ill as well. After Dad got home in the late afternoon, Mother came to check on me. She was certain then that it wasn't a flu virus but brought Marie's bedding downstairs for her to bunk in my parents' room overnight.

All day, I laid in bed, flipping through the pages of my *Rodents and Reptiles Nature Guide*. I think I can recite every word in that book now. While Mother was in the garden, I sat on the stairs and listened to one of Marie's records playing in the living room. I couldn't hear all of the words since she had the door to the Mother and Dad's bedroom closed. I'm sure Mother had told her to stay quiet while I rested. The songs are childish and repetitive anyway. I was finally able to nap in the afternoon. Getting so little sleep the night before, I was still as a rock but probably slept too long and too close to my regular bedtime. Not that it mattered to me if I was awake at night and asleep during the day.

It had already been dark outside for over an hour when I saw a beam of light flicker over the window. As it came back for a second pass, I was already moving to open the window. I pulled the handle, and the window swung back. Patja was sitting in the window in the house opposite mine, swinging the flashlight back and forth.

"I knew you wouldn't be sleeping," Patja said.

Best friends just know. I glanced down to my parents' window below my own and noticed it was cracked ajar. I pointed cautiously at the window for Patja to see. I didn't want my parents to join in our midnight conversation. Patja pointed at the fence that enclosed our properties from the road. I

73

nodded in agreement to meet there. Patja swung out onto the sloped roof next to the window and scooted over the shingles to the corner. I watched Patja grip the edge of the roof doing a reverse pull-up to descend onto a stack of wood. Somehow, Patja had stacked the logs into a perfect staircase without raising any suspicions from parents or neighbors. I congratulated my friend on the successful escape and knew I somehow had to manage to leave without getting caught also. I slipped on a pair of overalls over my nightclothes, the left strap loosely fell over my shoulder. Then, as quietly as I could, I tiptoed down the stairs. I made it down with limited creaks of the floorboards and prided myself in one the quietest escapes I have made yet, but my joy came before the chickens had hatched.

"What are you doing?" came a groggy whisper from behind — Marie.

I spun around. "I'm going to make tea," I lied.

"For your stomach?"

Clutching my abdomen, I faked a groan, "Yeah."

"Maybe I should wake up Mother." Marie seemed genuinely concerned.

"It's nothing, Marie. Mother would just give me tea and send me to bed anyway. I'll do it myself."

"Alright," Marie yawned. "I'm going to the toilet."

I waited in the kitchen until I heard Marie come out of the bathroom. I quickly grabbed a mug as she peeked her head around the kitchen doorway.

"Goodnight, Niky. Feel better." She gave a little wave before shuffling back across the hall to Mother and Dad's

room. Placing the mug on the counter, I pushed open the window above the sink and in one swift motion, crouched into the window frame and silently leaped out.

It was only a couple of steps before I was through the gate and found Patja sitting, leaned up against the fence on the other side.

"I was starting to think I should have brought something to do while I waited," Patja teased. I stuck out my tongue.

Then, I said, "Marie saw me. I had to make an excuse."

"Aha! And you still made it out of the mouth of the lion. I applaud you, knight of valor!"

"Stop mocking!" I shoved Patja, who shoved me back.

We sat there quietly for a moment listening to the croaks of the frogs that hid around the banks of the river. Finally, Patja asked, "You haven't been around for a couple of days. You took the news about the village pretty hard, huh?"

I rested my head against the fence and sighed, "I can't imagine this all underwater. Why isn't everyone else more upset?"

"I guess they've had more time to process it all. The politicians told them of the plans to flood the valley last April. My dad said that most people knew four months ago, but that many of the parents had decided to wait to tell the kids until it was completely necessary."

I exploded, "They've known since April! I hate that they treat us like kids." I pounded my fist on the soft earth and then continued, "I don't understand why they have to flood the river here. Can't they get electricity another way?"

"Electricity? I guess that is in the future plan, but my parents told me that they are making the dam now because our river feeds into a bigger one in Letovice. That river goes all the way to the southern border of Czechoslovakia, and they have had a lot of problems with flooding in the past, so the government decided to dam our river since it is one of the biggest feeders into the main river."

"They are flooding our village to prevent flooding of other villages?" I grew furious. No wonder Mother and Dad didn't tell me that part. The logic seemed flawed in my book.

"You make a good argument," Patja agreed. "Except that the villages along the river aren't villages, but cities with many more people than in Lazinov."

"Whose side are you on?" I condescendingly asked.

Patja's head bobbled, looking for the option of lesser evil.

"Why don't they just dam the big river somewhere along the way?"

"I asked my dad that too, and he said besides the major cities along this river, there is also the main railway line between Prague and Austria, so they can't dam the water there because it would block the railways and cities."

"Pathetic," I huffed. "We have to try to do something about it."

"Like what?"

"I don't know. Maybe we can change the minds of the villagers? Protest?"

"Nik, I don't think any of the villagers are entirely happy about this right now, but we can't change it. The government decided, not us."

Patja tossed a stone across the road, and a frightened field mouse darted up the path and through a space in the fence. Neither of us spoke for a while.

"I've decided then," I finally stated. "I will not be here to watch my home flooded."

"It'll probably take them years to complete."

"Then, I guess I have years to prepare."

"Prepare for what?"

"Running away."

"Where? Things like this are happening to villages all over the country, not just in Lazinov."

"Running away from all of this. Out of the country," I clarified. "I'm fed up with these communist rules and limitations on everything we do, and now they destroy villages that are centuries old. It's appalling the control they have on us." I looked at my best friend, waiting for Patja to give some excuse or tell me that I'm crazy, that I hadn't thought through all the consequences of what I was saying; all valid statements, but Patja sat still. "Well?" I raised my eyebrows.

It was silent for a few moments longer. Finally, I heard Patja's teeth grind before asking, "You really want to leave?"

I nodded.

Patja's eyes focused on mine before saying three little words, "Count me in."

June 19, 1994
— Krista

The sun streamed into the living room through the thin lace curtains and beams of sunlight draped over the sofa onto the carpeted floor. Krista shielded her sleepy eyes with her right hand as her left arm rolled over the edge of the couch. Her eyes nudged open with the realization she had fallen asleep in Zofie's living room after dinner last night. Someone had covered her with a knitted beige blanket that she had successfully kicked off her right leg. Krista had been tired after their day at the dam, but she hadn't expected to fall asleep on the couch so shortly after arriving back at Zofie and Jakub's house.

She recalled Kai fell asleep after pulling out of the parking lot, his head bobbing with the movement of the car. Madla had been unusually quiet as she rubbed a smooth stone from the lake in the palm of her hands. The day of fun had worn off her chatter. Karel flipped on the radio as they drove back into the city. It wasn't long before Karel pulled into Zofie and Jakub's driveway, and Krista hopped out. Madla gave a wave followed by an adamant "goodbye," and Karel promised another trip to the lake the following weekend.

As Krista closed the car door, Kai awoke and mumbled something from the backseat, but Krista saw his head bobble again as Karel steered down the sloped street to Letovice's center. She noticed the sky was already fading to pink as sunset approached, and Krista wondered how the day had escaped so fast. Krista found the adults sitting around the kitchen table just as she had left them, though this time, instead of drinking coffee, they were finishing dinner. Krista dropped her knapsack on the floor and slid into the empty seat at the table. Though she had eaten a picnic lunch at the lake, Krista realized her stomach was once again telling her it was time to recharge.

The adults all welcomed her back, and Doma kissed Krista's forehead before grabbing another plate from the cupboard for Krista's dinner. Krista shoveled pasta salad and a pile of cucumbers onto the plate and mixed it around with the dressing before taking a bite. Though their conversation had been in Czech before Krista's return, they naturally switched over to English for Krista's comfort.

"Did you enjoy the reservoir, dear?" Zofie smiled.

Through spoonfuls of food, Krista shared, "We were swimming the whole afternoon! Dad was right; it does drop off quickly, but Madla's a good swimmer, and Kai used a floaty to rest his arms above the water when it was deeper. Kai also found a stick that floated on the water, and he would throw it out a little way, so Madla and I would race to see who could swim to it first. Sometimes, I let Madla have a head-start."

"It sounds like you had a nice time," Doma said from the sink, where she was washing the dinner plates.

"I bet it was busy at the lake. It was boiling hot here. We just sat in the shade in the garden and drank lemonade all afternoon," said Jakub.

"It was busy after lunch. We set up a picnic on the shore, and after we finished the sandwiches and fruit salad, the water was full of people! I was surprised how quickly everyone arrived," Krista shared.

"Did you go swimming before lunch too?" Zofie questioned.

"The water was still cool in the morning, so we soaked our feet but didn't go swimming until later. Kai and Karel watched the sailboats and looked for colorful rocks while Madla and I walked along the shore to a place where they keep all the rowboats. We played a game there and even met a fisherman!"

"Ah! The fishermen love that spot on the lake. I often see them sitting there when I drive past," stated Jakub.

"There was only one fisherman near the rowboats, but I saw more sitting further down the cove," Krista explained. "The fisherman was very friendly, and maybe he just wanted someone to talk with. He told me and Madla we remind him of some kids from his village, and then he shared a fisherman's legend with us." Though her eyes drooped from exhaustion, Krista was excited to tell her parents and hosts about the day's activities.

"That all sounds wonderful, Krista," said Doma. Turning to the rest of the adults, she continued, "I think I will turn in for the evening. I have some letters I need to finish." She excused herself from the room and squeezed Rick's shoulder on the way out the door. Zofie stacked the remaining dishes on the table to be washed as Krista scooped the last spoonful of pasta salad into her mouth.

"Is Mom tired too?" Krista asked Rick, yet wondering if she had said something to make her mom turn in earlier than normal.

"It was a hot day. The heat makes us all tired," Rick consoled.

Remembering the question she wanted to ask that Madla had stirred within her, Krista inquired, "Dad? Why is Mom called Doma? Madla told me today that it is just a word meaning 'home.' I already knew it meant 'home,' but I thought it was a name too."

Rick rocked his head in contemplation as Krista twirled her hair around the tip of her finger.

"Your mom knows it isn't a Czech name, but it was easier just to be called Doma when we moved to America," offered Rick.

Taking a step of courage, Krista continued, "Can you tell me more about when you moved to America?"

Rick smiled at his daughter. "You know we moved to the US with the help of Pastor Everson and the church. They sponsored us to come to America and supported your mother and me when we needed help at the start."

This wasn't new information for Krista. This is the part of the story she already knew. It was the pieces before that didn't come together. Though, she hesitated to ask any more questions sensing her dad had given her only so much for a reason.

Zofie jumped in before Krista had worked up the courage to ask further, "Krista, have a seat on the sofa. I'll bring you some honey cake for dessert."

"I can bring it to her," said Jakub, licking his lips.

"I am sure Krista doesn't want a bite out of her slice from your greedy sweet tooth!" teased Zofie as she tucked a strand of silvering hair under her bandana. In the kitchen, she got the last slice of honey cake from a plate in the refrigerator.

Krista added her dishes to the stack on the table and moved over to the sofa. She was convinced her dad sidestepped telling more of his past and wondered if her mom had not only chosen the shortened name for simplicity in English but if there was a deeper meaning to the nickname she carried.

It seemed Jakub enjoyed Krista's dessert after all because, by morning, an empty plate sat on the coffee table. Though, Krista wasn't thinking of the honey cake when she embraced an early bedtime. As she pulled her feet up on the sofa cushions, she was jumping between two thoughts: the untold mystery of her parents' past and how to make *Freezies* for Kai and Madla.

September 1, 1972
— Niky

The bus only comes to Lazinov three times a day — once in the morning, once in the afternoon, and once late in the evening. Mainly to bring us students to and from school and the occasional worker to Letovice. Last year, Ms. Novak came with us in the morning because she worked at the post office, but she is very pregnant now and wobbles so much that she said herself it is good there are no little ducklings this time of year, or they would surely follow her around the village! She was a bit worried this morning since little Katerina is starting her first year at school, but we all promised to watch out for her in the hallways and make sure she got on the bus back home after the school bell rang. *Lazinov is a long and narrow village, and while it is written that there is only one bus stop on the schedule, the bus driver is kind and makes an extra stop at the end of the street next to Dvorak's farm.*

We stood in line, waiting for the bus: Viktor, followed closely by his twin Vojta (those two will never change habits), Katerina who clung to Marie's hand, me, Patja, and lastly, Karel — who almost missed the bus because he spent too much time begging Filip for a ride to school in his dad's truck.

We sat on the bus in a similar fashion: Viktor and Vojta, Katerina and Marie, me and Patja, and Karel behind us, pouting that he had to ride the bus. Patja sat uncharacteristically still, staring out the window.

"Are you dreading school already?" I pried.

Patja's head shook.

"Then, what's wrong?"

"You're not going to like it."

"Come on, Patja, just tell me what's bothering you."

Patja looked at me with eyes that only a best friend could read. This was bad.

"I can handle it," my voice shook, wondering what news laid before me.

Patja started, "This morning, my parents told me we wouldn't be rebuilding our house in the new Lazinov location for after the flooding. They said we would move to Letovice. Once the dam's built, they're going to destroy the mill. My dad said it'd take too long to rebuild the mill, and they're not even sure if they would rebuild it, so it's best if we move before the dam is finished."

My mouth went dry. No words formed on my lips. It was the worst first-day-of-school, and it had just begun.

Patja stumbled over the words, "Dad said we don't have to move soon, but my parents are starting to look at some real-estate in Letovice. I guess I'll still be close, Nik, just not like living next door."

"Hey! I'm moving to Letovice too," Karel jumped in our private conversation.

"What?" I couldn't believe both Patja's and Karel's families are leaving just because of the dam. I felt if we all stayed together, we could make it work, but then again, I'm planning to leave too, aren't I?

"Yeah, my dad said the same thing to my mom about the mill closing, but I'll be moving much sooner. My older sister, Zofie, just got married a year ago. She and her husband have been living in a tiny apartment, but just found a nice, two-level home that is really like two separate apartments. Since my parents told them last April about what would be happening to Lazinov, my brother-in-law found the place for all of us to live together."

I slouched in my seat and gripped the armrest until my fingers were stiff.

After school, I made sure Marie walked Katerina home while Patja and I headed to the climbing tree. We dropped our backpacks at the edge of Dvorak's fence, and Patja, in a general fashion, declared, "Race me." I won — again. We stayed there for hours, just me and Patja, as if nothing was different. It made me almost forget about the terrible news from the bus ride. Patja went back to the fence for our backpacks filled with homework — the reward for being second place in the race. We finished most of our homework together. Patja read the chapter of our history textbook faster; I got distracted by a tiny spider that crawled over my knuckles like little mountains. I stayed at the tree until the evening bell; Patja had gone home earlier to help prepare for dinner. As I slipped my books into the backpack, my fingers touched the spine of the journal.

I knew I needed to write about today, to get it out of my head and onto the paper. It's okay if I'm a little late today. It's likely Mother saw Patja come home and asked where I was. Maybe Mother also knows of the plans our neighbors have to move. She'd understand why I'm a little late coming home today; at least, I hope she understands.

June 25, 1994
— Krista

Krista thought weekdays trudged along like a lost snail. She often joined Zofie in the garden, though occasionally still accompanied her parents to the nursing home. While Krista's grandmother greeted her by name, she often asked questions Krista had already answered. She wasn't sure if her grandmother had forgotten what she had already asked or if she simply couldn't think of any other conversation starters. After all, what should she ask a granddaughter she never met before? The walk to the nursing home had been exciting for the first week. Each cottage-like house and every rock that formed the cobblestone streets grabbed Krista's interest all the way to the door of the old monastery, but she had long since memorized each little home and the cobblestones now hurt her feet. Spending mornings with Zofie in the garden had proven to entertain Krista a bit more than the long walk through the city to the sterile nursing home.

She'd help Zofie weed and water the vegetable garden, tend to the flowers, and collect plums that had fallen from the tree for jam. It wasn't the tedious tasks that thrilled Krista, but conversations with Zofie in Czech was more than her grandmother could offer. While Krista's ability to understand had already been pretty well mastered before arriving, her speaking skills had extended to bounds she herself didn't know she was capable of. Zofie would only say, "I knew a smart girl like you would catch onto speaking quickly. When one listens as well as you do, speaking is just as natural."

Besides the mornings with Zofie, two other things helped Krista get through the long days; knowing that the weekend would bring another day trip with Madla and finally receiving a letter from Ruthie. Krista's parents arrived home after lunch on Wednesday with the letter. The corners were smushed, and the stamps looped around part of the backside of the envelope. Krista knew right away Ruthie had sent the letter from camp because there was a stamp on the seal that read "Love from Camp Pinewood." She took the letter and rushed to the balcony to read it in the summer breeze while her parents retreated to their regular afternoon coffee chat in the dining room. Krista sat with her knees up to her chest on the cool wooden planks of the balcony as she tugged the seal on the envelope, successfully splitting the Camp Pinewood logo in two.

Krista pulled out a folded-up piece of notebook paper that was covered with Ruthie's handwriting. The envelope also included a sew-on patch of Camp Pinewood's logo and a postcard picture of the campgrounds. On the back of the postcard, Ruthie had written in big block letters, *"I wish you were here!"* Krista smiled as she set the patch and postcard to the side, knowing Ruthie had chosen them from the souvenir shop. She unfolded the note from Ruthie, bending the creases backward to flatten the page.

Hello Krista!

I like to think that, while everyone else at camp is writing letters back home that they will see on their dining room table in three days, my letter will still be traveling across the ocean to reach you! Camp has been so much fun this year (of course, not at fun as when you are here too, but it will have to do). I'm in Cabin 4, the one on the little hill that overlooks the lake. When I got to the cabin on the first day, some girls were already unrolling their sleeping bags and sliding suitcases underneath the bunks. I chose the bottom bed of the bunk bed closest to the front door since there is a light on the doorstep that shines through the window.

Although, I did bring my own flashlight this year and sleep with it like one of the younger campers would cuddle a teddy bear! I share the bunk bed with Alice, you know, from our church? She's a good bunkmate, even if she doesn't stay up late whispering like we normally did after "lights out." We finally won Capture-the-Flag this year and they taught us how to make friendship bracelets in the craft hall. Everyone's wrists look like rainbows with all the colorful bracelets.

While we were in the craft hall, weaving bracelets, one of the campers spilled the whole bottle of glitter. We were all immediately infected. When the camper accidentally dropped the container, it didn't just spill over the floor; the bottle hit the ground, causing the glitter to explode upward like a volcano. The sparkly dust blanketed everyone's head with a fine layer! The counselors told us all to go to the showers, but the water only caused the glitter to stick to our scalps better. Now, the craft hall director says we are all prepared to be angels when we perform our cabin skits on the last day of camp.

The theme of camp this year was "Heroic," so the program speakers talked mostly about heroes. Sometimes, historical heroes, but also modern heroes who did the right thing when no one else did. I like listening to the stories at Program and talking more about it at the campfire in the evening with the counselors. I see Jack every day. All the boys in his cabin really like him, and they always win the competitions — I think we only won Capture-the-Flag because Jack's cabin was our Buddy Team for the competition, but don't tell Alice because she thinks it was our defense that won the game!

I miss you lots, Krista. I can't wait until the end of summer when you come back home again! Keep taking pictures for me.

Love,

Ruthie

P.S. I wear my Best Friend necklace every day! Do you too?

Krista automatically reached up to grab the chain around her neck and twisted the half-heart between her fingers. She refolded the letter, slipped it back into the envelope, and went to ask Zofie if she could sew the new patch on the front of her knapsack.

Ruthie's letter had arrived three days ago, but Krista reread the note every day as she composed a letter back to her best friend. She told Ruthie about Madla and her lopsided pigtails, about helping Zofie in the backyard, and she lavished out details of the Saturday she spent at the dam. Krista had already filled up two notebook pages of stories for Ruthie. She pulled the third piece of paper out from her notebook and picked away the rumpled edges that had held the spine of the notebook. She set the clean paper on her pillow next to the ones that were already scribbled with notes. It was all prepared for when she would come back from her day at the reservoir.

It was finally Saturday again. Krista had waited all week, even counted the hours until she returned to the banks of the lake with Madla. This Saturday started similar to the one before. Kai and Karel sat on the shore to watch sailboats glide over the glassy water while Madla and Krista ventured back to the cove.

Madla elaborated on her last days of school before asking, "How is it that you can be here so long before school finishes?"

"My school finishes in May," Krista explained and then added, "We have three months of summer."

Madla's envious eyes pierced Krista. "Lucky. I wish we had Summer Holiday for three months. How can your parents be off from work for so long? My dad works all summer, so Kai and I spend most of our days with Aunt Zofie. Do adults in America also have three months of holiday from work?"

Krista gave a little laugh. "No. Mom is a high school teacher of Earth Biology, and Dad works at a university to help students from other countries feel comfortable. They also have summer holidays, but this isn't normal in America." Krista mentally patted herself on the back. She had only stumbled over a few words, but the mornings of practicing with Zofie were evident.

They rounded the shore, and the girls noticed a familiar elderly man seated in the cove. "Mister Fisherman Dave is here!" exclaimed Madla.

Fisherman Dave heard the girls and gave a wave with one arm while still gripping his fishing pole in the other. Madla and Krista quickened their pace to reach the friend they had made the week before.

"Well! Hello, girls!" Fisherman Dave gave a kind smile. "I was hoping someone would come by and want to chat with an old fisherman like myself."

"We were hoping you would be here to tell us more stories too, Mister Fisherman Dave," Madla beamed. Madla, the one who normally does all the talking, had finally taken an interest in someone else's stories. Krista figured Madla just needed more material to talk about with Zofie and Jakub, who have heard all of her stories a dozen times. Fisherman Dave's grin widened, exposing his teeth.

"What do you want to hear?" he asked.

"Maybe more about the siblings from your village?" inquired Madla.

"Ah. Those two siblings, alright," said Fisherman Dave.

"What are their names?" asked Madla.

"They were called Niky and Marie," he stated.

Krista elbowed Madla and whispered, "I'm Kristyna Marie!"

"A very popular name. This Marie lived up to her name," Fisherman Dave declared.

"What do you mean?" questioned Krista.

Fisherman Dave leaned back on his lawn chair, still holding onto his fishing pole. "The name 'Marie' has many meanings. Some people say it means 'a child that was wished for,' which she was. She came into the world as a surprise for many people in the village as her parents were already reaching an older age, but her parents had waited for another child for many years to be a friend to Niky. By the time Marie was born, Niky already had a best friend, though the two siblings still spent special moments together," Fisherman Dave explained. He started slowly reeling the fishing line to entice any patient trout lurking beneath the water.

"And? You said 'Marie' has many meanings," nudged Madla.

"Yes. Some people say it means 'rebellious,' though Marie hardly had a rebellious bone in her body. Niky was the rebellious one; possibly Marie learned some bit of rebellion from watching her older sibling." Fisherman Dave gave a soft chuckle before the corners of his lips drooped under his wrinkled cheeks. "Some people say 'Marie' means 'a sea of sorrow,' which fits the best as sadness came to Marie's family greatly when the valley was flooded."

"Why?" Krista ventured.

Fisherman Dave looked at the two girls sitting on the grass at his feet and quietly said, "When the valley was flooded, the family was torn apart, and what the parents did was unforgivable."

Krista's eyes widened. Her voice reached for words to ask more about what could have caused such heartache in the family, but it was Madla who jumped in, "Does Niky's name mean something too?"

"Niky's father chose the nickname because he had a good friend from long ago, Nicholas Winton, but to all his friends he was known as Nicky," Fisherman Dave shrugged.

"Who is he?" questioned Madla.

Fisherman Dave's eyebrows scrunched together. "I'm not surprised you haven't heard of him. Nicholas never saw himself as a hero, and people are just beginning to learn all that he did. Some people are like that, they don't know they are heroes, or maybe they don't want to be prideful. I'll tell you two, but are you sure you want to listen?"

Both girls nodded their heads; Madla's pigtails helicoptered. They were intrigued by the story of the unknown hero. Fisherman Dave took a deep breath and began, a spark caught on the surface of his eyes for a moment as he prepared to tell the girls one of the greatest stories he knew.

"I knew Niky's father well. Most people knew him by his last name, Vesely. Over the years, many people used the German spelling of the name Vesely and wrote it W-E-S-S-E-L-Y. With some Czechoslovakian roots tied into the Austro-Hungarian Empire, the spelling still clung. Even growing up, Wessely's friends simply called him Wes," Fisherman Dave began.

"Vesely means cheerful!" Madla jumped in.

Krista grinned as she had secretly guessed early on that Madla wouldn't last long before having at least a few words of input to Fisherman Dave's story.

"Yes, it does," nodded Fisherman Dave. "Wes was living with a relative in Prague to study at a special high school for students with great linguistic abilities. Wes had an ear for languages. It was his high school teacher who said it would be a mistake if he didn't transfer to the school in Prague, so Wes started school in the last year of high school at the age of eighteen with hopes of continuing to a language university. The year was 1938, when Wes started at his new school in September. It didn't take him long before he found a routine of going to school and helping his great-aunt in her apartment in the afternoon, but Wes didn't stay in Prague long enough to practice what he had learned in school that year." Fisherman Dave paused to take a sip of coffee from his thermos. Even on the hottest day, a fisherman must always bring along his favorite beverage.

"Why didn't Wes get to stay in Prague to practice all the languages?" asked Madla.

"Because, by March of 1939, linguist students weren't advancing in multiple languages. The whole country was only practicing one; German."

November 9, 1972
— Niky

It should be a law that missing school on your birthday is permissible. For my fifteenth birthday, my chemistry teacher gave me a test, and my literature teacher gave me a book report. On the bus ride home, Patja displayed a roughly wrapped gift. It didn't matter to me how it was wrapped, though the torn paper looked like a dog had chewed it. The tattered paper hid a head flashlight with an elastic strap around the back. I had mentioned once the struggle of gripping my flashlight under my chin while trying to journal at night. I was so excited to try out the new gift, which is why I waited until after sunset to journal tonight.

Mom baked a cake with preserves of blueberries and strawberries covering the top layer — my traditional birthday cake. We brought the cake into the living room. I sat in an armchair with the plate balanced on my knees as I ate my slice, Mother and Dad sat on the sofa, and Marie sat like an Indian on the floor with the cake at eye-level on the coffee table in front of her. Mother gave me the biggest piece of cake, but Marie ate her piece in record time to get a second slice. I put one piece back in the refrigerator to give to Patja tomorrow.

After finishing her second slice of cake, Marie disappeared from the room. I heard the creak of the stairs as she ran up to the bedroom and back down again. She returned to the living room with a small package clutched in her fingers. She extended the gift to me, giving me birthday wishes and luck in the next year. A pink ribbon held the paper around the gift — the same ribbon that had held the pen to my journal on the day I learned of what is to become of Lazinov. The ribbon started to become faded from the many times Marie has tied her curls back with it countless mornings before school. I untied the bow and let it fall back into Marie's little hand; she will wear it in her hair again tomorrow. The paper around the gift slipped off, revealing a new black-ink pen. I know Marie bought the pen with the money she had earned helping Mr. Pokorny gather plums from his trees last month. Marie bubbled as she told me she knew I was writing a lot and how she thought I could use a good pen for journaling. I thanked her for the thoughtful gift, and Marie is right; this pen is great for journaling.

Mother pulled a package from under the bed in the corner that revealed itself before being opened. I had held the Rodents and Reptiles Nature Guide in my hands so many times that I knew it was a new nature guide under the wrapping. I tore back the paper to reveal the title: Plants and Fungi. I flipped through the pages that are loaded with different kinds of trees, forest plants, flowers, and mushrooms. I paused on a page of mushrooms, and Marie grimaced as she looked over my shoulder. She has never liked the taste of mushrooms. She would join us in the forest when we go hunting for mushrooms, but that is where the fun stops for the picky eater.

While Marie and I were distracted with the Nature Guide, Dad slipped from the room and returned with another gift. When he reentered, he was holding a squirmy, noisy kitten, whose fur looked as if she had rolled in the ash of a fire pit. Dad placed the kitten on my lap.

Mother smiled, "What do you think, Bug?"

I looked at the frizzy ball of fur on my lap. I wished it was a bug, it would be more interesting to observe, but I gave a gracious smile back to my parents.

"She's cute. Thanks."

Marie squealed with delight as she scratched the kitten's forehead. "She is adorable!" Marie paused after each syllable, emphasizing her excitement in staccato. The kitten really is more of a gift for Marie. Maybe I would have liked a kitten more if I was nine years old, like Marie, not exactly a fifteenth birthday present if you ask me. Although, maybe it is just Mother and Dad's way of telling me that I'm of an age to have even more responsibilities.

Marie picked up the kitten from my lap and cradled it like a doll. The cat gave a defiant "meow," climbed up to Marie's shoulder, and draped her front paws over Marie's back. The kitten seemed pleased with the new position but continued giving occasional meows announcing her presence.

"Let's call her Cutie or Sweetheart because she is darling," Marie coddled.

"Niky gets to decide the name," stated Mother, and then all eyes were on me. I looked again at the kitten draped over Marie's shoulder and knew it definitely wouldn't be called Cutie or Sweetheart — not that it mattered so much to me. The

kitten's gray fur stood from either static or fear, making her look like a dust bunny under the bed, but I didn't think it would be so clever to name the kitten "Bunny."

"Ash," I said aloud so quickly I surprised myself.

"That suites her color," Dad nodded.

"Ash," said Marie, testing out the name. The kitten didn't acknowledge we were talking about her; she continued to lick her paw as if she cared less whether she was called Ash or Cutie. Marie set Ash on the floor, who quickly darted under the sofa. We let her explore the room while we finished the cake, and then all four of us corralled little Ash until Dad was finally able to grab the darting kitten. Ash squirmed a little in Dad's big hands but quickly gave in to her captor.

"We have a box for her outside," he said and began walking to the door.

"Dad! There are dogs outside! And she might run away. Ash doesn't know her way home yet," cried Marie. "Can she stay in our room?"

I rolled my eyes. She's a quick kitten; she could probably outrun a dog — at least fast enough to climb a tree. As for getting lost, well, Lazinov isn't that big of a village. Ash would end up in some barn, or under a doorstep, and through the neighborhood networking system of babbling grandmothers and tattling toddlers, we'd get our kitten back in a day or two. I didn't believe Dad would give in for a second until...

"A kitten still needs to learn to use a box. It can be a problem in the night," Dad replied, "but if we put a small box at the top of the stairs, I think she will find it even in the dark. Alright. Just until she gets used to it here."

My jaw disconnected as it gaped at how quickly Dad had given into Marie. It's true, Dad has never been the arguing type, but whenever I begged something from Dad, he always firmly said, "End of discussion, Niky."

Marie cheered and took the kitten to see her room, introducing Ash to all her stuffed animals and dolls piled on her bed. I'm sure the little, furry kitten would get lost among all the cuddly toys under Marie's covers.

That's how my birthday present ended up sleeping in Marie's bed tonight. For a tiny kitten, she purrs rather loudly. (I should have named her "Locomotive.") I'm surprised the purring hasn't woken up Marie. I know Ash won't stay curled up and purring all night. She is active and still exploring her new home, but I won't be doing any babysitting throughout the night. If the kitten wants to stay inside, she'll have to take her midnight rouses up with Marie because I'd be more than happy to put her box outside tomorrow.

June 26, 1994
— Krista

Krista sat on her bed with her chin resting atop her knees as she reread the letter she had composed to Ruthie the evening before. She and Madla had joined Karel and Kai after Fisherman Dave packed his tackle box and folded his lawn chair. Karel, Kai, Madla, and Krista enjoyed lunch on the lake's shore before going swimming in the heat of the afternoon. They hadn't stayed as long as the time before because Madla needed to finish some homework before the final week of school. Madla dragged her feet all the way to the car, pleading with Karel for another half-hour of swimming. An agreement was made between father and daughter that if she did well on these last days of school, she could return to the reservoir with Krista the following weekend.

When Krista arrived back at Zofie and Jakub's home, she retreated to the bedroom to write Ruthie all about her day. Though the paper had started, "Dear Ruthie," Krista felt the words she wrote were also for herself. She was beginning to understand how her mom could fill pages of a journal so easily. However, words came naturally for Doma, whereas Krista often found herself flipping through the thin pages of a thesaurus and toying over words when teachers asked for creative writing pieces. She sometimes lazily asked Doma to revise her essays, knowing her mom would spice up the bland sentences. Thankfully, writing letters to Ruthie was easier than writing an essay for school, but out of habit, Krista frequently reminded herself to add descriptive words. Often, she thought of a word too late, and descriptive words were squeezed into the margins and linked to the sentence with arrows. Krista noticed how her handwriting tilted to the right side as it swept over the pages in rough lines like waves of the sea with parenthesized adjectives creating bubble inserts.

... Fisherman Dave told us about one boy he knew called Wes, who was originally from his village — Lazinov, but Wes lived in Prague right before the Second World War started. He studied languages at a university in Prague and already knew Czech, Slovak, Polish, and Russian — which Fisherman Dave

said are all pretty similar, besides the lettering in Russian — though, Wes was quickly learning and practicing English, French, and German. Every morning, Wes would walk down the street to catch the tram that rolled over the cobblestones through the (old) city. The (rattling) tram would lull him for the twenty-minute journey as he dozed in and out of sleep before reaching his stop. The (morning) autumn air instantly cured any drowsiness as he stepped out of the tram and walked around the (narrow) city roads to reach the (linguist) school. It was a four-story building with tall windows and a (large double) door that opened to a courtyard where the students would gather between classes. Wes's first class was on the fourth floor overlooking the courtyard. He didn't have any friends since he had just transferred to the school and hadn't lived in Prague for more than a couple of weeks, but Wes didn't have time in the morning to talk to anyone in the courtyard seeing that he had four staircases to climb before the bell rang signaling the start of First Period. Fisherman Dave said Wes always had a knack for learning and enjoyed attending school. He would bounce between language and linguist classes in the morning hours, filling his notebook with notes to review later. At the (lunch) bell, he would rush back to the tram and meet his great-aunt at the apartment for (a home-cooked) lunch. On Tuesdays and Thursdays, Wes had mathematics in the afternoon and would hurry through lunch to make it back for the afternoon class. The teachers at the school (highly) encouraged the students to use the afternoons on Monday, Wednesday, and Friday to be involved in activities where they could practice the languages first-hand. Some students jumped into cleaning jobs at international offices, while the lucky ones emptied the trash at embassies with only a hope for the opportunity to translate. Others roamed around the city center offering (short) tours to foreigners for pocket change, and some volunteered in kindergartens to read (picture) books to refugee children from Austria. Since Wes was new to Prague and his great-aunt had no connection with foreign offices, Wes couldn't be found giving tours through the city center or emptying trash bins outside an embassy. Fisherman Dave didn't tell us what Wes did yet, but he said that an opportunity just fell into Wes's lap one day...

"There you are," Doma said from the doorway of the bedroom. "I thought you would be in the garden helping Zofie pick more strawberries for jam."

"I'm just reading over my letter to Ruthie," Krista signed her name at the bottom and squeezed in one last line below her signature that read, *P.S. I always wear the necklace.*

"Can you come with me for a few minutes? I have something I want to show you. It's a secret," Doma said the last sentence with a hint of taunting.

Krista left the messy notebook papers on her bed as she followed her mom through the hallway and down the stairs to the first-floor apartment. Doma pushed open the door of the first bedroom, which had become a storage room for all the old kitchen appliances as Zofie and Jakub remodeled the kitchen on the first floor. Old cupboards were stacked haphazardly against the left wall, and a rusted oven leaned against the faded-white refrigerator on the right wall. An assortment of mismatched teacups and saucers trimmed the windowsill. Three wooden chairs that had obviously each belonged to a different kitchen set circled a small table and looked as if Goldilocks was about to make her appearance to test each one. Krista had explored this room before, but one new item sat in the center. The frame of a bicycle was impossibly disguised as a ghost beneath a white sheet that draped over the seat and handlebars, leaving the base of the tires exposed. Doma pulled back the sheet revealing a new red and white bike with golden ribbon tassels dangling from either side of the handlebars. A decorated piece of paper was taped to the front of the bike that read, *Happy Birthday Madla!*

"Madla's birthday is on Friday, so Karel asked if we can keep this here. Madla and Kai finish their last day of school on Thursday, so we will celebrate on Friday. Make sure Madla doesn't find the bike before then," Doma impressed the task of secrecy upon her daughter.

Krista ran her fingers over the handlebars and through the tassels. "It's a lovely gift! Madla will really like it," Krista smiled with excitement, imaging Madla unveiling the present.

Doma straightened the sheet back over the bike and said, "Good. Now come with me; there's still more."

Krista again followed her mom, wondering what other gifts they had hidden for Madla in the various rooms throughout the house. Doma led Krista out the back door into the garden, where Zofie was picking strawberries. Her bandana was loose and slowly sliding off her head. A basket of bright red strawberries was just in reach as she knelt between the rows of short, leafy strawberry patches.

"Did you see the surprise for my lucky niece?" Zofie asked as she knelt in the dirt around the strawberry patch.

"Yes. It is a very nice gift. Madla will like it a lot! She told me she needed a new bike," Krista replied.

Zofie laughed, "Yes, Madla told this to everyone. Even our mailman knows her knees are hitting the handlebars on her old bike!" Zofie stood up and brushed the soil from her knees before saying, "There is something more to the surprise. Let me show you." Zofie walked into the garden shed, and Doma held the door open. A moment later, Zofie reappeared, pushing a second bike with a scratched black frame and faded gray seat. The rubber on the end of one handlebar was peeled, but the bike looked as if it had been recently cleaned.

"Madla is going to need someone to ride with, and Kai can't keep up. This is my bike. I've had it for twenty years, but I haven't ridden it very much recently. The hills were a lot easier twenty years ago! I was wondering why I was hanging onto it; now I'm glad I did." Zofie pushed the bike over to where Krista stood. Krista grabbed onto the handlebars as Zofie hit the kickstand with the heel of her shoe. The kickstand gave a defiant "squeak," but solidly propped the bike on the lawn. Zofie's bike frame didn't look like it was created for races, and Krista didn't know if there was a way to change the gears on the curved handlebars, but it looked like a sturdy bicycle.

"You mean, the second part of the surprise was for me?" Krista looked from her mom to Zofie, who both eagerly nodded their heads.

"Well? Try it out," Doma encouraged.

Krista pulled her right leg over the frame and straddled the seat. Zofie was a bit taller, but Krista gave a little hop, and her feet reached the pedals nicely. She preferred being higher on the bicycle anyway. She pushed on the pedals with her feet and caught her balance as she easily maneuvered around the plum trees and strawberry patch before returning to where Zofie and Doma stood watching by the garden shed.

"It's great! I think I'm getting the hang of it. Thank you so much!" exclaimed Krista. She leaped off the bike and mimicked Zofie's heel-kick on the kickstand before embracing both her mom and Zofie in a hug.

"I'm glad you like it," Zofie said.

"Now, the only thing is that we don't have a helmet." Doma bit the corner of her lip.

"She's clearly skilled on the bicycle! She doesn't need a helmet," Zofie assured.

Still looking concerned, Doma said, "Krista, it isn't necessary for kids to wear helmets here like it is in America, so it isn't possible to buy one in Letovice. Promise me that you'll be careful."

"I'll be safe; I promise. This is a great surprise! I can't wait to try it out with Madla!"

"Good," both Zofie and Doma said simultaneously in different languages. Krista laughed before pushing her bike through the yard and out the front gate. She let the slope of the road pull her down before she turned onto the path to the city square. Krista quickly got a feel for the brakes and was soon rolling over the bumpy cobblestoned streets in the center of the city. The bike looked like an antique with the fourteen-year-old seated atop it, but Krista immediately felt as if the bike was ready for an adventure again. It caused Krista to wonder where the bike had traveled many years before.

November 25, 1972
— Niky

I was right about the kitten that first night. Hours before the sun came up, I was woken by the persistent meowing and opened my eyes to see a dust bunny running around the room. It took me a moment to remember that the dust-like ball of fur was my birthday present. Ash bumped into one of the bedposts and leaped frantically onto my bed. I quickly shoved her back onto the floor, and she landed on all four feet with ease. I watched as she bounced up onto Marie's bed, waking my little sister. Marie didn't seem to mind. She pulled the kitten up to her cheek and cuddled with the squirming, meowing ball of fur. Ash wiggled her way out of Marie's hold and curled up once again at the base of the bedspread. I rolled over and went to sleep, convinced Marie wouldn't let the kitten stay a second night in the bedroom.

When I got up for school the next morning, Marie's bed was already made, and she was slipping on a sweater. I noticed one of her dolls laid on the edge of her bed — the dress of the doll was shredded from little claws.

"Did Ash do that?" I stupidly asked. Of course, it was the kitten; it's not like Marie had gone savage in the night. I was certain now that Marie wouldn't let the kitten back into our

room. I pursed my lips together to hide my grinning teeth in knowing Marie would ban Ash from sleeping upstairs.

"I didn't like that dress on that doll much anyway," Marie shrugged. My mouth gaped as she added, "Dolls are babyish."

Five months earlier, in the heart of summer, I didn't see Marie anywhere without the old baby doll pram. You could always hear Marie pushing the pram down the road as the front wheel squeaked from a loose screw. Many times, I had found it piled with all the dolls and plush toys that Marie could fit in. Once, I complained to Mother that the pram was taking up so much space in the bedroom, and I despised having to carry it up and down the stairs for Marie, but there simply wasn't space to leave it downstairs in the narrow hall either. Mother said, "It's just a phase. She'll grow out of it soon but let her enjoy the time pretending with her toys." I just hadn't realized she would outgrow playing with dolls so fast.

While I may be the one to dump out the kitten's box and put our food scraps in a bowl on the floor, Marie has quickly grown an attachment with Ash. The kitten purrs around her dangling feet at the kitchen table, waiting for Marie to casually drop a small treat from her plate. Most nights, Ash climbs into Marie's bed, and Marie scratches Ash's grey fur until she herself falls asleep. On occasion, Ash tried to climb into my bed after Marie submits to sleep, but the cat has quickly learned that climbing in my bed just means getting shoved back onto the floor. It isn't anything personal with Ash, but I don't share my bed with anyone. Not even when Marie has a nightmare; I make her walk downstairs to wake Mother. When we go camping, I sleep outside by the campfire so I don't have to share a tight tent with my parents or sister. I don't even keep more than one pillow and a quilt in my bed, unlike Marie, who barely has room enough on her bed for herself surrounded by a nest of plush toys, dolls, and every spare blanket in the house. Maybe Ash feels crowded in Marie's bed too, but there was no way a cat was going to be an exception on my bed.

I wasn't surprised that Ash chose Marie over me. Mother looks at me with sad eyes every time Ash chases after Marie's shoelaces as we leave the house for the bus. I think Mother feels bad that my birthday present chose Marie over me. I actually don't mind. I have Patja, and now Marie has Ash to play with, so she has stopped shadowing us so much. The kitten follows Marie around the house, keeping a close watch on her favorite human. Often, Marie has to run back to the house before the bus comes to lock the kitten inside, fearful that Ash will try to run under the large vehicle or may accidentally climb on the bus and go to school with us. When we get home in the afternoon, Ash is often soaking in the sun on the front step. Marie runs to her, and I leave for the climbing tree with Patja. We notoriously drop our backpacks at Dvorak's fence, and Patja always declares, "Race me" as if I don't expect it already, but humans are the greatest creatures of habit, just like I have a habit of winning the sprint.

Strangely, Ash will find her way to the climbing tree most days as well. At first, I didn't want to admit it, but I was happy the kitten had chosen to follow me. I had explained to Patja before how my birthday present prefers Marie, so when the kitten showed up at the climbing tree one afternoon I exclaimed, "Look, Patja! Ash followed me today!" The kitten darted around the tree, and I bent down to pet her. Just as my fingertips touched her spine, she galloped down the hill, nearly rolling as it sloped to the haystacks Farmer Dvorak had lined up for his goats. Ash darted in and around the haystacks until finally neither Patja nor I saw her anymore. Patja laughed, "I think Ash isn't following you. She's probably chasing some field mice in that haystack!" I rolled my eyes. Patja was probably right. Ash likely knew this place from exploring while we are at school all day. She must know her way home because she never follows me back to the house.

For many afternoons, our routine is just like that. Patja and I reach the edge of Dvorak's fence, fling our backpacks off our shoulders, race to the climbing tree, and Ash would come chasing after us from out of nowhere. She wouldn't stay long as she always ran into that pile of hay, likely to scout out a rodent. Patja and I would finish our homework and then kick around Patja's favorite tattered soccer ball. While some kids have worn-out pages of a book or a blanket from constant use, Patja's soccer ball has always been a priceless comfort item. For many years, that ball traveled with Patja nearly everywhere, as we'd put it in one of our backpacks in the morning to have the ball to kick back and forth as we waited for the bus to go home in the afternoon. Now that we are older, the space in our backpacks has been taken up by boring literature and pages of homework scratched in red, so we leave the ball tied to the tree in a cloth bag on the shortest branch. Most afternoons, we complete our homework and kick around the ball until Mrs. Kobzova faithfully sounds the *evening bell in our little village. Then, we tie the ball back onto the tree and head for our houses across the valley. I often arrive home to Mother setting the table for dinner and Marie sitting on the bench with Ash curled up in her lap. The kitten always finds her way back to Marie after completing her rounds to the climbing tree.*

The air is harsher now that winter is approaching. There is a chill that whispers for the coming snow. The leaves of the climbing tree have changed to a bright red and are falling at a rapid pace, creating an auburn carpet at the base of the trunk. The seasons are changing with such normality, and the kitten has found a routined pattern to the day that sometimes, I remember no one told the trees and the kittens there wouldn't be many autumns left in Lazinov.

July 2, 1994
— Krista

"Krista!" Madla called from the driveway. It was Saturday, only the second official day of summer for Czech students since school finished last Thursday. Krista appeared on the balcony and waved down to Madla, who proudly stood next to her new bike.

"I'll be right down! Hold on." Krista retreated into the bedroom, grabbing her knapsack from under the bed. Amazingly, the girls had convinced the adults the evening before that they could bike to the dam alone today.

It was just yesterday that they had finished the birthday cake Zofie baked for Madla, and her new birthday present was already strapped into the back of Karel's trunk. As much as the men tried putting the bike in the trunk of the car in different positions, they had reached the conclusion to simply let the back-wheel stick out. Jakub tied a red handkerchief to one of the spokes, and the men applauded themselves on their work well-done. Zofie and Doma glanced knowingly toward each other. They had said a half-hour earlier that the bike wouldn't fit in the car's trunk, but alas, they let the men try loading the bicycle in every angle like a toddler trying a square puzzle piece on a circle space. They were all seated in the kitchen with glasses of juice and tea. Madla, who had been overloaded with excitement and sugar, chattered more than normal.

"I'm excited to go biking tomorrow! We can go to the lake on our bikes. The past two Saturdays, we took Daddy's car, but now, we can all go by bicycle. Maybe it will be a little hard for Kai, but the way is mostly flat, and it isn't so far to bike to the dam. We can take breaks along the way if we need it anyway. I know some people even walk there if they don't have a car, so biking won't be too hard," said Madla.

"It sounds like a nice idea, Madla, but Kai has a soccer tournament all day tomorrow, so I need to be with him at the field. Maybe we can go another weekend," Karel consoled, trying not to disappoint his daughter in the last few hours of her twelfth birthday.

Madla's lower lip pouted. "Can't Aunt Zofie and Uncle Jakub be with Kai at the soccer tournament?"

"Of course we will come to watch one of the games in the day-long tournament," Jakub winked in Kai's direction, "but I'm afraid we can't stay the whole day at the field."

"I need to be at the tournament for Kai tomorrow, Madla. I'm sorry." Karel's gaze fell to his empty plate still before him at the kitchen table.

Zofie had been strumming her fingers on the kitchen table when mid-strum she clapped her hands satisfactorily together and declared in a matter-of-fact tone, "Well, there seems to be only one logical option then. Madla and Krista will go to the dam themselves."

The adults sat stunned, staring at Zofie.

"Zofie!" Doma whispered through her teeth, but it was too late, the girls had already acknowledged the idea. Krista and Madla looked at each other and nodded excitely.

"Wait, wait. I'm not sure the girls are ready for that." Karel looked around the table at the adults, each of who were giving mixed expressions, their reactions changing as they considered the idea further.

"Why not?" Zofie asked but before Karel could answer, she added, "The girls have been there many times with you and know their way there and back well by now. It's one road, they can't get lost. They also know the area and have proven they can be trusted and safe in the water." Looking around the table to the other adults, she continued, "They're big girls now. Besides, we all used to bike down that street when we were their age."

Still whispering through her teeth, Doma interjected, "You know why that was different."

"Sure," Karel agreed. "We grew up there, spent our childhoods there."

Krista couldn't keep up with the conversation as the adults talked over each other, discussing the risks and advantages of letting the two girls venture to the reservoir on their own. Madla tugged on Karel's sleeve, repeating, "Please, please, Daddy, please." Kai had zoned out of the conversation completely as he blew bubbles into his chocolate milk.

Rick had remained an observer in the debate as he gathered the opinions of Doma, Karel, Zofie, and Jakub.

Finally, Rick cleared his throat, bringing the rest of the adults' discussion to a lull as they looked to him. He had decided. Addressing both the girls, he stated, "You will stay together the whole time. You will be back before sunset, and you will not swim out farther than you can touch the bottom of the lake. You will not talk to strangers, and if you need help for any reason, you will go to the bus stop in front of the dam and use the payphone to call Zofie and then take the bus back to Letovice immediately. Do you understand and agree to the conditions?"

Both girls nodded fervently, and Madla gave a military salute for added measure.

"Good," Rick smiled.

He knew he'd have to talk with his wife after Krista went to bed in the evening, but he also knew Doma's hesitation wasn't because she didn't think Krista was capable of the journey by bike. After all, Zofie's old bike knew that particular trail to the dam well.

Both Madla and Krista had woken excited for their adventure and reviewed the conditions with Rick in the driveway before they headed out on their own. All the adults waved the girls off with Rick standing in front of the house, Jakub from the open garage, Zofie in the doorway while holding a dishtowel, and Doma leaning over the rail of the balcony. They each called a final warning to be careful and to have fun, but Madla and Krista were already swiftly moving down the sloped street. The roads were clear as most of the city spent the first Saturday morning of the summer relaxing behind closed doors of their homes. Krista hugged the right curb, and Madla's bike rattled over the cobblestone sidewalk as they rode side by side. They weaved along the edge of the road through the forest to the dam. Stopping once on the slow incline to take a quick drink of water before continuing on their quest. Krista took the lead and wasn't surprised that Madla chatted most of the journey, though she could only make out part of Madla's monologue.

"This bike is amazing! I like that…," the wind took Madla's voice in all other directions, "and it is great to… I think… again sometime… and see Fisherman Dave."

Krista wondered how Madla had the energy to bike all the way to the dam while talking most of the trip. Krista noticed that she could smell the sweet, musty pine trees when she turned her face to the left. When she faced the right, she caught the fishy smell of the lake just beyond a row of trees. As the girls went over the bridge, Krista slowed and hopped off the seat of her bike.

"What are you doing?" Madla asked. "We're almost there."

"Let's see if Fisherman Dave is in the cove," Krista said.

Madla leaped off her bike with a satisfying grin. The girls looked down the empty street and quickly pushed their bikes to the other side of the bridge. Leaning the bikes against the guard rail, they peered over the edge of the bridge and saw the top of the beige fisherman's hat below.

"Hello! Mister Fisherman Dave!" Madla called.

"Up here!" Krista added.

Fisherman Dave looked up as the two girls waved their arms over their heads.

"We will be right there!" Madla called, her voice echoed through the valley of the cove.

Krista and Madla gripped the handles of their bikes and waited for a white car to pass on the road before pushing off on their pedals to continue over the bridge. They turned into the gravel parking lot by the lake's shore and continued on the path that rounded the bend to the cove. The path faded, and the girls hobbled along on the grassy terrain before pushing their transportation the rest of the way to Fisherman Dave's spot.

"Such talented girls! You are to come today by bicycle," Fisherman Dave applauded.

Madla's bike leaned as she set the kickstand in place, and Krista noticed the tassels on Madla's bike handles resembled her little friend's crooked pigtails. Krista leaned her bike against one of the overturned rowboats.

"Do you like my new bike, Mister Fisherman Dave?" Madla grinned. "It was my birthday yesterday. I am twelve years old now."

"Well, happy belated birthday!" Fisherman Dave's voice sang.

"We came all by ourselves today. We have our lunches in our backpacks with our towels and swimsuits! It will be a great day. Right, Krista?" Madla asked rhetorically.

Krista nodded. She was suddenly very thankful to have met Fisherman Dave so that Madla didn't drain her out by talking all day.

"Did you catch anything today, Fisherman Dave?" Krista politely asked.

"I had a few bites earlier, but a fisherman must be patient," he answered.

"I don't like being patient," Madla added.

"Ah, but sometimes when we are patient, life has a way of giving us exactly what we didn't know we were looking for," Fisherman Dave grinned.

"Huh? How could we find what we aren't looking for?" Madla said as she sat on the ground. Krista pushed herself up onto a rowboat and pulled her knees under her chin to listen as she was certain the fisherman would continue the story.

Fisherman Dave's grin widened as he asked, "Do you remember where our story left off last time?"

"You said Wes found a great opportunity to use his translating skills," Krista recalled.

"Not only that, but this opportunity came to Wes when he wasn't looking for it. He was patient and knew he would find some way to use and practice his language skills, but the project he was a part of was not something he had expected."

"Did he find some treasure and needed to travel the world on a treasure hunt to return it to the owner?" curiosity sparked Madla.

"You don't go on a treasure hunt to return the treasure. You go on a treasure hunt to find treasure. Now, shh." Krista anxiously waited for Fisherman Dave to continue.

"Then, I bet Mister Wessely meets a girl from another country, and they have to speak a foreign language that he knows, and they fall in love," Madla's eyelashes batted.

"Madla, shh!" Krista tried again.

Madla covered her mouth with both hands and muffled, "Please continue."

Fisherman Dave chuckled as he leaned back on his sagging lawn chair, a gesture that catapulted the aging fisherman's thoughts like a time machine.

December 22, 1938 — Wes

The Nazis were already moving closer to Prague, the heart of Europe, shortly after Wes had started his new school. On the last day in the month of September, four powerful European leaders met to discuss political matters that could no longer be avoided. They signed an agreement in the city of Munich, allowing Germany to legally begin taking over Czechoslovakia. Interestingly, President Benes, the beloved president of Czechoslovakia, wasn't invited to this social gathering with Hitler, Mussolini, Chamberlain, and Daladier even though it determined the fate of his country. It was no surprise then that the Nazis had control of the mountain range around the edges of Czechoslovakia that border Germany by the first week in October. Many Germans were already living in this region called Sudetenland, known for being German-inhabited Czechlands. The leaders of Italy, England, and France should have known Hitler wouldn't stop forces in the Sudetenland as it only took him another five months to have complete control of Czechoslovakia. In those five months, the Czech people all sat on the edges of their seats as they flipped the dials of radios and read newspaper alerts looking for any bit of gossip to help them prepare for the inevitable.

Wes juggled through the first months of school, trying to focus on his schoolwork, but the whispers from the teachers in the hall and the never-ending worried conversations of citizens in the streets surrounded him. Some evenings, he tried to talk about his worries with his great-aunt, but Wes didn't want to frighten her with the graveness of the situation. She had witnessed the events of the First World War, and Wes feared the repetition of history was too close for comfort for his fragile great-aunt.

It was a cold day near the end of December when Wes fell into an opportunity he was never looking for. The bell rang, signaling the end of his final class. Students rushed and chattered with the excitement of Christmas Break, making plans to meet with their friends before the new year arrived. Wes and his great-aunt, whom he now affectionately called "Auntie," had plans to take the train the following day to Wes's home in Lazinov to celebrate Christmas with all their family. Wes was anxious to see his parents and the farm. He was sure the calves born last spring would be nearly full-grown by now, and he tried to imagine how the rabbits had multiplied. Excitement grew within him, and Wes was convinced he could already taste his mother's Christmas rolls. Wes eagerly closed his books, slipped on his coat, and wrapped a scarf around his neck. He pulled his hat over his ears and slid wool mittens on his hands before tucking his schoolbooks under his arm to head out to meet the tram. The brisk, frozen air caught his breath as he exited the front doors of the school building causing Wes to pull his scarf a little tighter under his chin. Leafless trees were frosted with a silver layer of ice that reflected the afternoon sun's low glow through the winter mist. Wes fell into a rhythm behind the other bundled students also headed for home. At the end of the street, Wes turned the corner to the tram stop, and at that moment, the student walking just feet in front of him slipped on a patch of icy cobblestones and fell onto the sidewalk as if he was collapsing on his home sofa. Wes quickly rushed to the fallen schoolmate; however, he was cautious to weave around the ice the student hadn't noticed before.

"Are you okay?" Wes knelt next to the fallen boy. He reached out to save the wire-rimmed glasses that had flown from the student's face in the fall.

"Oof! That is going to bruise!" The boy rubbed his backside before placing his glasses firmly back on the bridge of his nose and tucked behind his ears. "At least the glasses didn't break this time."

"This time?" Wes looked at the scattered papers and schoolbooks and began shuffling them into a stack.

"You wouldn't believe how clumsy I am."

"That ice could have been easily missed by anyone."

"Maybe, but somehow, it always knows how to find me before anyone else. Thanks for your help. I'm Sam."

"Wessely. Everyone calls me Wes," said Wes as he pulled Sam up from the sidewalk.

"You're the new kid in class 4A. I've heard about you," Sam reached out to shake Wes's hand.

Wes's eyebrows arched, unaware until that moment that he had a reputation at his new school. Seeing his reaction, Sam added, "We don't usually get new kids coming in for their last year of school. They say you must be pretty talented to get accepted into the program this late."

Wes gave a laugh, "Or so horrible that they let me in just for the final year."

"I don't think it works that way. I heard the guys in 4A talking in the halls. They say you've got skill."

Wanting to change the subject from himself Wes asked, "What class are you in?"

"1B."

"Well, Sam from 1B, where are you headed?"

Sam pointed down the street in the direction of his destination as he said, "I've got an internship on Wenceslaus Square. I'll be there just for a couple of hours today before I head home to enjoy the long winter break!"

"If I were you, I'd maybe avoid ice-skating."

Sam waved his hand in front of his face as if batting a fly. "Yeah, I've also cut skiing from the list long ago. Have you got an internship?"

"Haven't found one yet. To be honest, I haven't been actively searching."

"You can come and see if they'll let you in where I volunteer."

"What do you do exactly?"

"Well, it's a pretty high-end hotel for foreigners, so they already have great translators and staff there, but they let me translate room service messages for some of the cleaning and cooking staff who aren't trained in foreign languages. When there's nothing to do, I just sit in the lounge and listen to all the different languages and read through my studies. The guests often leave newspapers on the tables, so I am well rounded in current events in a few languages. It's not a bad experience. The hotel has a lot of class and doesn't normally have interns, but my teacher of French Language got me connected with the manager. He probably felt he had to look out for me since I am younger than the other kids in 1B. The manager agreed to try it out if I don't bother the customers; to be honest, the manager is so busy and has so many workers, I'm not even sure he remembers he has an intern! Most of the afternoon staff know me at least, and Josef at the front desk gives me little tasks to do."

Wes shrugged, "It doesn't sound half-bad. I suppose if the manager doesn't remember he has one intern, maybe he wouldn't remember if he had two! I will tag along today, at least."

Wes followed Sam through the streets of the city. He concluded Sam could be no older than fifteen and likely accepted into 1B early due to incredible potential with languages. After living in Prague for four months, Wes started feeling comfortable with the narrow, winding streets surrounded by cascading buildings. Locals hustled between shops carrying last-minute presents and cough medicine from the pharmacist. Groups of Prague citizens huddled like penguins as they waited for the trams while munching on hot rolls from the nearby bakery. Sam weaved through the city with ease. Wes attributed this skill not only to Sam's familiarity with the streets but also to his thin, lanky figure. Wes, having grown up in the farming country, continued to bump his broad shoulders into fellow pedestrians. He mumbled apologies but never let his eyes leave the back of Sam's head in fear that he would lose him altogether.

"Here we are," said Sam as he paused for a second in front of a gleaming yellow building. Wes gazed up, counting at least six stories with protruding balconies and grand bay windows adorned with green wrought iron railings. Sam pulled off his stocking cap and combed his hair back with his fingers. Wes imitated the actions of his new friend. Sam pulled open one side of the large, green double door at the front of the building, revealing a lobby even more majestic than the facade had led on. Rows of neatly arranged tables stretched to the back of the room where a barman stood at the counter engaged in a conversation with two of the guests. Tiles of marble adorned the floor and wove up the pillars on either side of the room. Rich oak dressed the counters and walls and trimmed the railing that overlooked the lobby from the second story. Wes's gaze lifted to see that the ceiling supported multiple dangling chandeliers. A red carpet guided the way from the front door to the main counter on the right side of the lobby, where a receptionist stood wearing a crisp vest and bowtie. Sam was already at the counter, though Wes hadn't moved far from the doorway, his mouth partially gaped as he took in the details of the room. As Wes's eyes continued to scan the elegance of the lobby, he noticed Sam's head jerk, motioning for him to join at the front desk.

"Josef," the receptionist introduced himself when Wes reached the desk.

Wes stuck out his arm. "Wessely." He shrugged and added, "Wes."

"Firm handshake," Josef applauded. "What can I do for you?"

Sam interjected on Wes's behalf, "Wes goes to my school; he's one of the top language students in the program."

Wes felt the tips of his ears burn. Growing up with the humble background of a village kid, Wes didn't know how to react to the praise Sam gave. Wes had only known hard work, and that also applied to his studies. He had never considered his language abilities to be raw talent.

Dealing with foreigners and guests regularly, Josef quickly caught onto Wes's mannerisms. "Where are you originally from, Wes?"

"Moravia. A little village called Lazinov," Wes confidently responded.

"Farm country, yes?" Josef inquired.

Wes gave a single nod.

"So, you're in Prague because you have a skill for languages and this little village of yours can't offer you more training, is that it?" Josef interrogated.

Again, Wes nodded.

"Most young men who want a chance to work here are quick to start showing off all their language abilities, but you're pretty quiet," remarked Josef.

Suddenly gaining confidence, Wes responded, "I don't need to prove myself. I bet you know more languages in a better accent than I do, but I study hard and learn quickly. I'm just looking for an opportunity to communicate in some of the languages I'm practicing."

Looking at Sam, Josef said, "Your new friend is not only smart; he's also clever." Josef's lips curled into a smile as he looked back to Wes. "We can talk to the manager about also giving you an internship, but Sam here already has such minimal work. I'm not sure what else we could pass off to you; however, if it is just opportunities to listen and converse in a different language, I might have a suggestion."

Wes's smile matched the receptionist's. He could tell why Sam liked Josef. He had a quick wit that made others easily feel comfortable.

Josef continued, "The lobby is technically a cafe. It is open to the public, though most people who visit are foreigners and guests of the hotel. You can come when you want and sit at these tables and mingle with other customers who want to strike up a conversation. Just don't intimidate the guests, but I don't think you will have a problem with that. Most of the guests are particularly keen on conversing."

Wes's smile deepened, revealing dimples on either side of his cheeks, "That is exactly the kind of opportunity I was looking for."

"Josef, why didn't you tell me to do it this way when I came for the internship?" questioned Sam.

"That's simple, Little Man. You came begging for work, so we gave you work!" Josef laughed.

Sam rolled his eyes. "Me and my big mouth."

An elevator ding was heard from down the corridor. Josef straightened his shoulders as a man appeared around the corner. His dark hair was slicked back, and a shadow of a beard was already starting to appear around the edges of his chin. The man approached the desk and greeted Josef. Wes quickly recognized the British accent from the man; he had listened to enough BBC on the radio to be able to decipher the accent and most of the language, though it was the first time hearing a native English speaker in person. Wes and Sam casually took a seat at a nearby table. Sam thumbed through a cafe menu that lay on the tabletop while Wes watched Josef interact with the Englishman.

"May I borrow a phone for a long-distance call? I must phone a friend in England. It is of extreme importance," the foreigner explained.

"Of course." Josef pulled a rotary phone onto the counter and called for a connection to England. He passed the phone to the gentleman asking, "Anything else, sir?"

"Pen and paper?" The Englishman leaned against the desk and crossed one leg in front of the other. Josef set a pad of hotel stationery and a pen on the counter. The Englishman nodded his thanks and then began speaking to a man on the other end of the line.

"Nicky, it's Martin Blake. I'm glad I caught you!" The Englishman listened to the man called Nicky on the other end. "Yes, I'm still in Prague working with the British Committee for Refugees. I know we were planning on that ski trip to Switzerland, but something's come up. I could use another hand here." Wes wished he could hear what the man called Nicky was saying. Of course, his parents had taught him not to eavesdrop, but listening to the English roll off the man's tongue was too tempting to recall social rules about minding one's own business. "Brilliant! The Sroubek Hotel on Wenceslaus Square. I'll hold a room for you," concluded the Englishman named Martin before he placed the receiver back on the dial and thanked Josef. Martin tore the page from the top of the stationery with his scratched notes and began making arrangements for another room to be prepared for his friend.

"For whom should I write this room accommodation?" asked Josef as he opened the desk ledger.

A name Wes would remember for the rest of his life fell from the lips of the Englishman, "Nicholas Winton."

March 7, 1973
— Niky

I'm convinced teachers meet together on the weekends, sitting in each others' gardens and drinking glasses of wine, planning how they can make our days in school more boring. It seems impossible, but after each boring class comes hours of even more torturous homework. Patja dropped out of the soccer league to have more time to study but still visits the field in Letovice once a week to kick the ball around with some of our classmates. I usually join in too.

Thankfully, we graduated out of Pioneers last summer, so Patja and I don't have to spend one afternoon each week reciting pledges to our government and defending our loyalty to the country by wearing a matching uniform. Enrollment in the Pioneer system is considered "highly encouraged" when a child turns six and starts school, so Mother and Dad registered Marie and me right away when we began first grade. When little Katerina Novak started first grade this year, we all assumed she would be attending Pioneers also.

As it turned out, her mother hadn't enrolled Katerina in the program in hopes that her daughter would be open-minded and come to understand values on her own. Katerina's classmates were too young to care that she didn't come with them on Tuesdays after school, but it wasn't long until little Katerina had been left out of conversations and birthday invites as her classmates formed friendships through the communist program. She rode the bus home one Friday crying as she had found out she hadn't been invited with the rest of the girls to go sledding that weekend. (Not that she would be able to join her classmates since her broken sled was still hidden in the ditch on the edge of the valley.)

I'm sure little Katerina begged Mrs. Novak that night to sign her up for Pioneers. I suppose being more occupied with a new baby at home and fearing Katerina had been teased and bullied by her peers is what caused Mrs. Novak to call the leaders of the program. Katerina came to school the next Tuesday with her new uniform neatly folded in her backpack. On regular Tuesdays, the older kids have an extra hour of class in school, so Katerina, Marie, Viktor, and Vojta go to Pioneers together and then join up with me, Patja, and Karel at the bus stop on the square to go back to Lazinov. (Of course, there are more students on the other side of our little village too, but Amalie, Theodor, Adam, Natalie, Denisa, Robert, Hana, Daniel, and Vilem are all cousins and a large gang on their own! They take over nearly the whole left side of the little bus and have secluded themselves from the start. They also crowd the little bus stop to go back to Lazinov after school, though they'd likely not notice if our whole neighborhood group was missing until the bus toppled onto its side from the disproportionate weight. The people in Lazinov call them the Cousin Club and us the Northside Neighborhood Gang. There are never any turf battles or anything like that — it's just how it's always been.)

Karel's family is taking longer to move in with his sister and brother-in-law than he had thought, but they finally finished packing the last of their house over the weekend. Karel says that, by next Monday, he won't be waiting at the bus stop anymore. He promised to have me and Patja come visit; I will probably be needing to visit Filip sometime soon anyway. Math, which had before just been an annoying mosquito, has now become a beast with rather sharp teeth. I could use a bit of Filip's tutoring again. Math comes so naturally for Karel and Patja that they don't know how to explain it; they just do it. I look at their notes and have a headache trying to understand.

I suppose I will be frequenting Letovice more when Patja finally moves there too. About two weeks ago, Patja's parents found an old, run-down house on the edge of the city. Patja told me about how the carpet is worn all the way to the floor planks underneath. The foundation is bowed, so the center of the room is a few centimeters higher than the edges, which has caused the wallpaper to peel from the top of the walls and cracks to form along the baseboards. Apparently, the lady living there is quite old and moving in with her son's family by next summer. The elderly lady is giving a good deal on the house since she knows it is in rough shape, but Patja's mother is most excited about the large garden that extends from the back of the house. I'm not sure why she is so pleased; it is nothing compared to the garden she has now in Lazinov, where the entire village is practically one big backyard. I think she's just trying to find the silver lining in the situation for Patja's sake. Patja says they will have to clean and renovate the house before moving in, which is the actual silver lining as it gives us more time in Lazinov together.

Two days ago, they started piling up soil where the dam will be on the edge of the valley. When I saw it from the bus window, it looked like a massive grave, piled high with dirt. Not one mourner stood there, only cheery construction workers who were unwrapping sandwiches and passing around a canister of (assumably) coffee. They also started digging a deep hole next to the mound of dirt, though I'm not sure why they want a hole in the center of the area they are *planning to flood. The hole went over the current road, so the construction workers routed a new trail for cars and buses. Now, the path is lower to the valley floor, which only a non-villager would have done because the workers stupidly routed the makeshift road next to the river. The whole point of them waiting to start work on the project was because the ground was still frozen in February, but all the locals know that the riverbanks bulge in March with water that seeps over the edges. With all the extra water from the melted snow and the rainstorm that hit last night, the banks of the river have moved further up the slope of the valley and are rushing at record speeds. The little road the workers made for us is inches underwater. I outright laughed this morning with the luck that the bus was unable to come and get us for school. I laughed because, for the first time, this insane dam project finally benefitted me.*

Of course, I realize I will have double the amount of homework tomorrow when they reroute the road again on the other side of the crater hole, but for today, I am enjoying the freedom.

The flooding river was a sight to see this morning. Out of the front kitchen window, I saw bales of Farmer Dvorak's hay bobble in the water like toy rubber ducks on a bathtub. There was even a goose sitting atop a smaller pile of hay where her nest was. The brave mother goose never left her eggs as the nest floated further down the river. I can see what Patja means about the creek flooding and feeding into other rivers; however, none of our homes are affected by the rising waters. We built our homes on the slopes, high above the banks of the rivers. Only the hay bales are impacted by the flooding current. If they'd had more sense in the bigger cities, they wouldn't have built their town squares so close to the river. Apparently, these city slickers aren't as clever as they thought, routing roads by rivers and building too close to the water. Why does the government think it is fair to punish us for their mistakes?

July 4, 1994
— Krista

Fisherman Dave was becoming accustomed to his two little visitors each weekend and had slid a bag of gummy worms into his lunchbox in hopes that Madla and Krista would be back at the cove this morning. He hadn't been at his fishing post for very long before the girls came around the bend on their bicycles. After responsibly returning home the Saturday before, their parents had given the girls the freedom to return to the dam again on their bicycles the following Monday. Madla and Krista were happy they didn't have to wait until the weekend to return to the lake, but with Summer Break finally in full swing, they could think of nothing else they wanted to do than sink their feet in the cool water and listen to Fisherman Dave's tales.

"Mister Fisherman Dave!" called Madla from down the shore of the cove. "We didn't know if you would be here on a weekday since we have only ever come on Saturdays," her voice echoed over the water and filled the still valley.

"There isn't much for a fisherman to do besides sitting at the shore each day," Fisherman Dave called back.

The girls were quickly at his side, hopping from their bikes and pulling off their knapsacks. Madla removed her sun cap; her iconic pigtails flattened from the hat she had worn on the ride to the reservoir.

"Do you ever fish anywhere else?" asked Krista as she looped her knapsack over the bike's handlebar.

"Oh, sure! My house is on the other side of the lake, I just need to walk a short way down the hill to the shore from my back door and I'm right at the water's edge," Fisherman Dave remarked. Rising from his lawn chair, he added, "Let me show you."

Madla and Krista propped their bikes against a flipped rowboat and followed Fisherman Dave back to the corner of the cove. They rounded the shore and walked past the swimming beach. Madla's endless list of questions followed as they strolled along the edge of the water.

"Are we going to walk all the way to your house?"; "How far must we go?"; "Do you walk here every day?"; "Can you bring your fishing pole on the bus?" Madla's endless questioning rambled.

Fisherman Dave politely answered all of Madla's questions, "No."; "A little further."; "I normally take the bus."; "Yes, I can."

Madla easily climbed and jumped from rock to rock along the shoreline. Krista walked close to Fisherman Dave, fearing the terrain was too much for the elderly man to handle. Madla bounded ahead as Fisherman Dave and Krista trailed closely behind. From a few feet in front of them, Madla's voice erupted, "I can see the roofs of the houses across the lake!"

Fisherman Dave and Krista were quickly at her side gazing across the water. From that spot, they could see the tips of the houses at the start of the little village of New Lazinov. Fisherman Dave pointed a steady finger across the lake. "You see the third house in? The pointy red roof? That's my home, the one I built after I gave my first home to the fish of this lake."

"If you live right on the lake, why do you come here to fish?" questioned Madla.

Fisherman Dave turned to look back in the direction of the cove. "The fish like the cove better, and the view from the cove is special for me. I can see the place where my home once was, and I like to imagine how life was back then. Plus, it is good for me to get out of my own home and backyard; it helps me meet new friends." He gave the girls each a wink. They began making their way back toward the cove, where the fishermen had forever claimed his spot.

"Fisherman Dave, where I live in America, many people will be at the lake today too," grinned Krista.

"Hmm, why's that?" asked Fisherman Dave.

"It's Independence Day!" Not knowing how to directly translate the holiday name, Krista motioned to the red and white striped tank top she wore with faded blue jean shorts. She kept a red, white, and blue tie-dye scrunchie around her wrist. She planned to use it to tie her hair back when she and Madla went swimming in the afternoon.

Fisherman Dave looked at Krista's outfit and said, "Yes, I see you are wearing red, white, and blue, but you could also be celebrating Czechoslovakia today! Our flag is also red, white, and blue."

"Wow! I didn't even realize that," Madla commented.

Fisherman Dave patted Madla gently on the top of her head. Turning back to Krista, he said, "Why are most people visiting the lake at your home today?"

"Where I live, there are many lakes. We go to the lake for a picnic and maybe to fish. We play games outside and watch fireworks in the evening. Madla and I brought food today for a picnic, too," Krista elaborated. The words came faster and comfortably through her lips. Though some letters still sounded like she had a stutter, Krista was beginning to master the art of speaking.

"It's nice to celebrate your country. I can imagine you feel a little homesick sometimes," Fisherman Dave consoled.

"Sometimes," admitted Krista.

Madla lifted her arm over Krista's shoulder and stood on her tiptoes. She said, "But now Krista's got me. She will be even more homesick for our friendship when she has to go back to America." As Madla's arm rested the back of Krista's neck, Krista felt the clasp of her Best Friend necklace rub against her skin. She missed home, and she definitely missed Ruthie, but Madla was right. She would also miss the friends she had made here when she returned to the states at the end of the summer. Zofie, Jakub, Karel, Kai, Fisherman Dave, and especially Madla had left an imprint on her heart.

Fisherman Dave noticed Krista's uneasiness. "It's sometimes difficult when you have a piece of home in different places."

Madla's questioning look gave away her question before words were ever said, "How can you have pieces of a home in different places?"

"A home doesn't have to be a building. Maybe a better way to describe 'home' is a feeling. A place where you feel loved, comfortable, and safe. Sometimes we don't truly know we are home until home ultimately finds us," Fisherman Dave spoke gently.

Krista instinctively pinched the half-heart dangling around her neck as she thought of how Ruthie must be celebrating the holiday back in America. Madla shrugged her shoulders, indifferent to the idea of having a home in multiple places considering all her family and friends lived in Letovice.

"Does your family celebrate any Czech holidays?" Fisherman Dave asked Krista.

"No. My parents didn't teach me Czech customs or even the language until five years ago. I still only speak in English with Mom. All I have ever known is how to be American," Krista replied.

The old fisherman nodded in understanding, "Sometimes it is easier for a person to cut the ties to their past because it makes them ache for a home that they know they cannot have at the moment." The fisherman bestowed wisdom like a fortune cookie.

"I bet that's why Mom doesn't tell me about her childhood," Krista said aloud, but more for herself to hear.

Fisherman Dave agreed as he sighed a compassionate, "Mhm." The conversation had brought them back to the quietness of the cove, and the fisherman easily slouched into his lawn chair. No sooner than the seat started sinking to the ground did he feel a drop of rain hit his forehead. Looking up at the sky, Fisherman Dave noticed the darkening clouds and the mist that followed.

"Interesting," commented the old fisherman as he glanced at his watch. "Normally, the summer rain comes at the heat of the day around three o'clock, but it looks like we will be getting a shower early today. I believe we will need to have Krista's Independence Day picnic under the bridge for the time being," Fisherman Dave stated. He pulled the lid over his tackle box and reeled in the line of his fishing pole. The sprinkling rain began forming ripples on the surface of the water. Holding the tackle box with one hand and the lawn chair the other, Fisherman Dave escorted the girls beneath the wide bridge. Krista and Madla each pushed their bikes to the new picnic spot and used the kickstands to keep the bikes from tipping over. Madla sprinted back to the fisherman's spot to grab his lunch pail and fishing rod. She made it back under the bridge before the rain started a regular rhythm, though her hair shone from the dampness it had acquired on the additional trip in the shower.

"Thank you, Madla," Fisherman Dave gleamed as he took the lunch pail and pole from her hands. Fisherman Dave unfolded his lawn chair, and each girl pulled a towel from their knapsacks to sit on.

"Aunt Zofie made sandwiches with egg salad. She sent along a container of watermelon and some chocolate-filled donuts too. Aunt Zofie is such a wonderful cook; she can make even a picnic from our knapsacks look like a feast," Madla rambled.

Fisherman Dave pulled out the bag of gummy worms, adding it to the pile of snacks and treats the girls laid before them. "I thought if I had worms to catch the fish, then I should have some worms to catch my listeners too," Fisherman Dave chuckled. Madla greedily tore open the bag of gummy worms and popped one into her mouth. She passed the bag to Krista, who did the same before she offered one to the generous fisherman.

"It doesn't look like we have much else to do but listen to more of Wes's story," Krista probed.

"It would seem that way, doesn't it?" smiled Fisherman Dave.

"So, what happens next to Mister Wessely?" Madla pressed.

Fisherman Dave lounged deeply in his chair. "It's amazing how one man pushed Wes into the person he became. Whether it was his interaction with Nicholas Winton or the tendency war has to raise boys into men at rapid speed, I guess only he will know. Yet, Nicky certainly had an impact on Wes's life in the limited time they knew each other. So much of an impact that he gave his first child the same nickname! However, the start of Wes's journey into manhood really began a few days before he met Nicky when he had a one-time encounter that launched the start of the war through his own eyes."

January 2, 1939
— Wes

Wes pressed his face against the frosted window. The ice tingled the tip of his nose. Though, the heat from his body left a melted mark that quickly froze again when he pulled his face away from the frosted pane. The sun tucked into bed early in the cold winter months, and on this night, the moon hid behind a curtain of fog and clouds. Even though it was only shortly after six in the evening, the darkness had teamed with the fog and frost to successfully hide any scenery from the view of the window. The train rocked as it plowed through a light layer of freshly fallen snow. The cabin lights in the train sparingly illuminated the compartment where Wes sat. Across from Wes sat Auntie, who fiddled in the dark with a ball of yarn and crochet hook. She had told Wes it would be a scarf, but the lack of light in the train cabin and his great-aunt's failing eyes altered her aspirations. The crochet project curved as Auntie accidentally skipped stitches, but Wes was certain she could make a nice hat instead. Wes's faded brown suitcase was packed full of Christmas gifts and sets of winter clothes he hadn't yet brought to Prague from home. Auntie's rug sack was overflowing with leftovers and preservatives from the farm stock. Jars of jams, applesauce, pumpkin compote, and sauerkraut clanked with the rhythm of the train. Wes knew they would arrive in Prague soon, but he was anxious to move from the spot where he had been planted for nearly three hours. He bounced his legs and tapped his feet, but he couldn't trick his legs into thinking they were moving. He simply needed a short walk, or he was sure he would jump from the train and sprint back to the apartment dragging his tired, old aunt from behind the moment the train stopped at the station.

"I'm going to find the restroom," he said to Auntie in desperation.

She mumbled something about getting back in time to help her take the luggage from the racks above their heads, but Wes was already sliding open the door of their train compartment into the narrow hallway. He held the railing that ran along the wall to balance with the swaying of the train. The dim lights on either end of the corridor guided his way. Though darkness remained fixated outside the window, Wes heard the echo of the train and knew they were passing through a tunnel. The sound was short-lived as the train soon came out of the hill on the other side, and the echoing ceased. Wes started in the direction toward the restrooms and noticed a group of businessmen who sat in the compartment next to his. Each sat with grave faces as they looked over different parts of the same newspaper. One man rubbed a hand over his chin, and another pulled the glasses from his face and blinked his eyes as he said something inaudible to the rest of the group. It was apparent that Christmas joy and merriness had been quickly forgotten as current affairs continued to pull the threads of social conversations. Wes looked away, hoping by distracting his mind, he could forget about the war that breathed down the back of his neck.

He moved a little further through the corridor and noticed a more peaceful scene in the next compartment. Two small children laid over the seats and had fallen asleep to the cradling movement of the train. A baby yawned in the arms of a mother and reached out to grab the beard of the father who sat next to his wife. The man wore a wide-brimmed top hat even in the confines of the train compartment. A doll lay on the floor where one of the sleeping children had dropped it, and a gold menorah extended its many arms from the top of one of their bags.

"They're Jewish," Wes whispered to himself.

With a thriving Jewish Quarter in Prague and a historical Jewish community near Wes's childhood home, he wasn't unfamiliar with the religious differences. He was simply surprised to see a Jewish family traveling with the height of concern in the news and the rumors they had inevitably heard. Wes reasoned from the number of bags of luggage they had stacked in the train compartment that the family wasn't going to Prague for a simple visitation. They obviously intended to stay for a while. Wes continued his short walk to the end of the hallway, the whole time thinking about how he wanted to avoid the talk of war; he wanted to forget about the displaced refugees who continued to flood into his country. He regularly sidestepped the newsstand and averted his eyes from seeing the bold titles that covered the papers. Yet, the war followed him closer than his own shadow, threatening him to pick a side and pay the consequences of the decision. Wes was never one to involve himself in confrontation. Like Switzerland, he often remained neutral and uninvolved.

The bathroom at the end of the corridor was locked and a sign tacked to the door read "Out of Order." Wes didn't hesitate as he pulled open the heavy doors of the next train car, revealing even worse lights in the second car. Wes saw the outline of the bathroom door and felt for the handle. As he took a step closer, his foot nudged something on the ground followed by a soft whimper and a series of sniffles.

Startled, Wes quickly retreated his step and whispered into the darkness, "Hello?"

The overhead light flickered, illuminating the end of the train car. On the floor next to the bathroom door, Wes saw who had made the sound. A child, no more than six years old, sat with his knees tucked under his chin and arms wrapped around his head, muffling his quiet sobs, obviously more frightened than Wes had been a moment before. Wes instantly dropped to his knees next to the boy and rested his hand over the little child's shoulder.

"Are you hurt? Lost?" Wes questioned.

The child peaked his eyes over his folded arms, his long eyelashes matted with tears. The curls on his head bounced with his infrequent sobs. The child mumbled something Wes didn't understand. Poking his head quickly around the corner, Wes looked to see if someone was in the corridor searching for the child. Seeing no one, Wes tried again, "Can I help?"

The boy took a breath and spoke a little more clearly, though Wes soon realized why he hadn't understood the boy before. He wasn't speaking Czech. Wes caught a few words that sounded German, but he knew the boy wasn't speaking exact German.

"Maybe a German dialect? Or Dutch?" thought Wes.

"Bathroom... afraid... dark," the boy stuttered.

Wes pieced it together and, in German, asked the boy, "Where is your mother?"

The boy pointed to the doors to the next train car that Wes had just come through and added, "Heavy doors... opened... ticket man... gone..."

With pieces of the story coming together, Wes reached to grab the shaking hand of the little boy.

"I'll help you find your mother," Wes said in German.

The boy pulled his hand back, not understanding Wes well enough. Wes pointed to the next train car. "Help you go to mother," Wes tried again. He held out his hand for the boy to voluntarily take. The boy wiped his nose and cheeks with the back of his sleeve before he reached out and grabbed Wes's hand. As Wes started pulling the boy to his feet, the cabin lights flickered and died once again. Wes's fingers lost circulation as the boy gripped with all his strength onto the hand of the stranger and slid back to the ground next to Wes's legs.

Leaning down, Wes comforted, "It's okay. We will go find your mother. Come on." He tried to loosen the grip of the child's fingers, surprised at the strength the little boy had. Grabbing the child under his arms, Wes pulled the boy up to his chest. The little boy wrapped his arms around Wes's neck, and his legs looped around his torso. Tears dripped from the boy's face and puddled onto Wes's shoulder. Wes saw the light coming through the edges of the train door and again felt for a handle. The boy tightened his hold on Wes's neck. After a little fumbling in the dark and balancing the added weight with the continuous rocking of the train, Wes felt the handle and pulled open the door with ease. They entered the train car with the boy still clinging to Wes like a monkey on a banana tree. Through the dim lights, Wes saw the Jewish gentleman step out from his family compartment.

"Feivel?" the man's rich voice boomed through the hallway.

The boy dropped from Wes and made a quick sprint lunging for his father's legs.

The father placed his hand over Feivel's curls as the child explained getting trapped in the next train car in the frightening dark. Pointing to Wes, Feivel continued to explain the crucial help of the stranger. The father tipped the brim of his hat to Wes in thanks before ushering his son back to his seat and sliding the door in place.

"Yiddish!" thought Wes, suddenly realizing the reason he only caught part of the language. Wes smiled to himself, feeling the joy that was contagious from reuniting the lost boy with his father.

The engine whistled as the train slowed to a stop. Passengers rushed to disembark and made their way to the warmth of the station. Wes balanced the rug sack and suitcase on one arm as he helped Auntie down to the platform of Prague's Central Station. She was tired from the long journey and leaned against Wes's broad frame for balance. As Wes helped her move slowly to the exit, he noticed the young Jewish mother standing on the platform, still holding the baby while one restless child tugged at her long skirt. The father held a sleeping child in one arm as he shuffled suitcases and trunks with the other. Finally, Wes saw Feivel. He was propped on a stack of three suitcases, his feet dangled, nearly touching the platform. A hat covered his head but failed to hide the curls that poked out around Feivel's ears. Feivel's head turned to catch Wes's gaze. His face was no longer damp with tears or red from sobbing. Feivel's cheeks lifted as he smiled in Wes's direction. He gave a small wave with his hand and then jumped off the stack of suitcases to help his mother with the little sibling that still tugged at her skirt.

Wes's attitude about the war changed at that moment. He knew then that the war wasn't something to avoid or avert from, but how he responded to the inevitable could only come from himself. Wes had seen the propaganda against the Jewish race. He had heard people already taking sides and making claims. Though he didn't know the Jewish community as a whole and had no further experiences to lay his opinions upon, Wes decided he knew Feivel: a gentle little boy frightened of the dark and not strong enough to open the door of a train. For Wes, that was enough to pick a side. He didn't make his decision on a whole nation of people or a long list of references; rather, his decision fell solely on a curly-haired boy with a smile and a name.

April 29, 1973
— Niky

Ash trailed after us as we hiked up the hill on the far side of the valley. Technically, I suppose Ash trailed after Marie, though I try to convince myself it is Marie's lack of shoe tying skills that causes the playful cat to chase the free laces. Mother carried a picnic basket over her arm, and I silently nibbled on a roll I had sneaked out of the basket before we left the house. Though Mother had invited Patja's family to join us on the endeavor, they regretfully declined, saying they needed to spend the weekend packing. I had seen Patja's room all stacked with boxes the day before. It made it impossible to find any of Patja's games, so we left the mess and went to play soccer at the climbing tree. At the fence corner, I automatically stopped and waited for Patja to announce, "Race me," but was surprised to see Patja continue hiking toward the tree.

"Getting a head start, are you?" I teased.

Patja looked back at me. "Don't you think we're a little old to keep racing to that tree, Nik?"

"You're just upset because, in the fourteen years of our friendship, you have never won," I smirked.

"I won that once!"

"Only because I tripped!" That blasted mole will forever be my greatest nemesis.

"I could win again if I wanted."

"Bet you couldn't."

Patja swiveled to face me straight on. With narrowed eyes, Patja announced, "Race me."

Of course, I won. Patja gave some lame excuse, "I didn't feel like winning is all."

The soccer ball had deflated over the winter months hanging from the tree. We kicked it around a bit, but I quickly lost interest as it limped over the grass. From out of nowhere, Ash appeared and batted her paws at the hobbling ball before she darted again to the receding pile of hay at the bottom of the hill.

"I'll have to inflate the soccer ball again," said Patja.

"Do you know where the air pump is?"

"At my house, I think."

"You think you can find the pump in the mess at your house?"

Patja shrugged, "It doesn't do much good to have a flat ball."

"It doesn't do much good to have a lost pump either."

Patja gave the ball a hard kick, and it flopped halfway down the hill. "I guess no more soccer today."

"So, let's race again," I suggested. "To the ball."

"That's just a sprint. We already sprinted today."

"I'm good at sprints."

"Right, and I like long distance. How about down the hill, around the goat fence, past Dvorak's farm, and back up to the tree from the backside."

I moaned, "Fine."

Patja won. I had a strong lead until we rounded the fence, and then a pinch came to my side. I slowed down a bit but was still close to Patja's heels. I pushed myself, but the distance between me and Patja kept getting wider. By the time I made it around Dvorak's farm, Patja was halfway up the backside of the hill to the tree. My legs felt like jelly, but in the final stretch, I gave all my energy and made the last sprint to the tree.

"I told you I could win if I wanted," Patja said as I collapsed to the ground.

"You can have long-distance. I'll keep the record in sprints," I said between breaths.

Patja sat down next to me with an outstretched arm, "Deal."

Though Patja had been able to slip away from packing yesterday, there was no pausing the boxing fiasco today. Patja's mother shuffled through narrow hallways of boxes, quickly scratching labels onto the sides with a black marker. I suppose we will soon be packing too, but today, we took a Sunday afternoon off from chores and schoolwork to enjoy a picnic together. Dad led the way through the streets of Lazinov and over the hills on the right side of the valley. The area was surrounded by forests, but an open field at the top of the hill gave the perfect look-out over our little village. The ground was still soft from the rain, and grass filled the open field in a sea of soft green. Mother laid out a blanket, and Marie followed Ash, who chased a grasshopper. I peeled off my jacket, the afternoon sun warmed me away from the shadows of the valley. As Mother set out the picnic, Dad laughed at Marie and Ash's parade. When the cat caught a whiff of Mother's toasted sandwiches, she quickly abandoned the grasshopper and tried to join us on the blanket. Mother scolded Ash and gave her a gentle shove off the blanket. Ash seemed to get the idea and laid down in the grass, though I saw Marie toss her a piece of ham from the basket. Our late lunch was over quickly as we were ravished from waiting and then devoured all of Mother's food. She asked if we enjoyed her cooking and Marie gave an enthusiastic, "Yes!"

I nodded in agreement. To be honest, I was so hungry, and I didn't wait to see how it tasted before I swallowed. Apparently, the roll I had confiscated from the basket earlier had only grown my appetite. As Mother put the empty containers back into the basket, Dad, Marie, and I played catch with a small ball that Dad had shoved into his coat pocket. Marie wanted to teach Dad a game she learned at school called Hot Potato. Of course, I already knew the game, and I'm positive Dad did too, but he listened intently as Marie explained the basic instructions.

It wasn't long before I was completely bored with the primitive game, so I purposely got myself out. Marie seemed pleased that she wasn't the first to lose, and Dad gave me a look that showed he understood the trick I had played. I sat down on the hill and looked across the valley. The river rushed vigorously as it carried the spring water and shimmered like scales of a fish in the sunlight. I traced the road with my finger through the village, following Filip's truck. Karel had said they would pick up the last of their things this weekend from the old house; they were all moved into the apartment below his sister and brother-in-law. Lazinov isn't the same without Karel and Filip. Patja can feel it too. As much as Patja and I tried to ignore Karel jumping into our conversations on the bus, we realized we actually miss his interruptions.

I didn't notice when Marie and Dad finished Hot Potato, but Marie was soon sitting next to me. Her hair looked lighter as the sun beamed down on it, and she scooped up Ash in her arms. The youthful cat didn't stay cradled in her lap for long and soon pounced over her shoulder after another grasshopper.

"Can you see our house?" asked Marie.

I followed the roads with my eyes. I almost felt the gravel beneath my feet having walked them hundreds of times before. My gaze traveled through the little center to the homes that sprinkled over the hillside.

"There," I pointed. "Can you see it, nestled in the side of that hill?"

Marie followed the direction of my finger. "Yes! There it is!"

I let my arm drop. I didn't want to look at Lazinov anymore. It was as if peering into an open coffin.

Dad spoke from behind us, "Isn't this a nice view?"

Marie's big curls bounced as she nodded.

"It will look different in a couple of years with the water all down there, but this place will stay dry and right near the water's edge," Mother commented.

"I think it will be beautiful with all the water," Marie resounded.

I didn't comment.

"You will like it here on the reservoir when they finally finish the dam," Dad grinned. The comment was probably more directed at me than Marie since he's already got her sold on moving.

That's when I realized why we were having the picnic on the hill. This is the place where Mother and Dad will rebuild our home in New Lazinov. I noticed then that some of the forest trees had been recently cut, and there was evidence that others had also visited the surrounding area. Dad had brought us there so we could become comfortable with the new location, but I wasn't falling for his prompts about how beautiful the view was or how great the water would be. The view was only wonderful because of the village that lay tucked into the valley. I tried to imagine the land covered with water, and in my imagination, it looked like how sea explorers predict the inside of the Titanic must look. Remnants of life frozen underwater — doors, windows, cupboards, staircases — all dripping with algae and deteriorating into the current.

As if the little village had read my thoughts, a faint echo of the bell resounded through the valley and drifted up the slope where we sat. I looked to Mother and Dad, who both had the same lamenting expression on their faces. Mother reached up and crossed herself as she must have learned from attending mass with her grandparents as a child. Though I have never seen her practice faith before, it seemed the bell this Sunday had reminded her of tradition. (Our government doesn't support religious practice, and those who attend church have strict restrictions. The only time I have stepped in a cathedral was for a tour — and it was unbelievably boring.)

Marie gave a confused look. "It's not morning, noon, or dinner. Why did the bell ring? Is there a fire?"

With no smoke in view, there wasn't a need to ring for our little fire brigade, which left only one other option for Mrs. Kobzova to pull the bell at this time. Someone in our village had died.

July 5, 1994
— Krista

The sound of the rain tapping against the window captured Krista's attention. She flipped over on her bed and watched the drops race down the glass. The solitary drops of rain followed the path of the one before them and then puddled at the bottom of the window frame before sliding off the windowsill. Though the rain had limited her activities for the day, Krista didn't mind an excuse to spend the morning reading. She had already made plans to help Zofie make desserts in the kitchen and practice new chords with Jakub on his guitar. Krista had taken an interest in learning guitar, and Jakub offered to teach a few basic tips. She heard him tuning the instrument in the living room and looked forward to their lesson, which Jakub said would begin at two o'clock, though that meant one-fifty since everyone knew the clock in the hall was notoriously ten minutes fast. Rick and Doma had taken the car to visit Rick's mother in the nursing home, which left Krista in the care of her hosts.

Normally, Krista knew her parents wouldn't have a problem if she wanted to take a walk with an umbrella on a rainy day, but after the events of last night, Krista decided to it was best to stay at the house. She easily recalled the commotion after returning from the dam the day before.

The sun had just begun its descent in the western sky when Krista arrived back at Zofie and Jakub's house after the day at the lake. The rainstorm hadn't let up until the afternoon, so Madla and Krista planted themselves under the bridge and listened to Fisherman Dave's unending story of Wes. Krista listened with more attention than she had given her school teachers all year and reasoned all educators should take a class from Fisherman Dave on storytelling. Most surprising was how the gripping tale even captured the attention of "Chatterbox Madla." Fisherman Dave's words spread the story like soft butter and kept Madla quiet for most of the story when she wasn't jumping in with a tale of her own.

When the rain finally stopped, Krista and Madla waded into the cool water before they laid their towels on the shore and let the rays of sunshine dry their skin. As the clouds shifted and the sun emerged, Fisherman Dave packed up his tackle box and folded his lawn chair. It had evidently not been a great day for fishing due to the rain, but storytelling had brightened the fisherman's day more than catching the biggest bass in the lake. Krista and Madla walked Fisherman Dave to the bus stop and waved goodbye with promises to come again soon. Truthfully, they were both anxious to hear what happened next in the journey of Wes. They had just gotten back to the shore to collect their bikes when the rain started again. The girls hustled once again under the bridge and waited out the shower. They passed the time by making up their own endings for the story of Wes. All of Madla's endings included a bride for the main character, and Krista rolled her eyes, wondering how many romance Hollywood movies Madla had actually seen. As the rain finally cleared, the girls hauled their bikes back onto the road home and set off.

Upon arriving back at the house, Krista first met Jakub, who was in the front entry tying his shoes. When he saw Krista enter through the door, the worried expression on his face relaxed. Before greeting her, he called up the stairs with relief, "She's back." Krista heard Zofie in the hall say, "Karel, Krista just walked in. You and Jakub won't need to take the cars out. Madla should be home soon." Krista heard the phone click on the receiver. The storm that followed was much worse than the one Krista had been trapped in at the dam.

"Where on Earth have you been?" Doma's voice bellowed from the hall before she saw Krista.

Krista was confused. Of course, her parents had known she and Madla had been to the dam again. She was back before sunset, just as she had promised, though the rain clouds still crowded the sky, mimicking an early dusk.

Jakub saw her perplexed look. "We were worried because of the storm."

"Your parents thought maybe you tried to bike in the rain," Zofie commented from the top of the stairs. Doma and Rick were quickly at Krista's side. Doma wrapped her arms around her daughter, "Since it cleared up and then started raining again so fast, we wondered if you had gotten stuck somewhere in the rain or if you or Madla had fallen on the slippery roads or if a car hadn't seen you in the downpour," Doma's voice drifted. She had clearly imagined every possible outcome.

"Madla and I waited at the dam for the rain to pass. We were going to leave earlier, but that's when the rain started again," Krista explained.

"Of course, we thought you would leave the bikes at the dam and take the bus home as we had discussed. When the bus came and neither you nor Madla got off, we called Karel and started preparing to set out for you," Rick finished explaining.

Krista looked at her feet. "I'm sorry, we honestly didn't mean to worry you. We just waited for the rain to pass."

"You didn't do anything wrong, dear," Zofie reassured Krista. Then, to the adults, Zofie calmly said, "I told you they'd be fine! They're clever girls. All this worrying wasted." Zofie wiped her hand through the air as if trying to clear the cloud of concern that had fallen over her house.

Krista felt guilty that she and Madla had caused five worrisome adults a stressful afternoon. The rest of the evening moved by quietly, and Doma tucked into bed early. Krista, fearful it was the added anxiety of the evening that had caused her mom's tiredness to advance, vocalized her concerns to her dad.

Rick looked at Krista sympathetically, "No, Krista, your mom is a little extra worried right now. We received an email from your brother today."

"Jack? What happened, Dad?"

Rick pointed to Zofie's computer on the desk in the corner of the living room. "The email is still up. Go ahead and read it. It arrived today just after lunch."

Krista sat in front of the boxy monitor and jiggled the mouse to wake the computer from its power nap. The screen slowly awoke with a dim glow, and Krista saw Pastor Everson's email address on the top of the screen and Jack's name printed at the bottom. The note started with *"Hi Mom,*

Don't worry," and Krista knew those first four words must have already sent her mom into a frenzy. She almost wanted to scold Jack for using careless words at the beginning of the email but wondered if maybe the email contained something to be worried about.

Hi Mom,

Don't worry, I had an accident at camp, but the doctor said I should recover quickly. I was at the beach with the campers during Free Time, and one of the campers swam out too far. He got scared and yelled for help because he didn't think he could swim back to the shore. I sprinted down the dock and dove into the water. Well, I stepped on a large sliver of wood that had come loose from the old dock. After I helped the kid get back to the dock, I noticed the thin trail of blood that had soaked into the boards and realized it was coming from my foot. The wood was still stuck in it, but another counselor quickly ran for the camp nurse. She called Mr. Everson and drove me to the hospital. Mr. Everson met me at the hospital and was already filling out all the forms. The doctors got the wood out and stitched up my foot. It's wrapped well, but it looks like I'll be on crutches for the rest of the summer. I've already switched my Free Time watch on the beach with another counselor who organizes card games in the mess hall, and Mr. Everson told me they are repairing the dock to prevent more injuries. I'll take the extra weekend to rest at the Eversons' house. Like I said, no need to worry! Just wanted to keep you informed.

Love,
Jack

P.S. Krista, Ruthie says hello! She is great at making sure I always have juice and the remote for the TV. I told her she could give you tips for serving on me when you get home —
just kidding!

Krista knew Mrs. Everson and Ruthie were taking good care of Jack. They were always the first to bring home-cooked meals to friends and neighbors after a tragedy. As Krista thought about Jack's injury, she could imagine how bad it must have been, though Jack hadn't let on to any pain in the email. She admired her big brother's strength and knew he probably didn't mention the pain the injury had caused so not to worry Doma more. Krista applauded his efforts in protecting their mother from greater apprehension, but Krista understood why Doma had been even more worrisome with the rain situation earlier.

"Mom must be pretty concerned," Krista said to Rick.

Rick nodded, "She has already written three emails with Pastor Everson, but he reassured her that Jack is doing all right and will be back at camp next week."

"That sounds like Mom," Krista replied.

Rick chuckled, "I thought it sounded like Jack to jump back into activities so quickly."

Krista smiled, "Yeah, Jack bounces back fast." Her eyebrows scrunched together as she asked, "What about Mom?"

"She'll probably be a little extra protective of you the next couple of days," Rick answered honestly. "Don't give her extra things to worry about," he added with a wink. Rick teased Krista with the last statement knowing his sweet, straight-A daughter was always a responsible child and had yet to present a rebellious stage.

Krista caught onto the joke and suppressed a laugh before asking, "So, why does Mom worry so easily?"

"Because she's a mom," Rick said.

"She worries more than other moms," Krista pressed.

Rick gestured for Krista to join him on the sofa. As she sat down on the cushion next to his, Rick started, "Your mom was a free and adventurous girl growing up. She didn't worry about hardly anything. She was a lot like Jack and would never show how she was truly feeling or hurting."

"So, what happened? Why did she change?" Krista inquired.

"I suppose having kids had something to do with it. We both worry about you and Jack because that's what parents do."

"But that's not all of it, is it?" Krista pried.

Rick looked into his daughter's eyes, which looked more green than hazel with the pale green sweater she wore. Taking a deep breath, Rick pushed through the next part of the story. "When your mom and I left Czechoslovakia, we had to leave everything behind. Our family and friends, our home, language — everything we knew that was familiar changed overnight. Suddenly, there were so many changes that your mom began having great uneasiness about things she couldn't change."

Krista hadn't thought about her mom's anxiety in much depth, but she realized that Doma's worrying attitude spiked in situations that she could not control, like in the event of Jack's injury.

"Your mom is learning not to get overwhelmed and stressed over things she can't control, though it is often difficult for her because many of the situations remind her of the anxiety first caused by leaving Czechoslovakia," Rick notified.

"I've learned in school about soldiers who have post-traumatic stress after a terrible situation, and when they are reminded of it, they relapse into reacting like they are in war again. Does Mom have something like this?" asked Krista. She was concerned for her mom, though also relieved for finally receiving some answers about Doma's reoccurring heightened nervousness.

"Maybe something like that," Rick concurred before he added, "Your mom is really strong, and she doesn't like to look back on the past, but sometimes the past still affects her."

Rick quickly wrapped up the discussion saying, "It's time for bed, Krista. Just remember to give Mom a little extra time in situations like this."

Krista looked to her dad, reluctant to leave. "I still have more questions, Dad."

"Maybe another time, kiddo," Rick patted her head. It was then that Krista realized it wasn't only her mom who held onto the pain of the past, but her dad, like an onion, revealed only a layer at a time. Which is more than she could say for her mom, who resembled more of a clam in conversations such as these. Krista gave Rick a weak smile whispering, "Goodnight, Dad."

She walked across the living room and got a glass of water from the kitchen before retreating to their shared bedroom, leaving Rick alone on the sofa.

For a few minutes, Rick remained planted where he sat with his head resting in his hands, his fingers blocking his vision. He heard Zofie enter the living room and sit across from him. Her fingers rhythmically tapped on the arm of the chair, giving away without a doubt that she had joined Rick. Without looking up from his hands, Rick said, "She's a curious one, my Krista."

"Mhm," Zofie grunted and continued to strum her fingers. For a few moments, they sat in silence. When Rick finally looked up from his hands, Zofie asked, "What all did you tell her?"

"You didn't hear enough from eavesdropping in the hall?"

Zofie shrugged, but her eyes gave away her stake-out in the corridor.

"You never change," Rick said with a small smile.

"On the contrary, old friend. It is you who has remained the same. Still trying to protect your girl from pain," Zofie truthfully stated.

"There's no easy way to tell Krista about what happened that night," Rick confessed, knowing Zofie understood clearly what he was referencing.

"By 'your girl,' I wasn't referring to Krista," Zofie clarified.

"Doma?"

Zofie nodded, "You're still trying to protect her from reliving the pain of the night you left Czechoslovakia, but I must tell you, friend, the thing that is hurting her the most is the fact that she has not released it."

Rick slid lower into the sofa. "I tried to help. I got her to write out her feelings from that night. I've talked with counselors on her behalf," Rick's voice trailed. He leaned his head on the back of the sofa and looked at the ceiling. "How can I help her if I don't even understand it myself?" he confessed.

"Healing isn't slapping on a bandage and saying everything is okay. It is hours of rehabilitation and learning to tug at the pain bit by bit because, in the end, you know it will only strengthen the site of injury." Gray hairs had brought words of wisdom to Zofie over the years.

Rick's face showed concern as he glanced in Zofie's direction, and Zofie read his thoughts before he could find the words. "I won't tell Krista. Jakub won't tell her either. We know this story must come from you and Doma," Zofie reassured.

Rick leaned forward on the sofa and grabbed Zofie's calloused hands between his own, expressing his thanks when he had no more words to offer.

June 16, 1973
— Niky

The days following Mr. Halas's death sent our little village into chaos. Many said Mr. Halas died from old age, though he was only just past the age of retirement. Others said it was an onset of pneumonia that began in the winter; however, I heard Doc

Daniel whisper to Dad that he had played cards with Mr. Halas only a few days before his death and showed no signs of even the slightest cough. Rather, Doc Daniel predicted Mr. Halas hit depression with full force. For the past seven years without Mrs. Halas, many of us neighbors have brought Mr. Halas meals, played cards in his kitchen, and sat with him on his doorstep, waiting for a storm to roll over the valley. Doc Daniel told Dad that when he visited Halas, there were many boxes half-filled and opened, displaying a relic of items. In the seven years after losing his wife, Halas hadn't changed one piece of the decoration in their little home. Doc said even the late wife's book still laid on the nightstand with the bookmark a quarter of the way through. While the elderly man had gone on with his life after his wife's death, it seemed that he had suppressed his loss and nearly imagined she had never left. As Halas packed her items, he realized Mrs. Halas would never return, which catapulted Mr. Halas into a deathly depression.

Marie asked Mother what would happen to Mr. Halas's home. Mother explained that the home would be given to one of his grandchildren from Prague, and they'd decide what to do with it. Not that his relatives have much of a choice in who'd inherit the house, seeing that the whole point of the packing tragedy was due to the fact that the generational home must be demolished. The Halas family had lived in that home for multiple generations. Dad told me before that he remembered visiting Papa Halas (how all the kids in Lazinov called Mr. Halas's father) for peppermint sticks on St. Nicholas Day. If children were ever disobedient, parents would walk out the front door of their homes and call across the valley to Papa

Halas to save the peppermint sticks for a different little boy or girl that year. The children straightened up right away!

Mr. Halas would always say he could feel a storm coming through his bones, and that is how he always knew when to pull the old rocking chair onto the porch. I believe Mr. Halas felt the biggest storm of his life with the news of the dam and the painful memories that came with finally packing his late wife's memories. It was too much for the man who firmly believed he had been born and would die in that home as his father and grandfather before him. Truth is, I've always adored Mr. Halas. He kept his father's tradition of passing out candy on St. Nicholas Day and knew each of the kids by name. (I don't think he ever mixed up Viktor and Vojta.) I wish I could tell him that I'm planning to escape too.

I never dreaded waking up on a Saturday until today. The sun gallantly splashed through the window, and I cursed Mother Nature for not making it mournfully rainy. I don't know where I found the will to get out of bed, but I peeled off the covers and shuffled over to the window. I combed my fingers through my unruly hair and noticed dirt still caked under my fingernails from when Patja and I met late last night by the fence. I had dug my fingers into the soil to see if I could grab some kind of lever that would freeze time so the morning wouldn't come. Obviously, a failed attempt.

Leaning over the windowsill, I saw Patja hauling another box to the back of the car. The box was then wedged between two others, and Patja gave it a final shove in place. I moaned, and my forehead hit the windowsill. For all the people who said a broken heart comes after the first relationship break-up have clearly never had their best friend and next-door neighbor move away. At that moment, I could feel the shards that poked at my heart as if it was made of glass and slowly cracking into itself.

Everything Mother and Dad said at breakfast was less than comforting.

"Patja will only be in Letovice. You can see each other easily."

"You are still in the same class at school."

"Patja's mother has already invited us to visit."

I stirred my oatmeal until it was cold and mushy. I had no desire to eat, but I didn't want to face what waited outside either. Part of me thought it would be best to just lay in bed and wait for today to be over, but somehow, I slid my shoes on my feet and went out to find Patja. There wasn't any more room in the family car, and I wondered if Patja would even fit in the backseat.

"Looks like your parents don't have room for you. You'll just have to stay at my place," I joked. My laugh caught in my throat.

"Nik, don't make this harder than it already is." Patja's shoulders fell forward.

I instinctively wrapped my arms around my best friend. Patja and I have never been the kind of friends who hug; we normally just give each other playful shoves or pats on the back, but when I wrapped my arms around Patja's waist, I felt Patja sag into my arms. A sniffle escaped, and I felt a hot tear marking a trail down my cheek. I quickly wiped it away. Patja held onto me tighter, and then, as quickly as we had reached *for each other, we slipped apart. Patja didn't say anything, only placed a small plastic bag in my hands before climbing between all the boxes in the back of the car. I watched as Patja's dad pulled the car onto the gravel road. Dust and my own cloudy vision made everything look like a Monet painting, but I still saw Patja's puddled eyes from behind the backseat window.*

For as long as I could, I stood on the road and watched the car weave down the narrow streets of the valley. I wished they'd suddenly turn around, declare there had been a mistake, and we could all help them unpack into the home next to mine again. When the car was finally out of view, I watched the dust settle that the wheels had kicked up and then turned back to the connected yard I had once shared with the best neighbor in the world. I sat on the edge of the broken sandbox, where Mother said Patja and I spent our toddler days together. Memories came pouring back as I imagined the sandcastles Patja worked so hard to make that I would jump on and let the sand sink into my shoes while our mothers dragged out baskets of laundry to hang. The laundry lines on Patja's side of the yard were forlornly bare. Mother had draped white dishcloths and pillowcases from our lines this morning, that now lapped in the breeze like surrendering flags. Sitting on the edge of that dilapidated sandbox, I exhaled slowly as I opened the bag Patja had placed in my hands.

I tried to gulp back my tears but completely lost control of the fountain that catapulted from my tear-ducts when I saw what Patja had placed in the plastic bag. Though it wasn't wrapped, I knew Patja had given me the greatest treasure because at the bottom of the bag laid the ball pump. At that moment, I knew my best friend had left me that tattered, priceless soccer ball at the climbing tree because a simple note was stuck on the pump with only two words, "Race me."

July 12, 1994
— Krista

Krista kept a low profile during the week as she knew Doma was still in a frenzy about Jack's condition. Doma continued to be vocally thankful for the gift of e-mail that connected them with Jack and the Eversons daily. Krista wondered if the e-mail was truly a gift since it was the quick technology that allowed her mom to know what happened to Jack and spiral her worried state, though Krista reasoned they would have found out sooner than later through the slow postal service. With Doma writing to Jack daily, Krista found the silver lining in the short notes Ruthie sent through Jack at the end of each e-mail.

P.S. Krista, Ruthie wants to know if you have any new friends there.

P.S. Krista, say hi to Madla from me! Any friend of Krista's is a friend of mine. Ruthie

P.S. Can you send me a recipe for Czech sweet buns? Ruthie

P.S. The sweet buns tasted great! I miss you. Are you wearing your necklace? Ruthie

Throughout the week, Doma frequently checked on Krista and bustled around the house, trying to keep herself from catching the next flight back to the United States. The e-mails had stopped arriving daily now that Jack was back at Camp Pinewood; although, Mrs. Everson had made an effort to visit Jack twice already, sending Rick and Doma encouraging updates about Jack's quick healing. With Jack on the mend, Doma naturally eased up on Krista as well. Madla and Kai had visited often during the week, as Zofie was not only their aunt but also their designated summer nanny. This summer, Zofie felt more freedom now that the kids were old enough to entertain themselves, and with Krista playing with Madla and Kai, there were fewer arguments to defuse. Krista, Madla, and Kai spent hours together playing backyard games and draping blankets from the tree branches to create teepees. However, after a week of playing within the confined area of the backyard, Krista ached for the freedom of her bike and the lake.

Madla and Kai hadn't come to Zofie's house today. Krista knew that Karel took more days off in the summer to be with his kids, but Krista also knew Madla would want to join her on a trip to the dam. Krista dialed Karel's number, which was conveniently tacked to the wall next to the phone, only to learn Madla was suffering from a consistent cough and had already emptied an entire box of tissues. Feeling defeated and trapped again, Krista slouched against the wall in the hallway. For a fleeting moment, she contemplated going to the dam alone but chased the thought away, knowing her mom would be frantic the moment she learned Krista had biked to the dam by herself.

Krista propped her elbow on her knee and twirled her hair around her finger. She heard Zofie's whistling echo up the staircase, followed by her heavy footsteps. As Zofie turned into the hallway with a clothes hamper balanced on her hip, she nearly tripped over Krista, who still sat under the phone.

"Dear girl! Why are you sitting on the floor? Are you planning to make me fall?" Zofie questioned.

Krista let her head lean against the wall as she looked up at Zofie. "I'm bored," she declared.

Still juggling the basket of clothes, Zofie chuckled, "When Madla says those words to me, I have a nice list of chores for her. She learns very quickly how to play nicely with Kai!"

Not fazed by the hanging threat of chores, Krista sighed, "Madla's sick."

Instantly, compassion filled Zofie as she set the basket of clothes at her feet and put her hands on her hips. "You know," Zofie started, "I was planning to go visit a good friend of mine today. Would you like to come with me?"

Krista shrugged, "Beats sitting around here all day, I suppose."

"Wonderful! After I get the clothes put away and box some biscuits for my friend, we can go."

Krista reached out and took the overflowing basket from Zofie's arms. "I might as well help since I'm bored anyway."

With Krista helping, they were ready to go in record time. Carrying a plastic container filled with sweet rolls, Krista walked out of the front gate and waited for Zofie on the road in front of the house. Zofie called to Jakub in the garage, saying she and Krista were headed out. Together, Zofie and Krista strolled down the sloping hill to the city center. Zofie glanced at her watch, "We'd better quicken our pace a bit!"

"Why?" Krista's brow scrunched.

"We'll miss the bus."

"The bus?"

"Oh, yes. My friend lives a little way out. It will be easier for us to travel by bus."

Krista hastened her step, suddenly a little more excited, knowing she would be taking the bus.

As Zofie paid the bus fare, Krista slid into a seat by the window. Zofie took an aisle seat and propped her bag on her knees. Krista still held onto the container of biscuits, silently wondering what else Zofie could be lugging around in the large bag, considering she didn't have more space for the container. Krista wasn't distracted by the contents of Zofie's bag for long as the view outside the window quickly captured her attention. The bus rounded the city square and headed slowly down a road she was quite familiar with.

"This is the way to the dam," Krista stated nonchalantly.

Zofie nodded and smiled. The bus was relatively empty, though Krista hardly noticed as her gaze was fixed out the window, watching the familiar landscape slide by. They rounded the curving street through the forest, and Krista caught a glimpse of the lake. Crossing over the bridge, she saw a group of fishermen in the cove. However, with the bus moving so quickly down the street, Krista didn't have the chance to pick out Fisherman Dave among the group. Krista wished she and Madla could have gone to the dam together; seeing it for a moment simply wasn't enough to fill Krista's desire to sink her toes in the water and listen to Fisherman Dave's continuous story of the boy named Wes.

Zofie interrupted Krista's thoughts, "Come on. This is our stop."

Krista shuffled over the seats and followed Zofie as they exited through the back door of the bus. The bus pulled away, and Krista immediately recognized the bus stop.

Krista pointed down the street to the little parking lot saying, "That's where Karel parked the car when we came to the lake together. I know this bus stop."

"Yes, I figured," smiled Zofie. "My friend lives there," said Zofie pointing in the opposite direction of the lake to a little village that wove up the hill and merged with the forest. "I will meet you back here in two hours to take the bus home."

Krista's wide eyes expressed her confusion, "You mean, I'm not going with you?"

Zofie unclasped her watch and wrapped it around Krista's wrist. "If you'd like to come, you may, but if you'd rather go to the reservoir, I think you can be trusted there alone. Just don't go too deep into the water," Zofie warned.

Krista laughed, realizing this had been Zofie's plan all along. "Don't worry, I can't go into the water higher than my knees, seeing that I don't have a swimsuit."

Zofie reached into her large bag, pulling out Krista's swimsuit and a towel. "Two hours," she reminded, pointing to the wristwatch on Krista's arm.

Krista grabbed the swimsuit and towel, certain she would have enjoyed the water even without the option to swim. She thanked Zofie and waved as she ran across the parking lot and down the grassy hill to the familiar shoreline. Kids squealed as the water receded and returned to lap at their toes and sailboats speckled the water with pure sails surrendering to the wind. Krista didn't pause as she rounded the shore and cut across to the cove. Her feet leaped over the rocks that littered the shoreline, her feathery hair chased after her. As she passed under the bridge, the mismatched assortment of rowboats and canoes came into view, and a handful of fishermen turned in her direction. One fisherman, who sat nearly on the ground in his sagging chair, dropped his pole to wave and called over to Krista.

"Just when I thought I should pack up for the day, you show up! I was itching to share the next part of Wes's story, so I started sharing it with the others already," Fisherman Dave's voice bellowed through the silent cove. Krista caught a glance at the other fishermen, who seemed pleased she had relieved them from the position of listening to the old man's tales.

"I suppose I will just have to start again from the beginning. That's okay, right, boys?" Fisherman Dave called over his shoulder. Krista heard one man groan, and two others slowly took steps deeper up the cove.

Looking past Krista in the direction she had arrived, Fisherman Dave asked, "Where's your other half?"

"Madla's sick today, but I'll tell her about what happens to Wes," Krista affirmed. She figured she could visit Madla during the week and tell her the next part of the story. Krista was already looking forward to surprising Madla with new knowledge of Wes's journey.

"You did not arrive by bicycle today?"

"I took the bus with Madla's aunt. I'm staying at her house, so I need to meet her back at the bus stop later," Krista explained as she laid the towel on the ground and sat atop the rocky soil.

"Well then, how much time do you have?" Fisherman Dave leaned forward, anxious to get on with the story.

Krista grinned and leaned forward to match Fisherman Dave, propped her elbows on her knees, and rested her chin in the cup of her hands. She heard the faint ticking of Zofie's watch on her wrist as she said, "Just enough time to travel back to 1939."

January 3, 1939
— Wes

With the holiday break over, many of the students came back through the doors of Language School with dragging feet and ambitions to make it to summer break. Yet, some students failed to return to school in the new year. Rumors circulated about the missing students ranging from those with distant Jewish relatives to others who had given up their careers as linguists to join Hitler's youth brigade. Truth be told, no one ultimately knew what had become of the students who were forever absent from the class lists. It seemed to Wes that the country was standing on cracked ice. Moving in any direction would cause the ice to snap inward, so the country remained cautiously balanced and calling for help on the brink of tragedy.

Wes joined in the cry of his countrymen as they made wishes in the schoolyard and pleaded on the streets for nations to recognize Hitler's bigger plans that unfolded around them. There was little Wes could do to stop the historical repetition at hand. However, falling under government restrictions of another country was an event Czechoslovakia had witnessed many times prior. Wes, a generally optimistic young man, never failed to find the silver lining. Unlike the rest of the country who talked circles around the problems that laid ahead for their nation, Wes let the little joys of each day guide his attitude. Whether it was a spontaneous snowball fight in the schoolyard, Auntie's apple strudel, or a letter from the farm back home, Wes never lost hold of the small joys each day faithfully presented.

On this day in the middle of the week, another little joy resurfaced. Sam had chased Wes down in the corridor at the start of the school day. "Wes! I'm going to the hotel after the last period. Josef told me to start coming again after the Christmas and New Year's crowds die down. They were overstaffed for the holidays, and I guess they didn't need a linguist student in the way of all the holiday events." Sam's shoulders shrugged as he couldn't understand why the hotel staff didn't need his talents during the busy season but was happy to comply with their request that gave him more time for leisure activities. "So, do you want to come along today?" Sam asked.

Wes didn't need any convincing. He had been looking forward all of Holiday Break to join Sam's trips to the hotel again. The two pushed their way through the hallway after the final bell, and whispers flooded in their wake as students commented on the unlikely pair of friends. Sam grew up as a city kid and Wes in the farming country. Sam's lanky figure and curly black hair appeared more evident next to Wes's broad frame and light hair. While Sam's scholarly glasses played a part of his personality, the slight crook on the bridge of Wes's nose gave him a mysterious look. Rumors had circled, saying it was a mark from a fight, while others claimed it was from falling off wild cattle, yet no schoolmate had dared to ask the new student and spoil the fun of imagining the life Wes had lived before.

Wes and Sam chatted idly about school and what they had done over the holidays, which for Wes included cramming everything he had missed from his childhood home into one week. He spent hours helping his dad and uncles with the farm animals and joined old friends for sledding races on many afternoons. The traditions of Christmas surrounded Wes as he explored the open markets with his family; he even found a sense of joy sitting in the cold cathedral for his yearly appearance on Christmas Eve mass. The threatening talk of war hadn't yet slithered into the daily life of the villagers.

Unfortunately, Sam had rarely ventured outside his home during the holiday for the rising fear that kept most families behind closed doors in the confines of their city apartments. Sam confessed he found some peace with school starting again as the routine of going to school brought comfort to his worried parents. The mismatched pair of friends arrived quickly to the hotel, yet the brisk walk was long enough to turn their cheeks rosy and kept their fingers shoved deep into their coat pockets to ward off the chill. They tugged open the doors to the hotel lobby to find all the tables full, and a small crowd gathered around one table in the left corner.

"I thought you said the holiday rush would be over," Wes commented as he unwrapped the scarf from his neck.

Also surprised by the small crowd of people in the lobby, Sam replied, "It is over a week after Christmas. I didn't think people would be staying this long. Especially now, with what is going on around Europe, people aren't taking holiday trips."

Both boys caught Josef's desperate look at the same moment. They rapidly moved to the aid of the receptionist.

"I was hoping you would both come today!" the receptionist frantically greeted as he simultaneously answered the request of a guest for a pen.

"Josef, what's going on?" Sam asked.

Josef waved a young woman in the directions of the restroom and handed a gentleman the cafe menu while answering Sam's question, "One of our guests has had visitors coming for a few days now like this. It started slowly, but in the past few hours, we have had a record number of guests in the lobby."

"What are they all doing here?" Sam questioned.

Before Josef could answer, a waitress passed by, balancing a tray with multiple cups of hot tea. She jumped in, "Thank God! Sam, go help Cook in the kitchen. You would not believe how many teacups there are to wash today."

Sam's shoulders dropped, and with eyes like a hurt puppy, he looked to Wes for reinforcement. "I can help wash," Wes confirmed. He was certain he wouldn't practice his language skills in the kitchen, but Wes's compassionate soul felt for his little friend.

"Wait, Wes." Josef stopped the boys before they made their way to the kitchen. "I've got to stay behind the desk, but the men organizing this mess are English. They're sitting in the middle of that crowd there." Josef pointed to the unseen table in the far-left corner. "Would you kindly ask them how long this chaos will take place today?" Wes was sure the receptionist had never had a crooked tie or messy desk before today.

Placing a hand on Sam's shoulder, Wes said, "I'll join you in the kitchen as soon as I can. I'll bring you the story."

Wes sidestepped past one family and rounded his way to the little crowd that circled the table in the far-left corner. Tapping a few people on their shoulders, he politely shuffled his way up to the head of the table where two men sat, a large scrapbook lay open on the tabletop between them. Wes recognized one of the men as the Englishman Martin who had made the interesting phone call a few weeks before. From his wide range of reasoning skills, Wes assumed the second man had to be the man on the other end of the line, Nicholas Winton. Nicholas's round face complimented the round glasses that fit on his face as if he was born with them attached behind his ears. His hair flatly parted to the side of his head, and a tie snugly looped his collar. The two Englishmen looked at Wes, waiting to learn the reason for his interruption.

Wes cleared his throat and began in proper English, "Excuse me, fine gentleman. I was sent to you from Josef, the receptionist, to ask if..." Wes didn't get a chance to finish Josef's request.

"Brilliant! Martin, look, they've sent a translator to help us," Nicholas beamed.

"Actually," Wes tried again.

"Get this young man a chair!" Martin called over the crowd.

The people around the table shuffled clockwise to make room for the added chair that slid in next to the Englishmen.

"But, actually, I was just sent here to see how long this commotion will be taking place," Wes finally completed his sentence.

"With your help, hopefully, a bit faster now," Nicholas stated. "What's your name, kid?" He motioned for Wes to sit in the chair.

Wes introduced himself with his full name before adding, "Most everyone just calls me Wes."

"Well, Wes, nearly everyone calls me Nicky," smiled the Englishman, "and this is Martin." Nicky waved his hand to indicate his friend, who thumbed through a small stack of papers.

Wes glanced at the open scrapbook on the table and briefly studied a map of Europe that was taped onto the pages. He fearfully voiced his thoughts, "Do you believe in this 'One People, One Empire, One Leader for the Greater Germany'?"

"You can read German?" Nicky looked at Wes in amazement.

Wes nodded.

"Scary to think what they are planning," Nicky said as he looked over his shoulder and then whispered to Wes, "We're trying to prevent it."

A shiver flooded through Wes's veins as he realized the Englishman was a part of risky business. The small crowd that had been gathered around the table quietly dispersed like rain trickling off the awning of a house, except for a young mother who sat at the other end of the table, bouncing a toddler on her knees while quietly talking with Martin.

"They'll be back," Nicky referenced the small crowd. "They haven't stopped coming in today."

"What exactly are you doing here?" curiosity tugged at Wes.

Nicky's glasses slid down to the tip of his nose as his eyes narrowed in on Wes. Wes, taken slightly aback from the inquisitive gesture, pondered if he had used incorrect English grammar. Nicky slid his glasses back onto the bridge of his nose and pressed his lips together before saying, "I'm going to assume you're not a spy. I've already seen two today, and you look nothing like them."

Wes's eyes widened as he observed the people sitting at the surrounding tables. None looked like spies in his opinion. Then again, he had never been aware to look for a spy before, though he assumed they wouldn't be sitting with children. It was then that Wes noticed every table had at least one child seated with the parents. He looked back across the table to see a smile on Nicky's face.

"No. You're not a spy," he concluded, "but tell me then, how do you know English and German?"

"I attend a language school. I know many different languages," Wes explained.

Nicky leaned back in his chair. "Well! You will definitely be useful seeing that this is my first time in Czechoslovakia, thus I have no grasp of the language, and some of the parents who come to us have little to no understanding of English. Just a few days ago, I was at a refugee center for displaced families due to the war, and the only phrase some of the people could say was 'I'm hungry; may I please have a piece of bread?'"

Wes's ears perked at the opportunity to practice his language skills with the Englishmen; however, he still wasn't sure what their operation truly entailed. Considering Nicky didn't regard him as a spy, Wes tried his original question again, "So, what are you doing exactly?"

Nicky flipped the page in the scrapbook. While the first page had been dominated by a German visionary map for Hitler's army, the second page was filled contrarily with pictures of young children. Names were printed atop each picture with surnames that were undeniably Jewish. Nicky tapped the page of pictures. "We're getting them out."

Wes's eyebrows lifted high into his forehead as he glanced over the pictures and names. Closing his eyes for a moment, he saw the image of another little Jewish boy, one who was afraid of the dark and had curly brown hair and wet, red cheeks. Feivel wasn't among the pictures in the scrapbook, but as Wes looked over the smiling pictures of dozens of little boys and girls, he saw children just like Feivel and his siblings. Their gentle faces showed no understanding of what dangers lurked around the corner. With the hope that he could practice his language skills and the possibility to help more kids like Feivel, or even Feivel himself, Wes looked up from the photos into the eyes of the man whose heart was evidently invested in this project. Wes didn't need a minute more to think before four little words catapulted from within him, "How can I help?"

Nicky slid a paper and pen under Wes's chin and then called into the crowd that slowly regathered, "Next please!"

October 27, 1973 — Niky

I've avoided journaling simply because, each time I think about writing, I am layered by another grievance. Lazinov isn't recognizable anymore. Nearly half of the residents have moved out or are planning to move before the new year. A long, obstructing bridge is being built over the south valley. Its height seems exaggerated to me, but they say when the valley is filled with water, the bridge's current height will be necessary. My heart feels like I'm falling from that bridge when I imagine the depth of the water that will soon flow beneath it. The leaders of Letovice have already begun to brag to the surrounding communities that the new dam will be the eighth largest reservoir in Moravia, with an estimated 28.5 meters deep and 126 meters across. They boast about the opportunities to sail, fish, and swim as if it was propaganda for a vacationing resort. When our little village is mentioned, most think it is a willing sacrifice for the sake of the dam. Only some click their tongues in condolences.

All the gardens in Lazinov are overgrown. No one has the heart to tend to the yards knowing it won't matter when the dam is finished. The same fate applies for any repairs on the little houses; though, somehow, Mother is still adamant about getting the squeaky side-door fixed. Some families have started taking apart their houses brick by brick to rebuild in the new location. When I go to the climbing tree, I don't look out over the valley anymore; rather, I turn and look at the hill on the other side. Truth be told, I haven't been at the climbing tree much unless Patja is visiting Lazinov. It's not the same when it is only me and Ash in a sprint to the tree. (And Ash beats me in the footrace, which cannot be counted as losing a sprint considering the feline has twice as many legs as I do.) Patja's family came for frequent visits throughout the summer, but with the start of the school year, there has been less time for our old neighbors to return. We are in high school now, after all. There's much more schoolwork to finish, leaving less time for fun and games.

Yet, I still figure out how to sneak away from it all. Yesterday, I told Mother and Dad that I would be staying in Letovice after school because Patja, Karel, and I were working on a history report for Friday. I told them we would be finishing the report late to have it perfect for the presentation in class, knowing the bus only goes back to Lazinov sparingly and curfew laws would finally play to my advantage.

Karel had invited us over because his parents were in Prague visiting Filip at required Military School, leaving Karel home alone for the night. Of course, his sister Zofie and her husband Jakub are in the apartment upstairs, who also knew of our plan to stay the night. Though, they didn't learn our parents hadn't approved the sleepover beforehand until later in the evening. We spent all afternoon at the soccer field, kicking Patja's ball around until sunset. (I had pumped it up and brought it to school in the morning. Marie questioned me, but I brushed it off telling her that it was for a gym class activity.) When we finally felt the evening chill, we went back to Karel's house. Patja's parents hadn't known before of our intent to stay at Karel's for the night either, but when Patja called and explained that we were all still working hard on the report and couldn't leave Karel to finish it alone, they agreed that Patja could spend the night. I was next on the phone to call home.

Marie answered, "Hello?"

"Marie, it's Niky. Put Mother on the phone."

"You should be on the bus."

I thought fast. "My watch was slow; I missed the bus. Get Mother, please."

I heard Marie call for Mother, and then, there was a moment of silence before Marie whispered again into the phone, "Your watch broke three weeks ago when you forgot to take it off before playing volleyball in the gymnasium. Come up with a better excuse for Mother."

Marie's detective skills are admirable, and I quickly adjusted my story.

"Niky?" Mother's voice shook.

"Mother, I missed the bus. The clock at Karel's house is slow."

Mother sighed, *"It's too close to curfew now for Dad to come get you. Are Karel's parents there?"*

"They're in Prague visiting Filip — but, Mother, Zofie is here with her husband."

Relief filled Mother's voice, *"Oh, lovely! Bug, listen to Zofie, and make sure you get on the bus in the morning for school. Mind you that clock is slow, don't miss the bus again before school. Do you need Marie to bring you anything in the morning?"*

"No, Mother. I'll buy my lunch at school tomorrow, and I have my backpack." I smiled at Patja and Karel, who both anxiously waited for the bait to catch.

"Don't stay up late. Goodnight, Bug." I made a face. Two *"bugs"* in one conversation. Mother was definitely pushing this nickname too long.

"Goodnight, Mother." I hung up the phone, and a series of high-fives passed between the three of us, though our rejoicing was interrupted by a series of tapping noises. We all turned at the same time at the sound of Zofie's fingers strumming on the stair railing. There, at the end of the hall, stood Zofie and Jakub. I hadn't known Zofie well, even though she also grew up in Lazinov, simply because she was fifteen years older. Ten years after Zofie was born, her parents were convinced they wouldn't have more children, only to be surprised with Filip. Four years later, they were shocked to be expecting once again, making Karel the baby of their family.

Zofie gave a weak smile, comprehending the little scam we pulled on our parents to spend one sleepover night together like we were little kids again.

"I'll make some tea and popcorn. Turn on the television and see what's playing. That is assuming you're all finished with that history report." Zofie cocked her head, showing she knew the report was also bluffed.

Karel thanked his sister for keeping our secret and ushered us into the living room. Patja flipped through the channels on the television before landing on a timeless fairytale. There was nothing else playing on the limited channels, so Cinderella was the only option. Though traditionally a Christmas film, no one objected. Zofie came in shortly with tea and popcorn, as promised. She and Jakub sat on one end of the sofa, and Karel stretched out on the other side. Patja curled up on the armchair, and I sat on the floor, leaning my back against Patja's chair. It was exactly what I had hoped for that night. Patja, Karel, and I didn't need to catch up talking, nor did we desire to whisper late into the night; we simply missed being together. Sitting in Karel's living room and passing around a bowl of popcorn was the perfect cure for our friendship deprivation.

Karel didn't last more than fifteen minutes. Patja and I both heard his breathing deepen and slow. Patja took the bowl of popcorn still on Karel's lap as Zofie draped a blanket over her sleeping brother.

"He was always the first one to fall asleep at camp, too," I told Zofie and Jakub.

"Did you play any pranks on him?" Jakub grinned.

Patja looked at me for approval before confessing, "Karel still thinks it was some other kids who drew a mustache on his face a few years back."

Jakub gave a silent laugh. "He notoriously falls asleep first when we watch late shows, though Zofie has forbidden me to play pranks on him. I'm relieved someone else has had their fun, at least!"

"I only forbid it because he would know it was you." Zofie ruffled Jakub's hair.

We sat in silence as Cinderella continued to play out on the television. When Cinderella broke the first acorn and made a wish, Jakub asked, "If you had a magic nut, what would you wish for?"

Looking back on it now, it was probably a question for his new wife, but I blurted out, "I'd wish we could magically transport out of this communist regime."

Patja's foot collided with the back of my head.

I yelped and instinctively rubbed the spot where Patja's foot left a mark. I glared at my best friend and then realized the intention to kick me was purposeful. I followed Patja's gaze to see that our hosts were carefully watching us. Jakub's eyes widened. Zofie's lips pursed together. I gulped. I've never been so careless before. This wasn't fibbing to Mother or skipping out on chores; speaking against the government is a federal crime. It doesn't matter that I'm not yet eighteen, I could be sent to a reform school or forced to a labor factory for this rebellious outburst. The only thanksgiving I had at that moment was that Patja could deny knowing anything. In the silent stress of the moment, I began saying the only thing I could think of in this situation — the recitation of Pioneer Laws.

"I am dedicated to the Socialistic country and the Communist Party of Czechoslovakia. I am a friend of the Soviet Union and a defender of advancement and peace across the entire world." I sat up straighter, the words slipped from my tongue faster, *"I admire heroism, hard work, and a battle. I do my part in advancing Socialistic lands by my own actions, by learning, and doing hard work."*

"Niky, I think...," Zofie started speaking, but I kept reciting.

"I am proud of the Pioneer organization."

"Really, Niky, it's okay. We understand," Jakub's deep voice reassured.

"I am preparing to enter the Union of Socialistic Youth," the sentence faded to a whisper as I finished the recitation.

We sat in silence for a long time; the fairy tale continued playing on the television, though no one was following Cinderella's journey.

Finally, it was Zofie who spoke, *"And do you have a second wish?"*

Silence again filled the room and the sound of the clock ticking on the wall became increasingly evident. I shrugged my shoulders, *"I don't know."*

Zofie cleared her throat. *"When someone's first wish is so strong on their heart, they don't wish beyond the first,"* Zofie's voice echoed in the silent room.

I stuttered, trying to somehow pull my way out of the mess, but my words failed me.

Looking then at Patja, Zofie bluntly asked, *"I suppose you agree with Niky? You've talked about it together?"*

Patja's head nodded; I cringed. I had hoped Patja would deny it all, but I should have known my best friend wouldn't let me sink alone.

"This government isn't for everyone," Jakub flatly stated.

"For some people, the desire for something different is so strong they feel the only way to get out is to escape the whole system," Zofie continued. Surprisingly, she added in a whisper, "We've even considered leaving."

My mind rattled, "Trap... trap... trap."

Patja spoke for us, "So, why don't you leave?"

"Safe question," I thought.

"Honestly," Zofie leaned into Jakub's arms, "I've found out I can't have children." She looked at Karel still sleeping on the sofa. "This is the only family we will have, and we can't leave them."

Jakub rested his arm reassuringly over his wife's shoulders before saying, "However, if this is something you are both serious about, maybe we can help."

It was my turn to be blunt, "How do we know we can trust you?"

Jakub got up and flipped through a notebook until he found a blank piece of paper. He tore it out, the ripped edge resembling a mountainous horizon. Jakub focused on writing something on the paper, and after a drawn-out minute, he passed the paper to me. Patja looked over my shoulder. A lightly sketched map took over the top of the page and listed notations about guard towers, electric fences, and army routines filled the lines beneath.

"How do you know all this?" My voice softened as I began trusting our hosts with this secret we didn't know we shared.

"Required military," Jakub stated before adding, "Something that may affect the pair of you from leaving together if you wait until after high school."

I hadn't considered how the two-year communist military requirement would affect our escape. We had only thought how slowly time moved for us to grow up so we could pursue the challenging journey. I suddenly realized that time was pressing on us as much as we pressed on it.

"What do we need to do?" Patja asked. Understanding and determination clouded our faces, though it was a relief to see real emotion as we were finally free from the facades.

"Keep the paper in a safe place. Look it over. Memorize it, and come visit us again if you are serious about this," Jakub replied.

"Come back for what?" I wondered aloud.

"Training."

"Suppose we don't wish to come back?" Patja ventured.

Jakub's gaze was firm. "Then, destroy that piece of paper or live with the consequences if anyone finds it in your possession."

With that final sentence, our hosts bid us goodnight and retreated to their room. I opened my backpack to slip the paper into my journal for safe-keeping. Truthfully, I would have opened the journal even without the need to hide the paper, but for the fact that sleep failed me tonight as anxiety, excitement, and questions clouded my mind ever since Zofie and Jakub had left the room hours ago; that and the wrestling desire to draw a mustache on Karel.

July 16, 1994
— Krista

Madla's contagious cold finally cleared up a few days after Krista returned from her solo visit to the dam. She was anxious to go to Madla's house to tell her the next part of Wes's story that Fisherman Dave had shared; however, even though Madla was feeling better, it seemed that Kai had now caught the sniffles. Zofie filled a jar with chicken broth to bring to Kai, but no sooner than Zofie was leaving to bring the thin soup to her nephew, did Madla appear at the door.

"Hi, Aunt Zofie! I'm feeling completely better now, but Kai caught my cold. He's at home with Daddy. Is that broth for him? When you brought it to me last Wednesday, it really helped my sore throat. Kai will be pleased to have it. Is Krista here? Can we play?" Madla had definitely recovered to her normal self again, and Zofie wondered if Karel hadn't shooed Madla out of the house so Kai could finally rest. Zofie pointed to the stairs calling, "Krista! Madla's here." Madla sprinted up the stairs, and Krista raced down the hall with squeals of delight.

Zofie called from the entryway, "I'll be back in a little while."

Krista and Madla hardly heard the door close behind Zofie as Madla was already telling Krista about all the board games and movies on TV she watched.

"It was so boring being sick, but I was too tired to do anything else. I beat Daddy so many times at Checkers, and I watched my favorite fairy tale over and over again until I didn't need to watch it to know what was happening," Madla elaborated.

"What movie was it?" asked Krista.

"Cinderella."

"Oh! My favorite part is when the mice sing, and the fairy godmother makes Cinderella a beautiful dress."

"What? That doesn't happen in Cinderella. Cinderella has magic acorns that she cracks to make wishes, like for her dress."

Both girls looked at each other visibly confused until a voice from behind them interrupted, "Actually, you are both correct." The girls spun around to see Doma standing in the bedroom doorway at the end of the hall. "Krista has only ever seen Disney's version of Cinderella, and that wasn't allowed in Czechoslovakia under communism, so Madla has only ever known the Czech version of Cinderella."

Madla beamed, "Wow! More than one version of Cinderella! That is so interesting. I heard about Disney before, but I haven't seen any of the videos. It is something with a mouse, right? We have a fairy tale with a Little Mole, so I guess it must be similar."

Krista looked at Doma, "Is it similar, Mom?"

"Not exactly, but it is the favorite cartoon fairytale of Czech children."

"What else is different between Czech and America?" Krista hoped the question would lead her mother to talk about her childhood in Czechoslovakia.

"You can answer that question for yourself now since you've seen both Czech and American culture," Doma reasoned.

"How about what life was like for you in Czechoslovakia and life in Czech now? How is that different?" It was Madla who innocently asked the question that Krista was building the courage to ask.

The thin smile on Doma's face fell into a line across her face. "It was completely different; and then again, completely the same." Doma looked back into the bedroom and said, "You two will start finding more inconsistencies, like Cinderella, the more you talk together. Then, you'll learn just how different the two cultures are."

Krista noticed her mom had gone back to present differences rather than differences between her childhood and now.

Doma leaned against the doorway frame. "I'm sorry, girls. I need to go lie down. My headache is back." She retreated to her room, slowly closing the door behind her.

Madla shrugged her shoulders, clearly not fazed by what Doma had said. For Krista, it was what Doma hadn't said that kept her thinking. "Where's your dad?" Madla asked.

"With Jakub at the mechanic's garage. Zofie?"

"She went to bring Kai some chicken broth."

The girls leaned against the wall for only a moment before a crooked smile pulled on one of Krista's cheeks, "Want to visit the dam?" Madla was already walking to the front door to tie her shoes.

The whole bike trip to the reservoir, Madla rattled questions at Krista, looking for the inconsistencies as Doma had suggested.

"Do you cook dumplings?"; "Do you have chickens?"; "Have you ever been to a festival?" The questions hit one after the other. During Madla's cultural investigation, Krista continued to think about her mom. Over the past week, Doma had rarely left the house and now hardly made it out of her room. It was a Doma that Krista was not used to. The shadows under her eyes grew wider by the day, and Krista noticed her already slim mother had lost weight since their arrival; a major task considering Zofie's non-stop kitchen hospitality. Doma had complained about countless migraines over the days and was often lethargic. Krista worried it wasn't due to the sleepless nights as Doma had explained.

"Unless maybe it has everything to do with the sleepless nights," Krista's realization was spoken aloud.

"What?" Madla asked from her bike.

Krista slowed down and pulled her bike off the road. "I think something is bothering my mom about being here in Czech. That's why she can't sleep at night, and it's causing her to be sick all the time."

"Just ask your mom what's bothering her," Madla twirled her pigtail.

"It's not that easy. I've tried asking Mom questions like this before, and she's a clam."

"Huh?"

"Like she doesn't open up about how she's feeling."

"Maybe there is someone else who you can talk to who can understand your mom."

Krista wondered. She had tried asking her dad, but Madla was right. There had to be someone else who knew more.

Madla hopped back on the seat of her bike. "Are you coming now? I want to know if Mister Wessely finally meets some girl and falls in love."

Krista's laughed, not because she thought Madla's comment was funny, but because she hoped there was something bigger to Wes's story than a simple romantic ending.

January 14, 1939
— Wes

Many days after school, Wes joined Sam, and the studious pair made their way through the crowds of Prague to the Sroubek Hotel lobby. Sam stopped by the table where Wes frequently sat with Nicky, but Sam never stayed for long as the staff regularly found tasks that required his attention. Wes pitied his little friend with all the mundane tasks he was given, though Sam rather enjoyed the busywork and short visits to see Wes and Nicky. Sam never told Wes, but he was happy his jobs didn't have the stress and anxiety that seemed to be associated with Nicky's work. Wes was convinced Nicky slept at the table in the left corner of the room as he always found him in the same place, impossibly surrounded by more paperwork than the day before, as if angels had brought more children to add to the stack in the silent nights. Though Nicky knew little of Wes's life beyond language school studies, he did share with his young translator how he had come to start the operation in the lobby of the hotel over a cup of the Englishman's habitual afternoon tea.

Nicky explained between sips, "I had visited the refugee camps for the Sudetenland Jewish families with Martin, and I began asking if there was an organization that deals with the children. After finding that there is no such organization, I began the British Committee for Refugee Children of Czechoslovakia." Nicky chuckled as he pulled off his glasses and rubbed his eyes. Leaning in close to Wes, he admitted, "When I say 'committee,' it's actually just a secretary I have in London, and I've appointed myself as the director."

Wes admired Nicky's determination. For a man not yet thirty years old, Nicky presented complete dedication to saving as many Jewish children in Czechoslovakia as possible.

"What made you decide to start the committee?" asked Wes.

"No one else had started it," Nicky stated plainly. "Honestly, it simply fell into my lap. After visiting the refugee camp with Martin, we came back here to the hotel. The next morning, we were sitting at this table for no more than two minutes with our morning tea when a lady approached us and asked for our help to save her son. It all just snowballed from there."

Wes wondered what "snowballed" meant, but he assumed it had to do with the battle Nicky felt inside himself, for the only reason Wes had used a snowball was in a neighborhood fight in the countryside of Lazinov.

Days sped past as if they were on an assembly line trying to meet a big deadline. Nicky's eyes became a shade of red that never completely cleared during his time in Prague. Many mornings, the scholarly gentleman was already working from his spot in the cafe at six-thirty in the morning. A five o'clock shadow slowly tinted his cheeks into the evening, and while Nicky retreated to his room late in the evening, he continued his work until after midnight before a pillow finally cushioned his head. For the little time he did lay in the hotel bed, he spent most of it pondering what more he had to do rather than sleeping. Undoubtedly, everyone noticed Nicky's lack of sleep, yet no one besides Wes urged him to rest. Everyone else with whom the Englishman met had problems of their own that also kept them awake at night.

The translation skills Wes administrated was an asset to the little team that kept them moving forward. He translated for young Jewish parents from Czech to English for Nicky's records, and sometimes even translated to German for the official paperwork that was being transcribed for each child to fit within the law requirements. However, this last task was frequently taken over by Nicky, who also had an understanding of German. Their little team included Nicky, Wes, Martin, the secretary back in London, and a few people the Englishmen had been in contact with at the refugee centers. Not one considered themselves heroic. There wasn't time to think selfishly when the lives of many children were already at stake. Wes continued to look for Feivel's name to appear on the list inside Nicky's scrapbook, but the little boy was lost in the mess of the city and his family hadn't requested the aid of the Englishman.

On one occasion, a curly-haired little boy exploded with a gust of wind through the doors of the lobby. With his hat pulled low over his face and a scarf that wrapped around his neck, only his hair and rosy cheeks were visible. The child's mother followed closely behind with a wailing baby in her arms. Over the past few weeks, Josef and the other workers of the hotel had become accustomed to the sound of children entering the lobby that the hotel staff hardly reacted to the noise of one more child. Wes, however, couldn't keep his eyes off the little boy, believing that Feivel had finally found his way to the hope of safety. Still juggling the wailing child in her arms, the mother reached down and pulled the hat off the little boy's head and ushered him toward a nearby table. It didn't take long for Wes to realize that the curly-haired child wasn't Feivel, though it didn't affect his eagerness to help the children and young mother who reminded him so much of the Jewish family he had encountered earlier that month.

Wes's growing dedication to the cause involved joining Nicky on Saturdays at the hotel lobby as well, and this morning presented an array of interesting guests, who were not their usual visitors.

Saturdays were generally calmer than most days since the Sabbath customs limited the actions of the Jewish community. It allowed Wes and Nicky to page through the scrapbook and make additional bookkeeping notes to ensure the placement of the Jewish children in good English homes. While Nicky had written many nations asking for asylum for the impressionable youth, only two countries had given their approval — Sweden and Nicky's home country, England. There were some countries Nicky never heard a response from as they flicked the letter into the trash in a similar fashion to Pontius Pilate rinsing his hands on the day of Christ's crucifixion. Some nations responded regretfully, as in the case of the United States of America. Nicky had hoped Roosevelt would open the nation for countless youth seeking refuge; alas, a letter from the States returned declining the request as it was unfit with the existing immigration laws. Wes shook his head as he looked over the letter he had pulled from the pages of the scrapbook, wondering how country leaders continued to ignore the crisis forming on Czechoslovakian soil. The letter was passed solemnly back to Nicky, who shoved it between the pages of the scrapbook with such vigor and resentment that Wes wondered why he even kept the letter at all. As if reading Wes's thoughts, Nicky cursed through his teeth, "It's proof that they turned their backs if nothing else."

Shortly after Nicky had ordered his cup of afternoon tea, a lady entered the lobby and, like most of Nicky's customers, walked directly toward the table that had since become his temporary residence. The lady walked with confidence, her heels clicking over the tiled floor. Wes watched as she didn't wait to be invited to sit as others had when visiting Nicky's makeshift office. Rather, she slid gracefully onto the free seat across from Nicky. Wes watched the lady curiously as she looked directly at a man at the table next to them, who was paging through a newspaper and sipping an espresso.

Still looking at the man, the lady spoke to Nicky, "Until that man behind the newspaper over there leaves, we'll just talk about the weather." Her eyes never left the back of the man's head as he quickly folded his newspaper, got up from the table, and exited the front doors of the lobby without paying the tab. Wes's eyes widened, but Nicky didn't look at all surprised.

Leaning over to Wes, Nicky whispered, "I told you the spies follow me everywhere. Actually, I'm so tired of telling them to leave me alone. It's nice someone else told them off for a change." He turned his attention to the clever lady on the opposite side of the table. Wes didn't hear much of the conversation as he focused on the other limited guests at the cafe, wondering if there was another spy among them.

Sunset came early on the cold Saturday, and with it, a bundled Sam catapulted into the lobby.

"Oy!" Sam exclaimed as he clapped his mittens together; light snow sprinkled off the wool and vanished on the floor. "It is chilly outside today."

Wes smiled at the sight of his friend. "Sam! What are you doing here?"

"I thought you'd be here. I couldn't come earlier... family stuff," Sam rolled his eyes. "I was thinking I could finally simply sit and enjoy some English conversation or help to translate like you do, without being interrupted by the staff to complete tasks."

A faint red tint colored Wes's cheeks in admiration realizing that Sam wanted to imitate him.

No sooner than Sam had unbuttoned his coat, a pair of darkly cloaked rabbis shuffled through the doors of the hotel. Wes was helping Nicky gather all the papers and stack the teacups that littered the table, evidence of their Saturday spent. The religious leaders stood out in the richly decorated lobby. Their ruffled beards were framed by long locks of hair that spiraled over their sideburns. If wrinkles and grey hairs measured wisdom, their faces contained a map of education. The rabbis hardly glanced around the room before approaching Nicky and Wes's table.

Nicky stood greeting the rabbis. "Gentlemen," he spoke kindly and gestured to the chairs at the table.

One of the rabbis shook his head. "We won't stay for long."

Nicky looked at Wes for a translation. Wes recognized the language as the same one he heard from Feivel on the train. He understood some, but before he had the chance to try the translation, Sam jumped in and translated the Yiddish.

"What can I do for you?" Nicky asked.

"Whispers have been circling from members of our synagogues about the work you are doing," the rabbi stated. Sam translated.

Nicky smiled, "I want to do everything to help these children find a good, safe home."

No smile appeared on the faces of the rabbis. "We will speak frankly, Mr. Winton. If you want them to have a good home, then you will avoid sending our children to Christian families in England, as we have been told you are planning to do so."

Sam gulped at the rabbi's bold words and blankly stared at Nicky. Even Wes had understood the harshness of the message.

"Didn't you understand them?" Nicky questioned. Sam nodded and glanced toward Wes before repeating the words of the Jewish elder in English.

The tips of Nicky's ears and his cheeks flushed hot with anger. He gripped his hands in fists below his waist. He didn't look at Sam to pass the next part of the conversation, and Sam didn't look up from intently studying the laces on his boots. Nicky's gaze bore through the rabbis who boldly spoke in his "office." Even through clenched teeth, his deep voice professionally articulated, "If you prefer a dead Jewish child in Prague to a Christian home, that is your problem. I refuse to stop my work." Gathering the scrapbook of children's names and placements protectively under his arm, Nicky retreated to his room with a muttered, "Goodnight, gentlemen." With that, he left Sam and Wes to finish translating for the Jewish leaders, who had nonetheless pieced together the response of the burdened Englishman.

Once again in the quietness of the lobby, Wes and Sam sat regathering the rough conversation they had just experienced. Wes's thick fingers combed through his hair, as he had often seen his father do in times of stress back on the farm; Sam's attention was still on his boot laces.

Wes finally spoke, "Nicky's doing good work to help these kids."

Sam looked up and folded his arms on the edge of the table. "Yes, that's true, but my father says that war isn't black and white —good and bad — that there is grey. Maybe we don't truly understand their position."

"You certainly understood them," Wes complimented. Wes recalled meeting Feivel on the train. The week following the chance encounter with Feivel, he had looked over the school courses, though there wasn't an educator specializing in teaching Yiddish at the language school; yet, Wes wondered if it was something the school may not have promoted in the course listings.

Curiously, Wes added, "How did you learn to speak Yiddish so well? I haven't been able to pick it up."

Sam smirked, "It isn't a hard language for me, Wes. I'm Jewish."

April 23, 1974
— Niky

Brick by brick, our new home is taking shape. I hate it. It resembles a lookout tower forming like a spike on the top of the hill. Dad says others will build their new homes nearby as well and, when the valley fills, the house won't seem out of place. Maybe it will look more like a lighthouse than a lookout tower when the flooding project is finally complete. Our house in Lazinov is hugged into the folds of the earth that sweep down into the valley, making the little home seem as if it always belonged. The new house doesn't need a light on top for a lighthouse to make it stand out more. (And it is incredibly windy at the top! How Mother expects to hang the laundry to dry without having the whole line pulled away like a kite, I've yet to understand.)

My schoolwork is slacking — not enough to make Mother or Dad worried. I've simply stopped putting effort into my lessons considering I'll likely not need to know the various dialects of Russian language and random facts regarding former Austro-Hungarian Imperial Royalty when Patja and I finally flee over these borders. Though my receding grades in Russian and History are frowned upon by my parents and teachers, it seems to be balancing out with my improving marks in Geography and Physical Education. Patja and I resolved to focus more on Geography to learn about the surrounding countries and terrain better. Knowledge of maps may prove to be helpful in our journey. I've always had good marks in Physical Education, though I'm also working to increase my strength for a trek over mountains or through miles of fields. My swimming endurance has also improved as a result. (We are unsure of which border we will choose for our attempted crossing, though it is good to be prepared for mountains or rivers.) My teacher is impressed with my added effort and stamina in the gymnasium, thus giving my parents very encouraging reports about the disciplined and hard-working child they've raised.

Patja and I ditch school early once a month — which isn't exactly helping our sinking Russian grades in any case. We catch the early bus to Letovice and meet with Zofie and Jakub for various training skills. They have taught us different map techniques and how to locate refugee shelters after crossing the border. When they asked us ultimately where we would like to settle after leaving Czechoslovakia, Patja and I both instinctively answered: America. In all the lectures our communist teachers tried to dilute the allures of the United States, I learned to equate "America" with terms such as Democracy and Freedom and Liberty. Beautiful words that contradicted everything I had grown up knowing in my own country with all the governmental boundaries.

It is difficult to imagine home being anywhere but Lazinov. I'm not sure I will ever be able to feel completely at home in America, or wherever Patja and I end up, knowing the home we will leave behind was nothing short of perfection — if I focus solely on the beauty of Lazinov and not the government that destroyed the land. For that is the greatest condolence I have; knowing that Lazinov will cease to exist. In a way, it makes leaving all the more necessary.

Last week, I really did miss the bus home. Even though Jakub had set the clock ten minutes fast for this exact purpose, it still failed me. Mother wouldn't be fooled twice, even if this time it actually did happen! Zofie came to my rescue.

"I have a bike in the garden shed."

The black-framed bike looked new, and I was hesitant to take it from Zofie. I guess Zofie saw my hesitation because she said, "Go! Bike fast, and you won't be long after the bus arrives. You still have time to make it home before curfew. Hide it somewhere in Lazinov and tell Karel tomorrow at school where it is. We'll get it."

I hopped on the bike, gripped the curved handlebars, and sped down the road through the city. I pedaled hard. The night air tickled my cheeks, and a misty rain breezed over my skin. I *imagined it must feel the same as an ocean spray if I had ever been to the ocean to experience it. I was almost to Lazinov before I glimpsed the taillights of the bus up ahead. I had caught up. I swerved onto a small path that cut through the narrow lanes between the houses and barns until I could see my house. Light flooded through the windows and a thin line of smoke rose from the chimney. It felt welcoming to see the little house like that; I had always seen it as more of a prison than a fairytale cottage. I nearly laughed imagining Mother scolding seven little dwarves for not tidying the beds.*

Hiding the bike was the next task, but I knew where I could put it. When people normally abandon a house, I think the house takes on the form of a mummy, with boarded-up windows and doors, but Patja's former house looked more like a skeleton. All the windows and doors were removed to be repurposed, as well as most of the shingles on the roof. I pulled up next to the opening in the wall that used to be a window that once looked into the Kopecky's living room. I hoisted the bike through the window so that it leaned against the wall underneath, out of sight — not that many people walking down this road who would be interested in the vacant house, considering there is an epidemic of skeleton homes throughout all of Lazinov.

Inside my own home, Marie was stretched out on the living room floor with Ash curled up next to her. Dad sat in his armchair listening to the music on the radio, while Mother added another log to the fire. When Mother saw my damp face and rosy cheeks, she quickly got me a bowl of warm soup for dinner. I liked it. Not just the soup, the whole warm evening together. For a moment, I thought about telling Mother and Dad of our plans to leave Czechoslovakia, so that they could come with, but I quickly lapped at the soup to keep myself from blurting. I know Mother and Dad can't make that kind of journey, and they don't despise the government restrictions like I do enough to risk everything. Besides that, if I don't tell Mother and Dad, they can plead innocent when the government questions them about my escape... or attempted escape. It is too close now to compromise the new future Patja and I have been working so hard to reach.

July 22, 1994
— Krista

It was talking with Madla that gave Krista the idea to visit her grandmother. She realized Doma was shutting down more each day and the only explanation Rick gave was that Doma wasn't used to the summer humidity with the absence of air conditioning. Krista knew it was more than the summer weather and wondered if her prying and curiosity about her parents' lives before moving to America was related to Doma's weariness.

Krista had tried talking with Zofie in hopes that she would have answers, but conversations with Zofie seemed to loop in circles more than a rollercoaster. Talking with her yesterday hadn't helped Krista in any revelations. It seemed that, for every question Krista asked, Zofie replied with a question of her own.

Zofie had her fingers deep in the soil as she pulled little roots from weeds that still hid underground. "If you don't get the roots, they always come back." Her fingertips worked like little tweezers around the patches of strawberry leaves.

Not really hearing Zofie, Krista asked, "Zofie, why is Mom so upset these days?"

"Why do you say she's upset?"

"She just stays in the house, and I just know she's fake smiling when I come to the room."

"She's not upset about you going on those bike trips if that's what you're thinking." Zofie leaned back on her heels and looked into Krista's eyes.

"So, what's she upset about?"

"Why don't you try asking your mother that question?"

Zofie had turned back to the garden and didn't see Krista's eyes roll and shoulders drop.

"You're Mom's best friend, you have to know."

Zofie gave a hard laugh and faced Krista again, who hadn't realized she'd said something funny.

"You think I'm Doma's best friend?" Zofie continued laughing.

Krista, not finding the joke, said flatly, "You knew each other when you were growing up."

"Do I look your mother's age? I'm a good decade older than her for sure! She grew up with Karel, you know that."

"Yeah, but why do we stay with you and Jakub if Mom and Dad were Karel's friends? Shouldn't we stay with Karel then?"

What Krista said made sense to her, but Zofie's laugh still filled the open garden.

"You think you can survive in the apartment with Kai and Madla all the time?" Zofie winked at Krista. "Your parents need some time to relax too. Besides, it's familiar for them here. When Jakub and I got married, we lived in the top apartment." Zofie pointed to the second level of the two-story house where Krista and her parents were staying. "Karel and my parents lived on the bottom level, so Rick and Doma were over all the time after school, visiting Karel and such. I just got used to seeing them around."

"So, you weren't friends?"

"Does it look like we were enemies?"

"You simply knew each other through Karel. Friends by convenience," Krista guessed, not willing to venture asking another question seeing that nothing was truly answered by Zofie.

"Something like that," Zofie responded before saying, "I think there are enough strawberries in our basket for about three jars of jam today!"

With that, the conversation Krista had hoped for diminished.

Krista thought she had reached the end of her search. She had tried asking her mom, dad, and Zofie if they could shine a light on Doma's past and to each no avail. She assumed Jakub would be even more rigid in speaking with her than Zofie had been. Krista always got a military-vibe from Jakub; the way he casually stood with his hands clasped behind his back and the repair skills he had for maintaining vehicles reminded her of movies with soldiers. Madla had said Karel didn't talk about anyone named Rick or Doma from the stories of his childhood even though Krista knew they had all been in the same class at school. Even Zofie had said Rick and Doma were over at the house visiting Karel frequently, so nothing added up. She had almost given up the hope of learning about her mom's past until she remembered there was one more person who could have known Doma as a child, Krista's grandmother.

Krista stood on the balcony as the summer sun warmed her porcelain, pale skin. She had learned there was little hope of tanning in the summer even with all the time she spent outdoors. While Krista would normally stand on the balcony and gaze at the palace on the hill and imagine all the royal parties that had once happened within their walls, today she watched the corner of the street, waiting for Madla to appear. The moment she saw Madla's bouncing pigtails coming up the road, Krista flung her knapsack over her shoulders and practically sprinted through the house.

"I'm going biking with Madla!" she called to anyone in the house who would hear her. Rick had been spending more time with Jakub at the maintenance garage as they tinkered on cars and motorcycles. She hoped Zofie or Doma had heard her yell, but she didn't wait for a response.

Zofie's old bike leaned against the fence. Krista swung open the gate and pushed the bike onto the road. She coasted to meet Madla halfway down the street.

"Where are you going?" Madla huffed.

"No, 'where are *we* going?'" Krista corrected.

"Okay, where are we going?"

"To visit my grandmother."

"Why?" Madla already looked bored with the idea of going to the nursing home.

"Because I think she might be the last person who can tell me what my mom was like as a child."

"Oh! I understand now. Didn't I suggest that earlier?"

Ignoring Madla's question, Krista asked, "Will you come with me?" Though Krista had visited the nursing home many times, she didn't want to go alone.

"Alright, but I just came from that way," Madla reluctantly agreed, wishing Krista had called to share the plan before she biked to the other side of town. Krista was already coasting down the rest of the little hill. Madla spun her bike around and followed Krista back the way she had just come.

The two pedaled through the streets and let their bikes rattle over the cobblestones. At the square, they could see the monastery peeking above the rooftops leading up to the hill where the palace sat at the very top. Even with the monastery in view to her right, Krista turned left at the square and continued down the road. Madla called from behind, "Krista! You're going the wrong way! The monastery is the other direction." They passed through the square and continued until they were near the edge of the city when Krista finally dismounted her bike. Madla pulled up beside her.

"I thought we were going to see your grandmother at the nursing home?" Madla shook her head wondering how anyone could be so directionally challenged to turn the opposite way when the destination was in sight.

"I thought so too, but when I started pedaling through the square I began thinking of Fisherman Dave and the next part of Wes's story. I didn't realize I was heading toward the dam. It's like this bike has a mind of its own and took a trail it's familiar with." Krista laughed at herself for thinking the bike could have ideas of its own.

Madla looked at Krista and then looked at the road ahead that led to the reservoir. She got a new wave of energy as she realized she didn't need to bike up the hill to the nursing home, at least not until she had to bike home later, but she was willing to go just about anywhere to put off the inevitable, beastly hill she knew would be her final ascent of the day.

"We can visit your grandmother later this week. We're already halfway to the lake, so let's go find Mister Fisherman Dave and hear what happens next to Mister Wessely!"

March 15, 1939
— Wes

Nicky Winton left Czechoslovakia shortly after the conversation with the Jewish elders. Before his departure, he told Wes, "I need to get back to London to help my mother prepare for the arrival of the refugee children. Plus, it is getting too dangerous for me here. I can see the war is coming, and it won't stop in Prague, Wes." Then, he added, "Sometimes, I think I know more than the politicians."

Just days before leaving the country, Nicky sent a group of twenty Jewish children by plane from Prague to Sweden. He knew flights would soon become impossible for evacuating the children and created a network of help in Prague to board the children on trains that would take them over German enemy lines, through the Netherlands, and finally across the channel into England. Nicky, confident in the team he had equipped back in Prague, commissioned one more person to the group. In the day before his departure, Nicky pulled Wes aside. "You have been a great help during this busy month, Wes, and you have been a friend to me in a time when people are mostly asking me for favors or trying to destroy my efforts. For that, I am truly grateful." He gripped one of Wes's broad shoulders as he continued, "I still need your help if you are willing. With so many children and the risk of war coming to Prague, I want to ask if you can join my team of leaders at the train station to make sure all the children get aboard the train safely."

Wes gave a single nod, "Sure."

"There is more, Wes. You and I both know it isn't safe for the Jewish community during this time, but it is important they believe this isn't a final goodbye. Parents might decide to pull their children from the train at the last minute. It will panic other parents and children during departure. Ultimately, they could cancel all the transports if chaos erupts on the platform," Nicky's eyes widened behind his glasses as he spoke. "You have a talent not only with languages, but your voice is reassuring; use it."

Wes nodded, understanding the risks that could be at stake if even one transport was not allowed to leave the station. Not only for the children on that transport, but the ones following.

"Will they ever get to come home?" Wes asked.

"I truly hope so, but where is home for these children without their parents, Wes?"

Wes understood, while Prague had become a temporary home for him during this year, it wasn't the farm in Lazinov with his parents.

"Any information I need to send you, I will send through Josef at the hotel. He has agreed to take messages. Lastly, take this," Nicky held out a woven handbag. Wes took the bag from Nicky's hand and peered inside. Papers with scribbled names of children and the plan for the first transport departure folded over in the bag from weight at the bottom. Wes lifted the papers to reveal what was causing the bag to slightly sag. Two bumpy grenades nested at the bottom of the woven sack, like turtle-dove eggs. Wes's eyes met Nicky's who had a finger pressed to his lips. "Don't ask me where I got them; honestly, I couldn't tell you anyway because it was passed to me this morning by a man I never met before. I can't risk carrying it any longer. When the spies hear that I'm going back to England, they will be close on my tail until I'm out of the country."

Wes wondered if the spies were following him as well. Though, it was the Englishman they were always after, not the farmer's son who got mixed up in the crowd on his extended stay in Prague. Wes knew Nicky wouldn't give him the package if he thought there was a large risk involved. He had grown a deep trust for the simple stockbroker who risked his life for the Jewish children. Now, Wes felt it was his turn to take a little risk.

Nicky continued, "When war does arrive here, make sure you stay safe, my friend. When the Nazis come, they will take over the train station first. Do whatever you must to make sure they don't stop these rescue transports." Nicky gave Wes a quick pat on the back as Wes let the papers fall back into the bag, concealing the grenades.

It had been months since Nicky left Prague, though his predictions about the war coming to the heart of Europe were nothing short of accurate. On March fourteenth, Wes arrived at the train station and helped usher a group of nearly one-hundred children onto the train carriages. While the other leaders ticked the children's names off the list, Wes guided the children into the train and settled them on the benches for the long journey. Many of the kids were too short to reach the racks above the seats to store their bags, so the task was given to Wes. He lifted the smaller children up the steep carriage steps as the parents passed bags of luggage through the doorway, followed by blowing kisses and promises of meeting up someday soon. Wes's arms ached, not from lifting children and suitcases onto the train, but from the tugging on his heart that exploded through the rest of his body. He knew it was his hands taking the child from their mother, maybe for a longer time than any of them realized, though Nicky's words echoed through his mind, "We're giving them a chance at life!"

The first transport had gone all too smoothly. Wes hadn't even brought the sack Nicky gave him. Rather, he removed the paper he needed for the day and hid the bag with the grenades under the bottom drawer of his dresser at Auntie's apartment. As the train pulled out of the station, mothers and fathers waved to sticky, little fingers pressed against the window glass, and all the support team remarked at how easy the first transport had been, but just as quickly as the train had left, a draft blew in from behind. Wes knew the winds of change were closer than anyone thought.

At ten-twenty on the morning of the very next day, March fifteenth, a parade of cars, motorcycles, bicycles, and tanks unwelcomely entered the city of Prague, each vehicle adorned with a boy playing "soldier" and a red flag displaying a crooked cross. It took them only three hours to make it from the border of Northern Czechoslovakia Sudetenland through a blizzard all the way to Prague. The parade march continued down the city streets as the cloned tin-soldiers clicked their heels rhythmically over the cobblestoned streets. Airplanes flew in formation overhead, momentarily drowning out the sound of the thousands of stomping boots. For a Wednesday, the turnout for the Nazi procession was overwhelming. Shop-owners closed their doors, and mothers with baby-carriages mixed with all the students unsure if school was still mandatory. Wes arrived at Wenceslaus Square as he often did in the mornings to check in with Josef at the Sroubek Hotel in hopes that Nicky had left a message late the evening before.

Sam also took to the habit of joining Wes at the base of the square before visiting Josef and then making their way dutifully to school. Today, something was different in the atmosphere as people lingered on the edges of the streets and whispered rumors played "telephone" down the sidewalk. Wes had felt the shift coming the day before, though he hadn't expected a change to arrive so quickly and drastically.

Sam also noticed the commotion of people and led the way into the already-forming crowd, easily weaving his narrow frame between civilians. He effortlessly arrived at the front of the mass of people where his vertically-challenged body type would be less limiting. Wes, on the other hand, apologetically bumped through the crowd as his broad shoulders and wide feet clumsily plowed the way until he was standing behind Sam. Glancing back to make sure he wasn't blocking anyone's line of sight, Wes saw Josef in the doorway of Sroubek Hotel, standing on a flowerpot for a better view. The sight of the professional desk clerk in his neatly pressed suit balanced on a potted plant should have made Wes laugh, and yet, it only caused him more concern as to the severity of the event at hand.

Sam's thick glasses widened his eyes even larger. "What are they doing here?" he leaned back, asking Wes. There was only one possible reason for the army of Nazis to be parading through the center of the city, both Wes and Sam already knew. For a while, they only stood in silence side by side with their fellow countrymen as swarms of soldiers continued to appear from around the corner until the wide street was filled with clicking feet and roaring motorcycles.

At last, Sam spun around to face Wes, "What do we do now?" Not waiting for an answer, Sam looked at his shoes saying, "What do *I* do now?"

There were no words Wes could think of to comfort his friend. At that moment, Wes wanted to pick Sam up over his shoulder and plow back through the crowd; he'd carry Sam back to Lazinov if that meant keeping his friend safe. Wes resisted the urge knowing it would draw more attention to the two as the crowd closed in tighter. Down the street, a soft song lifted through the brave onlookers above the sound of the soldier's hollers and stomping. The Czech national anthem flooded from thousands of voices. Wes's eyes met Sam's as he cleared his throat, and his rich voice joined the chorus.

From within the swarm of Czech nationals singing their beloved anthem, Wes heard the occasional curse thrown out as the rows of soldiers continued to promenade down the long square. Sam's glasses clouded as tears rolled over his round cheeks. For Wes, crying was a rare occurrence. Lazinov men grew through hardships and overcame with brute force, and while Wes's insides were burning to stand against this opposition, he truly was a lamb at heart. One by one, tears began sliding to his chin as well. Wes wondered if there would be enough tears from all the onlookers to create streams in the gutters and if the drains would even notice it wasn't raining.

Somewhere on the other side of the street, a fistfight broke out after a couple of men raised their arms in salute of the coming oppressors. Czech police were quick at the scene to break up the fight and roamed up and down the streets silently weeping along with their countrymen. As the march came to a close, the uniformed police quickly dismissed the crowds in fear of riots. Their wishes were answered, though the Nazis were not greeted in welcoming spirits, there was no riot of resistance that formed upon their arrival.

Wes held onto Sam's hand, determined not to lose the little friend as the crowd dispersed in all directions. Trucks with mounted speakers trailed after clusters of people on the streets declaring, "Do not be afraid! Follow all the rules of the National Socialist Party, and no harm will come to you." Radios in windows stated the start of an eight o'clock curfew, and posters on doorways declared similar propaganda statements by none other than Hitler himself. The two language schoolboys weaved up Wenceslaus Square and rounded the corner. After finally finding a clearing in waves of people, Sam released his clutch on Wes's hand.

"Do we go to school?" Sam's voice shook. Wes didn't believe anyone would be expecting them at school this late in the morning. He wished Nicky was here; Nicky would know what to do next. Sam seemed to understand what Wes was thinking and suddenly said, "Listen!"

Even with the chatter and wailing of bystanders leaving the square and the loudspeakers blasting through the morning air, there was one sound that was unmistakably missing. With the school and square so close to the train station, the boys had become used to hearing the rattling and whistling of trains coming and going from Prague's main hub. No screeching wheels and whistling rings pierced the air. "They've stopped the trains!" Wes's face drained white as he thought of all Nicky's work to free the children from what he knew was inevitable, and only one train transport made it out before the occupation.

"We need to get back to Josef to see if he has any information for us." Wes turned to see Sam slumped on a doorstep, his hands gripping his stomach. Fear and stress butterflied through Sam's insides, making him visibly ill. Sam mumbled something and rested his head against the cool cinderblock of the building where he sat.

"What is it, Sam?" Wes knelt closer. Sam's face had taken on a tint of green.

"I can't make it home."

Wes leaned over to pick up his friend, knowing Sam's small frame wouldn't be very difficult for him to carry.

Sam pushed away Wes's outstretched arms. "No, Wes. I can't make it home."

"I'll help you."

"You can't."

"I will."

"Wes, I live in the Jewish quarter."

"I know it's across the city, but we'll make it. You need to be in bed."

Sam groaned as he clutched his abdomen. "Wes, you don't want to be seen helping a *Jew* in the *Jewish* quarter. It won't be good for you. Not now. Not after today," Sam emphasized his nationality.

"As far as I'm concerned, I'm just helping a *friend* get *home*." Wes pulled Sam onto his feet and wrapped his arm around Sam's back to help him balance. It didn't matter how long it took to get Sam home, without school or Nicky, and with the trains all at a stand-still, Wes needed the task if only to allow him time to think of his next move.

March 28, 1975
— Niky

I thought it necessary to write a disclaimer before going any further in my writing, seeing that I am a year older now. I have wanted to sit and journal numerous times, but I will explain why the pages before this one are piled with scribbled notes, sketches, and lists rather than waves of words strung together.

Simply put, I haven't had the time to write out my thoughts, and I surprised myself by not journaling for nearly a year. Technically, I have been journaling — sort of — I guess it is more like note-taking on the previous dozen of pages. It is all scribbled papers of information that Patja and I have learned from Zofie and Jakub. We spend as much time as we can with our mentors to learn the art of escaping, and I jot notes to review again later with Patja. Because the journal contains military secrets from Jakub's time in forced service, we have kept the journal in utmost secrecy. I have hidden it in an old cigar box under a board around the edge of our empty sandbox in Lazinov. After each meeting with Zofie and Jakub, I slip the journal back into the cigar box and lay the board over the little hole I had dug in the ground. It had been harder to keep it hidden in the winter as I was afraid my footprints in the layer of snow had unknowingly revealed the hiding place of the little box, but when Mother asked me about the footprints to the corner of the sandbox, I explained that I stand at the edge of the sandbox when I'm missing Patja. It was the place we first met, after all. Mother's hands ruffled through my hair as she applauded me for handling all the new changes so well. She smothered layers of calling me "Bug" between all the encouragement. Marie stood skeptically in the hallway with crossed arms. Marie knows my special place is the tree, not the sandbox, though she never questioned me about it. Maybe she simply assumes I have multiple special places, or she's wisely chosen not to intervene.

There are many things I hadn't considered before we started meeting with Zofie and Jakub. Things they explained to us that had felt normal my whole life. Brainwashing had been implemented in our education from childhood by the communist government. A few months back, Zofie explained the Grandfather Frost character who brings good children gifts on Christmas was brought by the communists from Russian tradition to eliminate Baby Jesus — who was said to have brought gifts on Christmas Eve in Czech culture. Even though I have heard many elderly still slip and use Baby Jesus, Grandfather Frost has always been used in school and in the media. Apparently, Baby Jesus is too religious, though it seems to me that any character who magically appears on Christmas Eve with gifts is already made-up, religious or not.

When I'm not trying to keep up with my studies and secretly meeting with Zofie, Jakub, and Patja, I've been enlisted to help Dad with building the new house. While workers have it under control, Dad wants to double-check everything and insists we do some of the work our own to get the house up faster and cheaper. It was either spend weekends with Dad at the new house or help Mother begin packing boxes upon boxes. While both are terrible ways to spend my weekends, I chose the lesser of two evils. Since I never plan on living in the new house, I don't need to become attached to it, whereas packing boxes of memories from cabinets and attic spaces sends me into a mournful panic.

A few weekends over the winter, the weather was too cold to hike to the new house and work in the unheated building, so Mother somehow guilted me into boxing. While going through the crawlspace above the stairs, I found a box filled with a jumble of memories — old pictures Marie colored in preschool, photos of a birthday we celebrated with Patja's family, a ratted stuffed animal I'm surprised Marie hadn't adopted under her covers, an old hat my late grandfather once wore, a jar of feathers Mother and I collected together when I was young, and buckled picture books from when Dad would tuck me in at night. As I shuffled through the things in the box, the memories flooded my head, all the memories that give Lazinov the irreplaceable title of "home." I backed out of the crawl space and sat with my shoulders leaned against the wall. I closed my eyes and just focused on deep breathing. "It's just stuff," I kept telling myself. Though it wasn't the box of trinkets, it was the memories linked to those useless items that haunted me.

Marie was sorting through a box I had already pulled out of the crawlspace. She took one glance at me and hollered for Mother when I emerged from the little attic door at the point of my breakdown. I was gulping for air and felt the blood rush from my face as I sunk lower unto the floor. Mother flew up the staircase; I heard her feet hit only a few steps. She must have leaped over a nearly half.

"What happened?" Mother knelt next to me, instinctively placing her hand on my forehead as any concerned mother would do.

"There must have been a ghost in there! Look how white Niky's face is," Marie exclaimed.

"Just felt a bit claustrophobic," I fibbed between breaths. It wasn't a complete lie for I was claustrophobic, just with thoughts rather than spaces.

"That's enough work for today anyway," Mother said as she helped me to my feet and over to my bed.

"So, no ghosts?" Marie sat with her legs folded up on her bed.

"No," Mother said as she shut the opening to the crawlspace and pushed a box in front of the little door, probably more for Marie's peace-of-mind than anything.

"Either way, I'll be happy when we move out of here," Marie said. I know Marie is nearly thirteen years old, but I thought the incident would have frightened her more. By evening, she seemed to have forgotten about the whole thing. I suppose she isn't a little girl anymore and braver than I give her credit for. Though, Marie still does sleep in a cocoon of plush toys.

The bridge over the valley is completed, and they have created a building resembling a look-out tower in the middle of where the reservoir will be. They say it will manage water levels and store other information regarding the dam. Now, all the workers have moved their focus on constructing the actual *dam itself, which is going up faster than I had expected. A high wall of cement and soil imprisons the valley. The wind that used to ripple over the meadow through the crevasses of the hills is now stilled and silent. The wind is warning us, as if sent by the spirit of Mr. Halas, saying, "There is always a calm before the storm."*

I went to school as normal today. I ignored my mathematics teacher as normal today, I took a literature test as normal, I mouthed the words to the recitation of the Communist Pledge as normal, and I met with Patja and Karel after school to complete our Russian language homework as normal. However, upon arriving back home, nothing was normal. I noticed it first as the bus bumped more heavily down the old dirt road into Lazinov. I looked out the window and nearly dropped the nature guide I had been holding in my hands. (A new edition nature guide entitled "Insects" I had received for Christmas.) The ground all over Lazinov had been ripped apart! Bulldozers still lingered at the edge of the valley, admiring their sloppy work. Little mounds of earth that had once hosted gardens were completely flattened. Fenceposts uprooted like a child plucked dandelions and bushes that had once sheltered the front yards now left the homes naked and defenseless. The bus stopped abruptly.

"The road is too rough from the bulldozing. I have to turn around here. I'm sorry, everyone; you'll need to walk the rest of the way," the bus driver called back.

I followed Viktor and Vojta off the bus. (Marie and little Katerina Novak have short days at school on Friday in Elementary school and can come home with Ms. Novak after lunch by car. Ms. Novak has started working part-time at the post office again when she leaves baby Frankie in her mother's care.) The upturned ground clung to the edges of our shoes as the twins and I tried to follow the road into the village. The soil looked more red than brown as if Lazinov was slowly bleeding and had succumbed to her fate. I led the way, with Viktor followed by Vojta trailing behind. We zig-zagged over the street, trying to avoid the bigger piles of mud. Layers of the upturned soil that stuck to our shoes continued to weigh down our feet.

"Can you believe this mess?" asked Viktor.

"It's a disaster," replied Vojta.

"How will we get to school if the bus can't come to us?" asked Viktor.

It was silent for a moment before a unified twin-full voice said, "Niky?"

"I suppose we will need to walk further to meet the bus, or someone could drive us," I answered practically.

Thankfully, that was all the time the twins had for questions before they took the fork in the road to their home, calling goodbye as they marched in step to their front door. After losing the boys, I half-ran, half-slid on the mud further down the road. My teeth hurt from clenching my jaw, and my knuckles turned white in my gripped fists. I didn't want to be here for this. I didn't want to see my Lazinov stripped and dismembered. The creek was a muddy mess, stray fenceposts floated and piled up further down on a bank as if a beaver had been hard at work instead of bulldozers. Though, in this case, the beaver and bulldozer have the same end result in mind.

I didn't go straight home. I had to see all that had been taken and destroyed in my village. Dusk shadowed the streets and chilled the air. I wove my way around piles of soil until I reached Dvorak's farm. I could hear the goats inside the barn before I saw why they weren't outside in the field. Fenceposts littered the ground like a massacre of fallen soldiers who no longer kept the barricade strong. Some still bravely stuck sideways in the dirt in a final effort to complete their purpose. Without the fence, there was no starting line to race to the climbing tree, but that wasn't necessary because the climbing tree, like any good general, would have never retreated on his soldiers. My knees buckled, and my stomach flipped, and for the first time I can remember, I didn't run to my tree. Each solemn step became heavier with the weight of mud on my shoes and bitterness in my heart. I reached my hand out and touched a fallen limb of the tree. I knelt in the mud and cradled a branch in my arms. I tugged off a few leaves and slipped them into my pocket, knowing that was all I would have left to remember the dear friend by. I felt the gash in the trunk from the bulldozer's blade and pricked my finger on the split wood.

Finally, I hoisted myself onto the collapsed trunk and dangled my feet just inches from the ground. I looked out over Lazinov from my notorious place in the tree, though much lower than normal, for the last time. No tears fell from my eyes as a sadness greater than I had imagined for a piece of nature clouded through my thoughts and stiffened my body. I imagined all the times my hand hit the trunk of the tree before Patja's, all the days I spent balanced on the branches, all the seasons I saw change over the valley, all the ways the tree had been the pillar of my childhood. For it wasn't simply any old tree, it was my home after all. At that moment, I realized the truth of the whole situation: Lazinov was no longer my home.

I don't know how I made it back to my house. I don't remember saying goodbye to the tree. I simply left, my feet guided myself on a path that had been ingrained in my memory, and I somehow made it to the house. Our garden looked like the rest of Lazinov — the absence of grass, the fence and bushes flattened, and little heaps of dirt that matched the ridges of the bulldozer tires. The sandbox looked like an island in disarray. My body froze. The sandbox! I ran over to the edge of the sandbox, the tracks going around the little pit, but leaving it untouched. I stood puzzlingly on the corner of the old wooden frame wondering why the bulldozer hadn't ripped the useless little sandbox from the ground as well.

"I saved it," a voice from behind startled me. I spun around and saw Marie clutching a flashlight. "I got home just as the bulldozers were working their way up our road. I knew your climbing tree probably looked like the rest of the trees around here, so I sat on the edge of the sandbox when the bulldozers came."

My eyes widened as I stared at my little sister in disbelief and asked, "You sat on the sandbox when the bulldozers came?"

Marie nodded; her golden waves rippled over her shoulders.

"How?" I managed to squeak out.

"I remember you telling Mother that this is a special place for you because it is where you met Patja. I couldn't let them plow over it, so I just sat on the corner." Marie pointed to the board I knew was covering my most prized possession. Marie continued, *"When they came up the driveway, the men in the bulldozers told me to go inside. I told them I was staying. They said I was too old to play in a sandbox. I said I wasn't playing."*

I looked at Marie in disbelief, wondering how my little sister stood up to a team of bulldozers! My voice forced out a single word, *"And?"*

"One man stopped his machine and yelled, 'Hey, little girl! Stop fooling around!' So I yelled back, 'I already said I'm not playing.' They said something about a contract and removing me by force; I said something about child-handling and a lawsuit, and that pretty much ended the conversation and sent them back down the road after a quick sweep over the garden."

I clasped my hand over my mouth in amazement and to muffle my laughter as I imagined my sweet, never-say-a-bad-word-to-anyone Marie talking back to those workers. I reasoned I'd go back for the journal tonight when Marie fell asleep.

"Thanks, Marie," I smiled. *"I still can't believe you did that. How can I repay you?"*

Marie thrust a flashlight in my hand. *"The bulldozers scared Ash away, and I've already been all over Lazinov looking for her! Come on."*

So I joined the search squad. We went door-to-door asking if anyone had seen a dust-colored frightened kitty, but it seemed that everyone was inside behind closed curtains as the bulldozers made their ambush. Some of the Cousin Club from the other side of Lazinov helped us look through their barns for Ash, but our cat wasn't found among their swarm of felines. (I think the cats have taken lessons from the people in that family to repopulate so quickly!)

We looked for over an hour until I finally convinced Marie that Ash would find her way home. We had just crawled into bed when a persistent scratching came from the front door, followed by floods of meows. A very frightened and active cat spent the night waking me up. Maybe it wasn't entirely Ash's fault; I did stay awake long enough to make a secret late-night trek back to the edge of the last remaining sandbox in Lazinov.

July 25, 1994
— Krista

Krista and Madla had nearly made it up the hill to the nursing home, though both girls were pushing their bikes instead of riding them.

"This hill is horrible to bike up," Krista panted.

"You're telling me! I live in the apartments behind the nursing home. This is the way I have to go home every time I come visit you." Madla leaned her arms over her handlebars as she continued to push the bike further up the hill. "I keep telling Daddy we need to move closer to Aunt Zofie and Uncle Jakub because I really don't like this hill. Daddy says when

Aunt Zofie and Uncle Jakub finish the repairs on the lower level of the house, then we can move into the top apartment. Of course, after you go back to America. I told Daddy I'd be really happy to live there, but that means I'd need to walk up this hill to school every day, so I don't know what's worse." Madla had used all her breath and focused on pushing her bike rather than talking.

The girls finally reached the big wooden doors of the monastery. They propped up their bikes on the kickstands in the small gravel parking lot at the front of the monastery. They spent a moment leaning against the wall that divided the monastery grounds from the road. Krista pulled a water bottle out of her knapsack, took a drink, and handed the bottle to Madla, who chugged half of their supply.

"Just so you know, you are biking home alone after this. There is no way you'll get me to go up that hill twice in one day," Madla shook her head, letting her pigtails brush against the wall behind her.

The two girls moved softly through the corridors of the nursing home; the high ceilings and tiled floors echoed their little footsteps through the stairwells. Madla followed so closely behind Krista that, when Krista finally stopped in front of the door marked "L. Kopecka," Madla bumped into Krista's back.

"Sorry," she whispered.

Krista lightly tapped on the door and nudged it open. Her grandmother sat on the bed, propped up by three pillows stacked against the headboard. Grandmother's eyes opened and, seeing Krista, she smiled.

"Did I wake you, Grandmother?" Krista hesitated in the doorway.

"I didn't even realize I had fallen asleep," Grandmother's laugh turned into a yawn. She reached for the book on her lap and glanced around wondering where the bookmark had fallen. Madla noticed the paper bookmark lying on the floor and bent down to retrieve it.

"Here you go," Madla cheerily held out the bookmark.

"Who are you?" Grandmother's inquisitive voice seemed almost apologetic for asking. The elderly woman had met many young visitors over the past years at the nursing home. Children who came down the halls bringing scones, reading stories, and singing to the residents. She often forgot the faces of all the children who passed through the corridors year after year.

"Grandmother, this is Madla. Mom, Dad, and I are staying with her aunt and uncle," Krista introduced.

"Oh, of course, you're Karel's daughter. Kristyna's parents told me you've been spending time with my granddaughter," Grandmother said to Madla. Madla's pigtails bounced as she nodded.

"Are your parents coming up too, Kristyna?" Grandmother looked toward the open door and then back at Krista.

"It's just me and Madla today. We came on our bikes."

"How very kind of you to stop in and say hello on your bike trip!" Grandmother patted Krista's hand. Krista decided not to explain the sole purpose of the bike trip was to inquire about Doma's childhood in hopes that the idea of a general pop-in might make Grandmother more comfortable. Being that it was

Madla's first time in the room, she slowly spun around, looking at all the pictures pinned to the walls. She noticed on many of the pictures Krista stood with her brother Jack holding a birthday cake, but the smallest number of candles in all of Krista's birthday pictures was nine. There were no birthdays earlier than her ninth. On the wall across from the bed was a small poster, which Madla recognized as a picture from a famous Czech artist. A variety of picture frames held dried flowers frozen behind the glass rested on the nightstand, and a rocking chair sat on a colorful woven rug. A small wardrobe leaned against the corner of the room with a cane rested up against the side. Besides those items, there wasn't much else in the room. Madla realized how sad the room must look without the cheerful pictures and little memories on the wall, but the way Krista's grandmother had easily decorated the confined, white room had brought it a touch of life.

While Madla moved closer to see the pictures on the wall, Krista hesitantly started, "Actually, Grandmother, I was wondering if you would tell me what Mom was like when she was a child. Did you know Mom when she was growing up?"

"Of course I knew your mother!" Grandmother gave a single, dry laugh, which Krista almost mistook for a cough. "She was always getting your dad into all kinds of trouble. The two of them together were more mischievous than two alley cats at night."

Krista smiled. She was finally getting somewhere, though the description her grandmother gave was nothing like she imagined her parents.

"So, what was Mom like?" Krista asked again.

"She was nothing like you, Sweetie," Grandmother looked at her innocent, rule-following granddaughter. She turned to face the poster on the far wall and lifted her pale, thin finger to point across the room.

"Do you know who made this picture?" Grandmother asked.

At the same time that Krista shook her head, Madla nodded hers.

"Alphonse Mucha," replied Madla. "He was a famous Czech artist. I can tell it is his style. We studied his art in school." She smiled having successfully passed the spontaneous exam.

"Very good," Grandmother praised. "It is a copy of one Alphonse Mucha created. It isn't one of his more famous pieces, but it is my favorite."

"Why?" asked Madla. Krista was slightly annoyed to be off-topic yet again.

"Because it reminds me of your mother, Kristyna," Grandmother looked at Krista. All the times Krista had been in the room, she had seen the picture, but she had never taken the chance to really look at it. In the center of the drawing was a young girl, dressed in traditional Czech clothing and a colorful, embroidered bandana covered her head. Two unraveling braids fell over the young girl's chest. The girl sat in what Krista would describe as a dead tree. No leaves adorned the dark branches and a black raven perched in the corner of the picture on the tip of a branch. The girl in the tree looked to the side with one hand raised to her ear as if she heard something and the other hand resting near her chin where the girl appeared to be biting her nail. Krista pointed to the girl in the picture.

"This is how my mother looked?" she asked.

"More than you could know. It is as if Alphonse Mucha had prophesied your mother in this piece of art. The carefree, traditional little Czech girl sitting on the dead tree, nervously listening to the warning call of the raven."

While the girl in the drawing should have been the attention of the picture, considering she took up the most space and was directly in the center of the piece of art, Krista's eye was continually pulled to the dark raven in the corner.

"You said 'the warning call of the raven.' What warning?" Madla asked Grandmother.

"Artists put clues in their pictures to tell us more about the story. In this picture, the raven is telling us more through symbolism," Grandmother taught her two curious students.

"Then, what does a raven mean?" Krista ventured.

"Loss."

Before Krista could ask what kind of loss her young mother had experienced, a nurse appeared in the open doorway saying Mrs. Kopecka needed her rest and scolded the girls for not coming with an adult. Krista and Madla shuffled past the nurse and retreated to their bicycles. Thoughts in Krista's head swam with more questions about the girl in Alphonse Mucha's picture and her mother.

"Tomorrow, let's visit Mister Fisherman Dave," Madla interrupted Krista's thoughts.

"Yes, that's a good plan," she quickly responded before they parted ways and biked home. Truthfully, Krista welcomed the idea of being distracted by Fisherman Dave's story. Between trying to learn more about her mother and wondering what would happen next to Wes, Krista was getting used to the feeling of uncertain curiosity.

May 20, 1939
— Wes

The breeze whistled over the narrow cobblestone streets, and Wes let the wind lift his sweater into flapping wings behind his back. The musty smell of rain hung in the air, and thick clouds shadowed the morning sun. Every couple of days, Wes still left Auntie's apartment early to check in with Josef before continuing on his way to school. Even though there had been little contact from Nicky, the train transports still functioned as Nicky's team worked hard to ensure the cabins were filled with children. Wes figured they were averaging a train transport of children about every three weeks.

While the trains had been stopped the day the Nazis overtook Prague, it was only a momentary precaution to eliminate any quick deserters. These days, trains continued to leave from Prague Central Station filled with passengers; of course, only the passengers who were able to display the proper traveling documents. Nicky had considered this in advance, and the arrangements for the children were already accounted for. When Nicky had left in January, the list of refugee children was a mere seven hundred and sixty; now, the total tallied over five thousand waiting and registered children. Wes quickly recalled a conversation with Nicky in between all the meetings at the Sroubek Hotel, "The British government is also considering evacuating their London children to the countryside, so we just need to get the government to also include Jewish refugee children into the mix." He had certainly accomplished just that.

School was still in session, though most of Sam's and Wes's language classes were being replaced with mathematics and literature. It was obvious the Nazis were only supportive of languages spoken by the Axis power. Each day, class sizes dwindled as students joined relatives in the countryside or began learning at traditional schools in their neighborhood; without the special draw of languages, there was no need for the students to travel across the city for an education they could receive down the street. Auntie had already begun packing up the small apartment. Wes had convinced her to stay through the end of the school year, claiming he wanted to finish his final year at the language school. In all truth, Wes could care less about the school; now, his focus was centered on these children and the transports. There was one name on the list of evacuees he wanted to see off the platform: Samuel Levy.

Sam, not yet sixteen years of age, still qualified for the children's transports, though he had to be on the train before his birthday at the end of summer. Sam's help at Sroubek Hotel ceased the day after the Nazis came. Josef dismissed Sam from his internship entirely based on his heritage. Though, the dismissal was not in hate of Sam's race, rather out of deep concern for Sam himself as many of the new residents in the internationally known hotel were decorated officers of the Third Reich.

Wes was caught up in reflecting on all the changes over the past short two months that he hardly noticed he had arrived at the door of the Sroubek Hotel. The destination had become automatic over the past few months as he passed mothers pushing baby carriages, locals standing in line for fresh bread, and pairs of soldiers clambering down streets. Wes was greeted by smells of coffee and fresh pastries for breakfast in the hotel lobby. Uniformed Nazi leaders cheerfully ate their rich breakfast as a muffled chatter echoed throughout the large space. Wes stared straight ahead to the receptionist's desk, where Josef was certainly growing roots into the floor. Josef gave a single nod of his head in greeting when he noticed Wes approaching.

"Did your shoes get glued to the floor? With everything changing in Prague day after day, I can always count on finding you here," Wes teased.

Josef gave a half-smile back, "For a village-kid, you sure have stayed in Prague longer than I would have expected."

Wes leaned against the desk and raised his eyebrows.

"You'll be leaving then," Josef concluded.

"Not yet."

"How's Sam?" Josef's voice lowered as he asked about the little intern he had grown accustomed to seeing over the first half of the school year.

"Hopefully, also leaving soon."

"Hopefully."

Josef's attention was diverted to an SS officer who swiftly stepped up to the desk. Josef switched to German, "May I help you?"

The officer complained about a light fixture in his hotel room that was dim and in need of replacement.

"I will make sure we have maintenance repair that before the evening," Josef stated as he jotted a reminder.

The officer, satisfied with the answer, looked over at Wes and continued talking to Josef, "This young man is a friend of yours. I've seen him here before."

"More of a nuisance than a friend," Josef chuckled.

The SS officer grinned. "Can he understand us?"

Wes glanced at the ceiling and Josef took the hint. "If he doesn't learn fast, he'll be the stupidest child in all of Prague."

"Not such a child. He must be nearly an adult. Certainly, we have men younger than him joining our army each day! If this young man was from German stock, I would have enlisted him myself. See how thick his arms are? A strong, hard-working young man. Even his light hair and chiseled figures could clearly be of German descent."

Wes looked at the officer's clean-shaven face. His black hair sprinkled with grey at the temples and creases around the corners of his eyes. He was slightly rounder in the waist, though his uniform hid the bulge. Wes imagined he carried a picture of his wife and children in his coat pocket. If Wes hadn't felt so much like an auction horse at that moment, he might have thanked the officer for the vanity compliments. He simply looked at the officer and forcefully stumbled over a German sentence, "I no good in German; I speaking learn."

Wes wanted to cringe at his own grammatical mistakes but hoped the officer had fallen for the bit.

The officer gave a firm chuckle, "Well! He certainly is not a fast learner like you said. That would be the clear difference between a German soldier and this young man. While he may be able to pass on his Aryan looks, a German soldier is clever; adaptable!"

"Very true, sir," replied Josef. "This boy just comes to take delivery messages on occasion. Though, without a grasp on language, he is frankly rather useless here for deliveries and will be going soon." Josef hoped Wes wouldn't take his criticism to heart as they both knew it was a full-faced lie.

"Perhaps he can change the light in my room then," the officer laughed at his own joke.

"Perhaps."

The officer pointed at Wes and shouted as if Wes was deaf and that yelling was the remedy for not knowing a language, "You learn German! And quickly! We are here to stay." He turned and stamped his feet together; raising his arm, he declared, "Heil Hitler!" The men at the table nearest the desk rose and saluted back before the officer pulled over a chair and called the waitress to deliver the breakfast menu.

Josef looked apologetically at Wes.

"Don't," Wes said. "I know you were protecting me."

"I'm going to protect you more now. Don't come back."

"Josef," Wes started, but Josef interrupted in hushed tones.

"Look, Wes. I sent Sam away because I didn't want him to get hurt. Now, I'm doing the same for you. That officer could have sent you to work for him just because he thought you looked like a strong worker. If he had known you speak German; forget it. You may have been serving him hand-and-foot like a pack mule until the war is over. No, you mustn't come anymore."

"How will I get messages from Nicky?"

"This is the last one." Josef slipped a paper around the edge of the desk for Wes to stuff into his pocket. "Mr. Winton won't be calling here anymore. He knows the phones are bugged. With the entire guest list of Nazi officers, we expect as much. I was able to get this last message feigning it was a mistaken number. He'll contact his evacuation team directly. Perhaps they will get word to you."

"Thanks, Josef," was all Wes could manage to say.

"You understand why it has to be this way."

Wes nodded.

"Promise me you'll never come back here. Avoid Wenceslaus Square completely."

"I promise."

Wes knew Josef was not a man of goodbyes, but his eyes said the words for him.

"One more thing," said Josef before Wes turned to leave. "Get Sam out."

"He's on the list."

Josef swore through his teeth. "I know he's on the list. Get him out!"

At that moment, Wes understood that Josef knew more than what he had said. Of course, Josef had heard and understood all that the officers were talking about in the lobby and halls of the hotel. He could possibly even tap into the phone calls as the Nazis had done to hear their private calls. It all pieced together in Wes's mind. Josef knows Sam is Jewish, and he knows what the Nazis are planning for the Jews. Josef cares about Sam. He cares about Sam so much that he has dismissed not only Sam but now Wes in an effort to save one of the only links Sam has to reaching safety, even if it means Josef must cut himself off from contact with everyone associated with the operation. It was all for Sam.

Wes's shoulders arched back, and he stood a little taller. "You know I'll do all I can."

"Let's hope that's enough."

Josef began stacking and arranging the papers on his desk. Wes knew it was his cue to leave as the desk had been immaculate from the start. He longed to shake Josef's hand, to thank him, to tell him he'd come back after the war was over, but he let the image of Josef growing roots into the tiles beneath his feet be the hope he had for seeing the beloved receptionist again someday right where he could always be found.

Wes, as unnoticeable as a shadow, exited the hotel and blended into the morning street crowd. His long strides quickly brought him across the square. Wes tucked around the corner of a pastry market, away from curious eyes, before unfolding the message of encouragement in his pocket.

Tales of violence and war, concentration camps and social ostracism have become so commonplace...that the average person has completely lost his normal moral standard... But there is a difference between passive goodness and active goodness; which is the giving of one's time and energy in the alleviation of pain and suffering. It entails going out, finding and helping those suffering and in danger, not merely living an exemplary life.[1]

Yours,

Nicky

July 16, 1975
— Niky

My nails are all stubs. I bit them down in a fit of anxiety. The dam is complete, and the river is flooding faster than anyone expected! Winter snow had long melted away and spring rains poured for months creating an already heavy flow in the river. However, for the first time, the river rushed through the valley in its usual vigor only to be greeted by a barricade blocking the stream's yearly pilgrimage. Liquid curved around every part of the dam, looking for an escape route to continue its journey. Finding none, the water began expanding out in the middle of the valley, frantically widening its search in every direction.

The villagers went into a panic, transferring final items from their homes to their cars to take to New Lazinov. Some of the men had moved our village bell and its little house last week, which we are all now grateful for as it would have already been surrounded by four feet of water if they had left it until today. Our bell has seen Lazinov through many days. It was first created for the fire brigade in 1832 but has been used

---

[1] direct quote from Nicholas Winton's moral & ethical code written May 1939.

to mark time and deaths over the years. During the First World War, our prized bell was taken to melt the copper and use it for the war effort. During that time, Grandfather told me they would just look at the sun to tell the time because the bell no longer sang each morning, afternoon, and evening. A new bell was placed in the little bell-house in 1922, which is the one we have used until today. It would have been a great loss for Lazinov to drown our little, beating heart of the village.

It's impossible to cross the river to the other side of the valley, so each side has its own driving trail on opposite slopes of the valley into New Lazinov. Marie waved at little Katerina Novak across the valley, shouting, "See you soon!" as Mrs. Novak ushered Katerina into the backseat of their car while safely clutching baby Frank.

Mother called Marie and me back into the house. "Grab all the boxes left in the attic and bring them to Dad to load into the car!"

Marie bolted back into the house and began pulling boxes down the stairs. They thumped and smashed on each step, and I began to wonder why even bother if all the items will be broken by the time we get to the new house. I took the box from Marie. "Go grab something lighter." She crawled back into the attic space and pulled out a tattered, knitted sack.

"Niky? What's this?" asked Marie.

"How should I know?"

Marie was just about to open the bag when Dad came inside. "Marie! We don't have time for you to go through everything you bring down."

Ignoring Dad's comment, Marie asked, "What's in the bag, Dad?"

"It belonged to someone I knew long ago. There's nothing important in there."

Still holding the bag, Marie said, "It feels like there are two bumpy eggs in there!"

"Just some collectors rocks I've kept too long. Now hand it over, please. We don't have time to chat about it." Dad held out his arm and Marie reluctantly draped the handle of the sack over Dad's outstretched arm. "Go get something else," Dad said. Marie ducked back into the crawlspace.

I followed Dad outside with the box I was holding, but, instead of going to the car, Dad walked further down the slope of the valley until his feet nearly touched the advancing water. Then, I watched as Dad twirled the bag for a moment in his hand like a slingshot before he released the strap from his grasp. The bag briefly flew before catapulting into the growing lake, and slowly, the knitted sack sank with the weight of the water and whatever sort of egg-shaped items that were inside (I'm not buying that they were "collectors rocks." Who would keep that in the attic for years just to sink it?) Dad kept watch over the bag until it had disappeared into the murky water. I left the box I was holding next to the car and quickly ran back inside so Dad wouldn't know I had seen him throw the bag. Marie will forget about the one knitted sack with all the other treasures she will discover as we unpack the car at the new house. Though I am curious myself, I wonder how many more secrets this dam will hold before bubbling over.

Fifty-Five buildings were vacated and destroyed. Fifty-five buildings that will be consumed by the new-forming lake. Our little fire station, the mill, and many houses are slowly drowning.

The new house is filled with clutter and boxes. Mother looks tired already and Marie just wants to run and play outside with all the neighbors. Viktor and Vojta live right next door to us now, and little Katerina just four houses down. With all the adults running around to get things unpacked and ready to use, they hardly noticed the kids trekking their way back down the valley to watch the flooding. When Mrs. Novak found the kids all tossing sticks in the rushing water, she scolded the four children all the way back to the houses for being so careless near the rising current. Dad looked at Mother with her hands in her hair trying to decide where to begin with the mess and how to keep track of Marie during the whole process. Then, Dad looked at Marie, who'd maybe continue trying to get as close to the water as she could, never really understanding the danger of the water rising too quickly or the ground becoming too soft and sinking underneath her. Either that or she and the neighbor kids would all be playing in the streets, which wouldn't be any safer than the waterfront with all the moving trailers and construction vehicles. Finally, Dad looked at me as I chewed my nails, and my hallow eyes were already resenting this house. Dad reached over and grabbed a bag on the top of a pile of boxes.

"Go pack," he said. We all looked at him with confusion written on our faces. We needed to UN-pack. Dad held up the bag with our camping tent and repeated, "Go pack. Let's go

away this weekend. The kids are on summer break, and we need some time out of this mess. Grab what you need, and we'll leave for the campsite first thing in the morning."

A smile peeled over Marie's face; she has always liked camping. Mother looked even more stressed now thinking about preparing for a spontaneous camping trip AND unpacking the new house. My thoughts raced. The camping site we travel to every few summers is near the Austrian border. This could be our chance, but I needed Patja.

"Dad? Can the Kopeckys come with us?"

"That's a great idea! I'll call them up."

I waited near the phone as Dad talked with Patja's father. I heard them agree and confirm the time to leave in the morning.

I turned my head so Dad couldn't see the excitement spread on my face, followed by worry and then stress. I pulled back the boxes looking for all I would need. Not for the camping trip, but for crossing the border and leaving this place. How does one pack to leave forever? There was no time for me to tell Jakub and Zofie. No time for any last-minute pieces of wisdom for them to give us, but I hoped Patja would find a way to sneak over to Jakub and Zofie's house tonight to give them the news.

Tomorrow morning, I'll leave this place for good, and soon I'll be out of this communist controlling state forever. Either that, or I'll be in eternal handcuffs at a prisoner work camp. Or, I'll be dead. Only one outcome appeals to me, and for that to come true the other two also remain a frightening high possibility.

Though there are still many blank pages after this one, this is will be my last entry in the journal. It's impossible to take it with me over the border. If I was captured with the pages of notes and maps, it would also incriminate Zofie and Jakub. I hope Patja and I will remember it all. I've learned from Dad how to dispose of secrets, so tonight, I will cast the journal over the rushing water and let it sink into the depths of the widening river as I bury my most prized possession simultaneously with my home.

August 2, 1939
— Wes

The humidity in the midday heat curled the name tags clipped to the children's outfits. Steam from the incoming trains only aided to the discomfort as men wiped their brows, and women fanned their faces with folded newspapers. Platform One was the ideal example of organized chaos. Nicky's volunteer staff had successfully passed information to Wes, who continued to faithfully come to the train departures to help with the organization more than the chaos.

SS guards monitored the platform, balanced on rifles like walking sticks and chatting as if the hustle around them was not occurring. For the sake of everyone's safety, Wes had left the cloth sack with the two grenades tucked under his dresser. He wanted to forget about the destructive bag, though he reasoned he'd bring it back to the farm in Lazinov and hide it away in the crawl-space in the attic on the off chance he may need the weapon in their little village. Auntie had been slow to pack up the house, gifting items she no longer needed to neighbors as she wasn't planning to return to Prague. Wes didn't rush Auntie in her packing, each month he stayed was another transport he provided with help. The staff of the transport organization had quickly learned his name.

"Wes! Can you help lift bags onto the fourth car?"

"Wes! I need a translator!"

"Wes! The kids in the first car got their window stuck. Can you pull it closed?"

Wes had become familiar with running up and down Platform One, lifting kids and bags onto cars, counting and recounting the moving children, and consoling parents who feared their children were too young to be sent away.

This day was like all the others. The commotion and the occasional glare from the SS officers caused Wes to tense, but seeing the trains successfully leave the station filled with children headed to the safety of England was a sight unexplainable. He focused on getting to the end goal and seeing the train pull away from the platform as soon as possible before anyone had a chance to change their minds.

Though, it seemed that wish was already too late today. Wes heard the cry of the little girl before he saw her face. The child had climbed onto the seat and was leaning out the window with outstretched arms screaming for her mother. Her cheeks were rosy and damp, the ribbon that had been neatly tied in her hair now drooped from the side of her head. Wes watched as some men helped the mother pull the little girl from the open window until her sobs were muffled in her mother's neck. Wes quickly approached the mother and young girl.

"Can I help? They will be wanting to leave here shortly."

The mother held the girl tighter. "I've changed my mind. She won't go. Not today. She'll be ready later."

Wes wanted to speak truthfully to the mother; yet, he didn't want to alarm her or any of the other waiting parents. Wes knew more transports were in the plan, and they were hopeful for many more, though the guarantee was forever impossible. With compassion flooding his eyes, Wes stated, "There are more transports planned, of course, but your daughter is here now. This train is leaving for the journey to London today. There are many more anxious children waiting to go on future trains, and this will only push back their departure as well."

"She is only one little girl," the mother sighed, though she knew Wes was right. She took a deep breath and pulled her daughter's arms from around her neck so she could see her face. "Ilse, remember what Mommy told you? That you will get to go on an adventure today! And Mommy wishes she could come too, but this adventure is only for children. Mommy will come soon, but first, the children must explore this adventure. Do you understand?"

Ilse shook her head and mumbled, "I don't want an adventure, Mommy."

"Look at all the other little boys and girls excited for their adventure! Wouldn't you like to see England with them?" her mother coaxed. She put Ilse's feet on the ground, though the little girl wrapped her arms tightly around the waistline of her mother's skirt. The mother shuffled with the little girl back to the door of the train car and, with some final promises and a nudge, Ilse stepped again through the door of the train.

Wes smiled at the mother, who had replaced her fear with a mask of bravery. She nodded to Wes, who then returned to his work and scrambled up the steps of the last train car to lift the suitcases onto the overhead racks. As Wes was lifting the packs, the children skittered between seats and eagerly chatted about the adventure of traveling to England. It seemed all the parents had told their children a similar exciting adventure was awaiting them across the Channel. Throughout all the hustle of children, there was one child who stood out. He wasn't too young, perhaps eight years old, though his posture reflected someone beyond his years. His white shirt was buttoned to the collar and tucked into his pants. The boy's hair was cleanly parted and combed to one side, and he held his hands neatly folded in his lap. The boy looked ready for the journey to begin, and, at the same time, he looked completely unready.

"I'm Wes." Wes had learned from experience that the kids would be more open with him after they know his name.

"Tomas," the boy replied.

"Are you okay?" Wes cautiously asked the boy.

"Quite."

Wes glanced at the boy's tag hanging around his neck, number 652. The seat next to the boy was free, and the girl across the aisle was pinned with number 654.

"Tomas, do you know where number 653 is? The bathroom perhaps?"

"He isn't in the bathroom. That's my brother, Antonin," Tomas pointed to a boy of about five years old resting his head against his mother's shoulder on a bench on the platform.

The separation issues in this group were higher than Wes had experienced before. He sighed, "I know it is hard for Antonin to leave your mother, but he has you here, Tomas. Can you convince him to get on the train?"

Tomas's voice cracked, "He's sick — has a fever."

It was then that Wes noticed the flushed face of the boy on the bench underneath the black-rimmed glasses that were sliding down his nose.

Tomas continued, "Mother says Antonin can come on the next train when he is well, but Mother wants me to go without him today since I am healthy." Clearly, Tomas was fighting all the emotions that pulled him away from not only his mother but his little brother as well.

"Yes, I am sure he will be able to join you in England shortly," Wes tried the comforting words. "You are a very brave young man," he added.

The left side of Tomas's mouth curled up in a half-smile for only a moment.

"My friend should travel on the next train as well. Hopefully, the next train will leave before my pal turns sixteen. Maybe he will travel with Antonin," Wes continued. The idea hit Wes so suddenly that he nearly collapsed over, "Tomas, would it be okay if my friend, Sam, took Antonin's spot on the train?"

Tomas gave three quick little shrugs. "No one else will use it."

"My friend lives on the other side of the city, I only hope we make it in time!"

"Good luck!" Tomas called as Wes leaped onto the platform. He nearly plowed into one of the volunteers coming to check on the children in the car.

"I'm going to get one more! There's an empty seat!" Wes called.

"Run fast! We can't hold the train."

Cars honked as Wes cut over streets, and the tram's bell noisily sounded when Wes didn't stop to look if the rails were clear. He only had one thought on his mind, *"Get Sam, and get back!"* He slalomed through people in the streets as if he was a downhill skier. Finally giving up on politely weaving, Wes began shouting, "Move!" to the people in his path. As if a canon had blasted Wes, he catapulted through the open square and into the sunken streets of the Jewish quarter. Wes realized if he hadn't helped Sam get home on the day of the occupation, he wouldn't have the slightest guess as to which home could be his.

While Wes had considered this part of Prague the "other side of the city," it was truly closer to the train station in comparison to many other parts of Prague. He didn't even need to cross the river that divides the city in half; something Wes was familiar with from growing up in Lazinov, though on a smaller scale. However, growing up in the little village had also altered Wes's idea of traveling across the city, which he interpreted as simply reaching another neighborhood district. Thankfully, the Jewish Quarter had been engulfed into the Old

Town district and Old Town bordered up to New Town district, which is where the train station waited.

The tall ornate buildings provided some shade from the August sun, though Wes's clothes were already damp with sweat. The humidity that hung in the air pulled at Wes's lungs as his breath huffed. One of the many synagogues flew past Wes's view, a landmark he knew was near Sam's house. He slid into the door of Sam's apartment, and the hinges flew open. Wes's strides up the stairs to the third-floor apartment made so much noise in the hallow stairwell that Sam's father was already standing in the doorway, a look of uncertainty and a hint of fear etched over his face.

Panting from the second-floor landing, Wes heaved out words that barely fit into a sentence, "Train... leaving soon... extra spot... Sam!"

Sam's father quickly spun into action. As if taking the baton from Wes, he called into the house, "Sam! Grab your shoes, and fast!" As Sam pulled his shoes on his feet, his father and mother bustled about throwing food and last-minute clothes into a bag. In less than three minutes, Sam kissed his mother and joined his father and Wes on a race back through the city. His father clutched Sam's transport papers in his hand, not willing to let them fly from a loose pocket and praying they will still be legible after a journey in his sweaty palm.

Sam's father took the lead. Having lived in Prague his whole life, he knew every short-cut through Old Town. Sam closely followed, a mini version of his father, tall and narrowly built with scholarly glasses that Sam frequently pushed up the bridge of his nose as sweat, gravity, and momentum slid the glasses further off his face. For the sophisticated look that both father and son held, Wes was surprised at how athletically they dodged and raced through the streets. Wes forced his energy to hold out as he trailed behind Sam. He let the sweat drip from his chin and shook his head to clear the black spots that formed over his vision. He wanted to yell to Sam to keep going even if he collapses, but the strength it would have taken to say those quick words while still running was too much to consider. They hardly noticed the people cursing at them and glaring as they disrupted the street crowds.

While Wes had encountered Nazi soldiers patrolling the streets on his long dash to Sam's house, the soldiers paid little attention to Wes, seeing that there was no one chasing him, likely assuming he was late for lunch or a job. Now, with the father-son duo trailed by Wes, the street patrolling Nazis took more of an interest, yelling, "You disruptive fools!" and "Look where you are going!" but they never declared "Halt!" So, the trio continued at the same speed. Perhaps if they had been racing through a forest away from the soldiers, their actions would have been different, but in the central streets of the closed-in city of Prague, there was little chance they were escaping. As they rounded the next corner, Sam's father sidestepped an SS officer who had just exited a restaurant; however, Sam wasn't so fast, and his little body's momentum was stopped by the standing officer.

"What on earth? You lunatics!" his voice bellowed, and anger flared on his face.

Sam's father skidded back and quickly pulled Sam from the narrowing eyes of the officer. "My deepest apologies, sir. My wife is in labor; my son and I are fetching the doctor." He pushed Sam ahead as if telling him to keep running. Sam moved a few more paces before looking to see where Wes had gone, but when his father quickly rejoined him. The race was again afoot before the SS officer could say anything more.

Wes had been losing speed, and when he turned the corner and saw Sam's father pull Sam away from the SS officer, he quickly sped ahead to the next street in hopes that this one joined up with the other street down the block. In Prague, he could never tell at a glance which winding streets join again. Wes had recognized the SS officer, the same one who had shamed him at the Sroubek Hotel. They were close to Wenceslaus Square, the main square in New Town, where the hotel is situated, so Wes shouldn't have been so surprised to see the same SS officer. He was glad he hadn't been following Sam too closely, or the officer may have recognized him, and the "wife's labor" story wouldn't have been so convincing.

The street Wes was on turned up ahead, and he could hear the echoing footsteps of Sam and his father followed by a few gasps and remarks from others on the path. Wes tried to quicken his pace, though he was already giving it all he had. He merged onto the street only moments behind Sam. Sam, hearing the oncoming footsteps behind him, glanced back.

"Go!" Wes shouted though it came out like more of a hoarse whisper. They were almost at the train station.

Once inside the station, the three raced through the corridor, pushing open the doors and leaping over steps to Platform One. The caboose of the train was just meters from the edge of the platform. Shock and disappointment immediately covered the three faces. A group of parents noticed the situation and quickly tried to call back the train with whistles and waves, but there was nothing to be done to stop the locomotive. Sam's father raked his fingers through his hair and looked painfully at his son. Sam was bent over, looking as if he might vomit from the exertion his body endured. Wes appeared no better as he staggered to a bench and collapsed. A few mothers began fanning him with folded newspapers, and someone splashed water on his forehead.

"We missed it," Wes wheezed. His eyes were squeezed shut, not willing to look where the train had been only moments before. Sam slid onto the bench next to Wes.

"It's okay, Wes. We tried."

Wes opened his eyes. His vision still slightly blurred made out Sam's long face, his father standing beside him.

"Without you, Wes, we wouldn't have even had a chance. You gave us a chance," Sam's father weakly smiled.

A social worker of the refugee committee approached the bench. "You three have certainly caused a commotion! You're Samuel Levy?"

Sam nodded.

"So, there's no need to worry. You are already on the list for the next transport," the woman smiled.

Sam's father interjected, "Sam turns sixteen on the thirty-first of this month. Will the next transport be before that?"

The woman looked over her list. "The next train should be scheduled to leave between August thirtieth and September first. The information will be sent directly to you."

"But if it leaves on the thirty-first or after, will I still be able to go?" Sam questioned.

The woman fumbled with the papers. "The government has agreed for those only under the age of sixteen. I will do the best I can."

"Thank you, Ma'am," was all Sam's father could say. She gave a compassionate smile before only the sound of her heels could be heard down the platform.

A little voice came from the bench next to where the boys sat, "Our glasses match!"

Wes recognized the little boy of about five years old with tousled hair and black-rimmed glasses to be Tomas's brother, Antonin. In the chaos of the moment, the child had only recognized the twinning pair of glasses.

Sam pushed his glasses up the bridge of his nose, now red from the wire-frame sliding up and down so much. "Yeah, I suppose they do," he calmly answered.

"Are you going on the next train too?" Antonin asked

"I hope so," Sam answered back.

"I'm going. I was also supposed to be on this train, but I have a fever. Are you sick too?" It seemed Antonin had noticed more than only Sam's glasses, but also his heaved over position and flushed cheeks upon arriving at the platform.

"No, I'm not ill," Sam gave a single laugh. "Though, I might be after all the running we just did."

"Your brother was on that train, right? Tomas?" Wes implored.

Antonin's mother brushed her hand over Antonin's head, checking his fever as he nodded. "I was supposed to go with

Tomas; I'll go on the next one." Then, looking at his feet Antonin continued, "But I'm a little afraid to travel without my big brother." His mother squeezed him a little tighter, whispering words of encouragement to her youngest son of how he would be brave just as Tomas had been to get on the train by himself.

A smile poured over Sam's face, "I'll hopefully be on the next train too if I don't get too old before then, and I'd like to have a traveling buddy. What do you say? Would you like to travel with me?"

"Gee, thanks! Then I won't be so scared."

"Now, we only need to hope the next train departs before my sixteenth birthday."

"Maybe Peter Pan can visit you, and you will stay a boy, so you can come with me."

Wes smiled at the innocence of little Antonin.

Even though Sam didn't have any younger siblings, it seemed he had practice talking with small children, "Maybe Peter Pan will visit you too, and instead of going to England, we will go to Neverland together."

"That'd be neat!"

"But if we can't meet for the journey to England, you find a star you think must be Neverland from the train window, and I'll travel alongside you all through the night, alright?"

"I guess that would be just as good," Antonin replied.

His mother thanked Sam and lifted Antonin onto her hip. He was too big to be carried, but Antonin didn't protest being carried off the platform. He looked over his mother's shoulder and gave Sam a little wave before he was out of view.

Finally, Wes spoke, "I'm so sorry, Sam. I know you're wishing you were on that train."

Still looking in the direction Antonin and his mother had walked off, Sam corrected Wes, "No, I wish *he* could have been on that train."

July 26, 1994
— Krista

Krista leaned forward, and Madla's eyes grew wider in anticipation for the fisherman to continue. Fisherman Dave swiveled on his lawn chair to face the water as he slowly reeled the line.

"Well?" Madla spoke first. "Sam got on the next train with Antonin, right? What happens next, Mister Fisherman Dave?" Madla tugged on one of her pigtails, causing it to droop further down the side of her head.

Fisherman Dave waited to speak until the line was completely wound. Krista and Madla patiently waited for their storyteller to continue. Fisherman Dave laid the fishing pole down at his feet and clasped his hands together but didn't face the girls. "Mr. Nicholas Winton saved 669 children from those transports. He almost lived his whole life without being recognized for his sacrifice and work with the children's refugee program. It wasn't until about five or six years ago that his wife was cleaning the attic and found Nicky's old scrapbook with all the children's pictures and names. When she asked her husband about it, he nonchalantly told her what he had done. The world is just starting to know his name, but he will never consider himself a hero for what he did."

There was an unsettling silence after Fisherman Dave had finished as the girls waited for the next part of the story that reluctantly came.

"It truly is wonderful all that Nicky did, but what about the next train? Did Wes see Sam and Antonin at the next train departure?" Krista ventured again with Madla's original question.

Fisherman Dave's eyes became cloudy as he breathed in and asked the girls, "Do you remember Tomas's tag number from the story?"

Madla looked to the sky, trying to grab the lost number from her memory.

"650-something?" guessed Krista.

"652," the fisherman recalled for them. "He was number 652. Now, can you remember how many children Nicky saved total?"

"669," Madla reiterated this number.

The fisherman's head nodded slowly. "Yes, very good," he praised though his voice did not contain the smallest bit of joy. "You see, Wes went back to Lazinov with Auntie before the next transport was supposed to run. He never got to see Sam off at the train station as he had hoped. Wes later learned that the next train had been scheduled to leave on September first, but on that day, the Nazis invaded Poland, and there were no more refugee children transports. Tomas was in one of the last seats on the last train that left Prague."

A tear slipped down Krista's cheek as she understood what the fisherman was saying. Madla, not understanding how all these bunny trails led to the conclusion of Sam and Antonin, asked again, "Mister Fisherman Dave, but what happened to Sam and Antonin?"

"Oh, Bug," Fisherman Dave coddled, "I don't know exactly what happened. You see, after Wes got back to Lazinov, there was no way to find out what had happened to Sam or Antonin. Wes was a man by the time the war had finished five years later. He went back to Prague to try to find Sam, but the Jewish quarter was desolate of all the previous residents. Josef no longer stood behind the counter of the Sroubek Hotel, and no one knew where the desk receptionist had gone during the years of war. Auntie had passed away during the last year of the war, surrounded by her family in Lazinov. So, you see, there was nothing left for Wes in Prague except unfinished memories. Thus, he returned to continue the only life he knew in Lazinov."

"So, we can never know what happened to Sam or Antonin? Why didn't Mister Wessely keep searching for them? Sam was lost forever?" Madla frantically asked. Krista wrapped her arm around her little friend's shoulder. This was not the romantic fairytale ending she had thought would conclude the story.

"But, Madla, Sam wasn't lost. Wes found Sam in another way. Every time he raced with his children through the village, he thought about racing down the streets of Prague with Sam and his father. Each winter when the first ice formed, he imagined the first day he met Sam when Sam slipped and catapulted his glasses off his face. Every train whistle caused

Wes to wonder if Sam had found his way to safety, and every trip to Prague, Wes searched faces in the crowd to no avail in hopes that Sam had come home again. Greater than all of that, every time he called Niky, his child's name, he was reminded of all Nicky Winton had done for him and the friendship that had started him to the greatest adventure of his life."

"So, Wes gave his child the nickname 'Niky' to honor the man who never recognized himself as a hero and to remember all the children, like Sam and Antonin, who Nicky Winton wanted to save but didn't get the chance?" Krista looked to Fisherman Dave for confirmation.

"Exactly," the fisherman's old eyes squinted in a smile. "Though Wes never knew what happened to all the people he had met during this adventure, his child Niky was his daily reminder that he would never forget how all the people — Nicky, Martin, Sam, Josef, Tomas, Antonin, and all the volunteers — had changed him."

Madla leaned onto Krista's shoulder. "I think it is so sad that Mister Wessely never saw any of his friends again, but he took all they had taught him home."

Fisherman Dave grinned, "You understand it now, Madla. That's the root of this story, that we meet people for a short time who change us and impact our lives."

"But, Fisherman Dave, you said at the start that Niky's parents made an unforgivable mistake that tore their family apart that could never be forgiven. What mistake did Wes make?" Krista curiously recalled.

Fisherman Dave began closing his tackle box as he said, "That is a different story altogether."

"Were you Wes's best friend after he couldn't find Sam? Is that how you know so much about Wes?" Krista asked.

"You could say that, and Wes's life changed after his family was torn apart. He didn't talk so much after that," the fisherman latched his box.

Krista noticed the elderly fisherman's cue not to ask further, but Madla had regained her perky chattiness, "What could Mister Wessely have done that was so bad anyway? You say he destroyed his family and that he didn't talk much after that, but that is the only part of your story that smells fishier than this lake because I talk too much for my own good to know that only one person can tell a detailed story about anyone as much as you talk about Mister Wessely. Mister Wessely didn't tell you this story. You lived his story. Isn't that right, Mister Fisherman Dave Wessely?"

written on November 4, 1975
about events from July 19, 1975
— Niky

The moon, an incomplete white flag, effortlessly appeared as a brave reminder opposite of the sun's fall. A noble surrender that should have equipped me for the heartache that followed in the shadow of that moon. Never again will I be able to look at the glowing full moon without seeing the rays that match the dusty blond hair that crowned her head; simply praying the nightmare will fade just as the moon renders to the cover of the Earth's shadow. Yet, one doesn't have to be in school for long to know that the moon religiously returns to its previous full state, which provides me no comfort.

And the stars will never out-glow the bold defiance in her teeth as she stared death in the face. While stars may twinkle and appear delicate, the burning power they represent to penetrate even the blackest of nights with a luminous glow will forever remind me of the snarl that curled over her lips to display the whites of her teeth. I was sheltered and ignorant to believe we were prepared; for nothing could have prepared me — not all the training in the world — for the events of that night.

Patja and I knew we would need to make a run for it that night. Our parents had decided to leave the campsite after lunch the next day due to Dad's impending work schedule, but with the Austrian border so close, we were positive we wouldn't get this chance again. Patja gave me a reassuring look that evening as we cocooned in our sleeping bags on opposite sides of the campfire. With our parents each in their respective tents and Marie sleeping soundly next to me, we both made wishes on the stars that someday they would understand. I knew it would be impossible to sleep, so I rolled onto my stomach and rested my chin atop my folded arms to watch the campfire turn from roaring gold to a majestic royal blue. I've never found the words to describe that color of blue produced by fire, and it is perhaps for that reason that I have always been drawn to the glow of the firelight the moment before the embers consume the indescribable blue into a burning scarlet. It must have been hours before the logs burned down to the fine ash layering the bottom of the fire pit, *but I hadn't noticed the time fade. Not until, suddenly, Patja's head emerged from the sleeping bag cocoon and, in the glow of the moon, our eyes caught. When I saw Patja's eyes, I knew mine mimicked the same fear and determination. We were going to do this, and we were going to do it together. If there was one thing we had trained for our whole life, it was the escape where we now found ourselves at the starting line.*

I shimmied out of the sleeping bag, not wanting to make any noise unzipping. My shoes were already tied on my feet. Even in layers of underclothes, I felt the night air cut through the fabric and raise goosebumps on my arms. Either the night air or nerves, I guess I can never be certain. I slung my backpack over my right shoulder and moved to join Patja, who draped a blanket over my shoulders and backpack. The underside of the blanket was slightly damp from being on the ground, but I knew we would need it if only we made it across the border. Patja's backpack was already filled with snacks and extra clothes. No one had suspected anything the night before when we said we would be going on a hike before sunrise to watch the deer in the meadow on the other side of the hill. Of course, it would give us a little more time if we needed to have our parents believe we were just on the other side of the hill and not making the most dangerous trek we would ever experience.

Patja's neck strained in a gesture to move to the cover of the trees, and from there, we followed the dirt trail out of the campgrounds and onto the road heading south. I didn't grant myself the luxury of looking back, for I was afraid if I saw my family soundly sleeping, I wouldn't be able to unroot my feet. Patja didn't look back either. It was just us in the world now, but maybe it had always been that way from the start. I grabbed onto the back of Patja's bag on the narrow path, not that I couldn't see the way, but I was afraid if I wasn't lead like an animal on a leash, I wouldn't surrender to the plan before me. As the path stretched up to the road, I felt for Patja's hand and gave a reassuring squeeze. Even though we were far out of earshot from any civilization, I couldn't talk for the sobs that had lodged in my throat. We moved down the side of the southern-faced road and knew we would be at the border within a couple of hours. We listened to the sounds of the night as we had so often done in Lazinov — the croaking chorus of frogs, the crickets playing a string quartet, and the occasional echo of our footsteps following us.

After the first hour, it felt natural walking with Patja in the night. Whether we were walking our final death-march or on the path to liberation, neither of us would have been able to say. Still, we were together, and hope was a strong fishing line that had hooked our hearts and pulled us the rest of the way. I could hear my heartbeat in my ears repeating, "Just one chance; just one chance." We only had one chance to get this right, one chance to have the lives of freedom we had only before dreamed could become reality. It was Patja who first broke the silence with a whisper so quiet I was uncertain if the whisper had been spoken or if I had imagined it. I glanced over and saw Patja's lips move congruent to the whisper I had heard.

"We will be to the border soon."

I nodded.

"We need to move off the road," Patja continued.

I nodded again.

I pulled Patja down into the ditch, where a few centimeters of water puddled around my feet, seeping into my once-dry shoes. We walked through the ditch a while alongside the road before I saw light coming from around the bend. I instinctively ducked my head behind my arms, afraid a car would come racing by, its headlights giving away our cover. Patja pulled my arms away from my face and pointed at the light. It wasn't moving. I knew then it must be rays of ambient light from a village. Just around the curve is the village before the border to Austria. Actually, the structural border was over four kilometers from the geographical border of Czechoslovakia and Austria to try preventing the very people we were about to become: refugees. I pointed toward the woods; Patja nodded. We moved through the forest, aware that there could be patrols lingering behind the trees waiting for unsuspecting escapees. I felt like Red Riding Hood, just trying to make it to the safe confines of Grandmother's house, where I knew I would be cared for and loved, but before arriving at Grandmother's house, one had to be prepared to meet the Wolf in the forest.

We followed along the edge of the forest to keep the glow of the village in our view before cutting through a narrow section of the wood. We knew getting lost in the mass of forest would not be helpful this close to the border. The forest thinned into a series of small meadows that widened the view. We cut through the pasture to the forest that extended on the other side. This part of the forest was quite narrow, and I could see the clearing peeking through the trees. It wasn't long before we reached the edge of the wooded area. Still under the cover of the trees, I could see a massive guard tower that growth-spurted all the surrounding trees. The spotlights on the tower, illuminated by high-voltage lightbulbs, blocked out the darkness and attracted every moth in a five-kilometer radius. There was a tall, wire fence that extended across the field, splicing the land in half. I had always known we were prisoners in our own country, but until that moment, I hadn't realized just how confined we were. Fields stretched on either side of the fence, giving minimal places for coverage, and a gravel path nestled between two wire fences on either side gave road access for patrols.

I knew from the maps we had studied before leaving that there were woods on the other side of the barricade, but, in the darkness, I couldn't see much further past the blinding lights. Patja moved to the edge of the forest and crouched down next to a stump. My fingers went to ice and my throat dried to a Sahara state. I felt my stomach cartwheel and a line of sweat delicately graced my hairline. I leaned up against a tree, more for balance than hiding coverage and felt the moss cool my cheek. I needed to compose myself. If not only for me but for Patja because it wasn't just my life at risk. I tried to close my eyes but was overwhelmed with a wave of nausea I thought would surely collapse me to the ground. I quickly wrapped my arms around the trunk of the tree and opened my eyes to see Patja slowly backing away from the stump toward my direction. I wondered how Patja could be so calm, but when we were close enough to see into each other's eyes once again, I saw the fear that was impossible to hide. I knew Patja recognized the fear in my eyes too. Best friends just know. I tried to swallow and muffled a cough in my sleeve. I gave Patja a single nod. We had to do this, and we had to do it now. I reassuringly gripped Patja's shoulders.

Then, Patja leaned in and whispered into my ear, "Wait for my signal," and with that, Patja moved back toward the outskirts of the forest.

I watched as the field grass swayed from Patja crawling toward the fence. I forced myself to move to the hiding spot by the stump. Even in the limited books I have read, I know a person's last words are the most memorable ones. As I sat on the forest floor next to the stump watching Patja, all I could think was that my best friend and I didn't have the chance to share any meaningful last words. It wasn't an option to have "wait for my signal" be the final parting words. It might sound silly but believing we would have a chance to say something more to each other, something to represent the decade and half of friendship, built my courage.

It was rumored that the wire fence barricades were no longer electric as they had been in the fifties and sixties. Apparently, the government concluded that it was "inhumane" to have the electric fences as if keeping us hostage in this country defined "humanity." Jakub and Zofie had warned us that even without the electric fence, there could be other electric trip-wires that would alarm the guard. Although the guards were known to be young, not much different than Patja and I, there was one thing that set them apart — their lack of training and loyalty to the invasive government gave them a dose of trigger-happy fingers. Amazingly, I recalled the conversations with Zofie one after another. How she had *encouraged, supported, and prepared me for this very journey. Before leaving on this endeavor, Patja had been able to make a quick visit to tell Zofie and Jakub "goodbye" from us both. Zofie sent some final words of encouragement with Patja for me — "Take the chance; take it for all of us who cannot." The image of her looking at Karel sleeping on the couch etched in my mind. Even though Zofie is nearly fifteen years older than I, there was a bond of friendship filled with anxieties, bravery, and thanksgiving that I would never be able to write into words. Jakub sent something with Patja too: wire clippers.*

I could see Patja's silhouette in the darkness, a phantom of the night, crawling through the grass that had been mowed to a height that made it difficult to hide, but Patja's slender frame rolled with the land in an effort of disguise. I heard the rumbling before I saw what made the noise, but I was unable to pull myself behind the stump. My stomach leaped into my throat as I watched a jeep appear through the trees on the service road between the four fences. The headlights as bright as the tower searchlight and sweeping wide to illuminate anything beyond the wired barricade. Patja's arms flung out to lay flat against the earth, the backpack creating a mound that resembled a large turtle shell with Patja hidden beneath. My fingers dug into the damp soil, and my teeth bit the inside of my cheek to keep from screaming out to my best friend. We had talked about moments like this. Moments when we could get separated. Moments where one would be caught and the other would need to continue; however, in all the conversations, I had assumed it would be me who was caught. I'm the one who relies on Patja's sense of direction, the one who has a record for getting caught (previously by Mother or Marie)... not Patja.

A lone bead of sweat dripped from my temple and cradled my ear before it glided down my neck. I knew I wasn't breathing; the air caught in my lungs, unwilling to escape. Though the stress of the moment likely lasted only a few seconds, it was an eternity of fear. The government vehicle continued down the path, crushing the gravel under the wide tires. My body sat frozen, but my head twisted like an owl's to watch the jeep continue its rumbling, destructive journey. As it passed under the wide legs of the guard tower, I snapped my head back to search the terrain for Patja. My eyes scanned the land, but I was lost, unable to locate my friend until a shadow appeared near the fence. I wondered how Patja had moved so fast to reach the barricade. From the distance, I couldn't see what was happening, but I knew Patja had the wire cutters from Jakub tucked into a deep pocket of the backpack. I concentrated on breathing, but my eyes dried as I was no longer blinking. The shadow near the fence moved along the edge, finding the perfect position to make the first cut. I waited for sirens or shouts to erupt. I waited for the military vehicle to come barreling back down the road. I squeezed my eyes shut — maybe because they stung from the lack of blinking, or maybe because I was afraid to see what came next as I imagined shouts and sirens, but the only thing I heard was a soft owl call.

My eyelids catapulted open, leaving behind a gentle rim of tears. My heartbeat skipped upon hearing Patja's signal, but I remained glued to the earth, unable to move. The owl called again, my conscience telling me over and over, "Go!" I heard my thoughts so clearly, it was as if a delicate little voice had whispered it from behind. I began crawling out from my hiding spot, dragging the blanket behind me.

Before, it felt as though my senses were compromised from the anxiety that surged through my body, but as I was moving across the field to where Patja waited for me, all my senses switched to alert. My lips tasted salty from the sweaty result of fear. Strands of hair fell across my forehead, still hinting at the smell of campfire. The soil up by the forest had been soft, but this ground was rocky and small divots cratered in the field. As I came closer to the fence, my sight that had been accustomed to the dark became limited again. I tried closing my eyes to maintain the night vision I had developed, but I only saw spots of light on the insides of my eyelids and needed my eyes open to keep moving down the field. I reached the fence and watched as Patja pulled back the area of the fence that had been previously cut by the wire clippers. Patja held the fence, and I went first through the hole in the wire. There were still three more wire-linked fences to clip before reaching the other side. I followed Patja, thankful for Jakub's wire clippers, and that the fences no longer surged with an electric current.

As Patja held the second fence back for me to crawl through, my backpack got caught on the fence and shook the wire against the cement poles like the sound of a conductor tapping his podium to bring attention from the band. I froze, but Patja unhooked my backpack and shoved me through the fence. We were in the middle of the four-fence barricade — half-way and standing on the road that the patrol car had used only minutes earlier. The gravel of the road crunched under my feet, like walking on a bag of potato chips. I worried someone would hear us and tried to shuffle my feet to control the crunching. The wires gave a satisfying "clip," and again, we moved through the fence with Patja pulling it back for me to crawl through, and then I would hold the fence for Patja from the other side. Just one more fence. One more before the race to freedom. I began believing we could make it. No longer did thoughts fill my head about what it would be like to be caught, but for a moment, I felt as though we had accomplished what we set out to do.

Then, the sirens started. Loud, unforgiving sirens. The wire-linked fence vibrated from the sound waves and jingled along with the alarm that stormed over the speakers atop a nearby fencepost. I looked at Patja and saw a fear I had never seen before in my best friend. In shock, I looked at my feet, trying to find the trip-wire that gave away my location. Patja pushed through the third fence and lunged around me to hastily clip the last fence. I was still looking at my feet when Patja pulled me through the last line of chain-links from the outside. That's when I realized this wasn't like when Mother or Marie had caught my attempts to escape home. There were real consequences at stake: being separated from everyone I care about, getting placed in a prison or labor factory, or they could kill us in this attempt for escape and no one would question if the soldiers were simply acting in the line of duty. Finally, it registered; there was still a chance we could outrun the soldiers. The blanket I had in my hand snagged on the wire as Patja pulled me through and wouldn't release.

"Leave it!" yelled Patja.

I turned and chased Patja up the slope on the side of freedom, though we were still quite far from freedom, being still over an hour away from the river that served as the dividing line.

"One problem first," I thought.

My feet slapped the ground, and my eyes tried to adjust back to the darkness. I felt my heart in my ears as if I was a ticking grenade. I heard threats yelling over the speakers and large cars on the dirt road we had just crossed over, but I didn't look back. I grabbed onto Patja's hand and sprinted with all the might I had. We could see the edge of the forest a few yards ahead. The cover of the trees providing some comfort to the situation we found ourselves still trapped in. The first gunshots caused me to flinch and drop to the ground with my hands covering my head.

Patja shouted, "They're shooting over our heads! Just a trick! Keep going!"

It didn't seem like a trick to me. I stumbled as I climbed back up, and then a screech from behind caused my heart to drop to my stomach.

"NIKY!"

Patja and I, still holding hands, whipped our heads around and faced the direction of captivity. There, only several feet in front of the oncoming soldiers, was Marie. Her honey-colored hair matched the moonbeams, and fear of the gunshots had also crumpled her to the ground. My head felt like a toy top — spinning and falling in a repeated pattern. Understanding hit me like a wave — the echoing footsteps on the walk to the border, the whisper that vocalized my thoughts in the woods, it wasn't in my head; it was Marie. She was there the whole time. Memories flashed through my head like a fast-motion slideshow; All my life, I thought Marie had always been able to find me, but she had always been following! My kitten, Ash, never followed me, she always trailed after Marie. Marie was there whenever the kitten appeared, though my little sister had hidden well. So many of the moments when I thought I was away in my own world, my Shadow, as Dad had so often called her, had followed close behind.

Instinct moved me toward my little sister. I needed to help her, to do something. Patja yanked my hand, refraining me from going to Marie. Marie had been like a little sister to Patja for so many years, and I could see the pain in Patja's eyes watching Marie just down the hill from where we stood.

"You can't go! The soldiers are too close. Marie has to come to us. We'll find her in the forest," Patja's voice was frantic. Realization continued to hit like waves on a shore.

"MARIE! RUN!" I had never heard Patja's voice pull such force.

Marie pulled herself up and flung forward up the hill. I gripped Patja's hand as if pulling an imaginary rope to move my sister faster. With each running step she took forward, Patja pulled me closer to the line of trees. My gaze never left Marie; my arm outstretched helplessly crossing the chasm still between us.

Marie's foot caught in one of the many holes, and she met the ground with a shout of pain. I tried letting go of Patja. I tried running back to my sister. I should have gone to her *sooner! The soldiers picked up speed on the injured thirteen-year-old, as unfair as a chase between a lion and a gazelle. Marie stood and lunged to the side in an effort to dodge the oncoming attack. The soldier grabbed her wrist and pulled her back to the ground with another cry, this time not in pain but defeat.*

"NO! MARIE!" my lungs bellowed. I collapsed to the ground and felt the same pull on my wrist as I watched the soldier pull my sister.

"We need to go! We need to go NOW!" Patja pulled me few steps further, and I watched as my sister, who had been a moment before so afraid of her captors, show a moment of bravery and strength.

Marie's face lifted to look into the soldier's eyes as he mercilessly held her to the ground. Even from where I was, I could see the defiance on her face. The whites of her teeth mocked the lion, though she knew there was nothing she could do. I remember those white teeth the most. How I saw them pierce the darkness, brighter than the golden locks that hung from her head. Those white teeth, that moment of strength and defiance from my little, goody-goody sister caused me to move with confidence once again. The soldier tried to pull at her teeth as if knowing the strength they represented. Marie twisted her head to the side as the soldier yanked harshly on her honey-colored curls. He pulled a pistol from his belt, and with a final warning, Marie's hands matted her disheveled hair in surrender. Her shoulders slumped forward in final defeat.

My limbs went numb from the pain that took over my heart and coursed through each vein, but I needed to finish this —

for Patja, for Zofie and Jakub, and now, more than anyone, for my Shadow. "I love you, Marie," my voice cracked as I gave my final parting cry. I was doubtful she could hear me. My eyes hosted a new geyser as I let that image of Marie etch into my memory. Her glaring teeth providing the last bit of strength I needed to stand.

Another three silhouettes of soldiers forced their way up the hill toward Patja and me. In the distance, I heard dogs barking over the wail of the sirens. I'm sure Patja would have dragged me the rest of the way to the trees, but I tried to keep up as I followed behind, tried to see around the tears that blinded my view and the stinging reality of Marie's capture. Patja looked over to me with compassionate eyes and cheeks wet from tears. I waited for my best friend to give me some reason or explanation of why we had to keep going, but there wasn't time to discuss and weigh the consequences. Glancing forward at the line of trees on the rim of the hill, Patja simply declared two little words, "Race me."

For my entire childhood, it had been those two words that brought fire to my legs. Patja knew. I picked a tree on the horizon of the forest, imagined it was my climbing tree, and I was suddenly miles away, back in Lazinov at the edge of Dvorak's farm. It was as if I could feel the sun warming my face, and the meadow grass brushing over my ankles. I imagined flinging my backpack over my shoulders to land against the fence. I eyed my competition, knowing I would leave Patja behind in the wake of my run. A gunshot exploded as if signaling a start, and then I ran. I sprinted as I had a thousand times before. I didn't feel as though I was running away from the grasp of the soldiers, I wasn't fleeing my homeland forever, I wasn't abandoning my little sister on the slope to freedom, it was just me and Patja racing as we had always done. With Patja close at my heels, I remembered the promise I had made to myself years before; I would never again lose another sprint.

later on July 26, 1994 — Krista

Krista gave up trying to figure out how Madla had pieced together that Fisherman Dave was Wes. Madla hadn't said her words to Fisherman Dave in accusation; rather, her revelation was more like figuring out that Santa Claus isn't the one hiding presents under the tree. While Krista's mouth had parted at the bold words, and her throat went dry, Fisherman Dave only smiled at Madla and said, "I always knew you were a clever girl." Then, he relaxed back into his lawn chair. Krista had been afraid the fisherman would become angry, but then she remembered all the times in the story that Fisherman Dave had said Wes was truly a lamb at heart.

Fisherman Dave rested his arm on one side of the lawn chair as he said, "I had two children, Niky and Marie, but I made a mistake. I couldn't protect them when they ran away and risked their lives for a chance at freedom." The fisherman's voice cracked, "I haven't been able to tell this story because it was forbidden to escape during communism, and my wife and I were always being watched. We had lost all contact with our two children because Marie never made it over the border, and Niky — well, I lost Niky altogether. I suppose Niky wants nothing to do with me, seeing that it is my fault that their escape was compromised. I took a risk, a sliver of a chance for the freedom of these children like I had back when I was helping Nicky Winton, but this time, it cost me my family."

During the whole time Fisherman Dave was talking, Madla inched her way closer to the fisherman's chair until she was finally close enough to wrap her arms around the elderly man as he let his heart break in front of two young girls. Fisherman Dave patted Madla lightly on the back, "Thank you, Madla, but I know now that some stories have happy endings, and some do not."

"And some still don't have endings," Krista whispered.

The fisherman nodded, "Truthfully, I don't know all that happened the day my children left, but I know I could have done something different, and every day, I wish I had."

Fisherman Dave looked back and forth between the girls before saying, "Thank you two. Though I may not be ready to share it all just yet, I am beginning to feel like a bird opening its wings for the first time. I think I will learn to soar soon enough, but, for now, I need to get used to the wind pushing against my feathers. If it is alright with you, we will stop there today, but Krista and Madla, do come back soon, and I will tell you more about Niky and Marie and the adventures they had growing up in Lazinov. I think talking is good medicine for my old soul, and you two are excellent listeners."

Madla beamed with pride, "You mean, I helped? And you said I'm a good listener? Can you tell my teachers this?"

Fisherman Dave chuckled, but Krista was still toying with one final thought in her head, *"How do I get Mom and Dad to start opening up with their stories too?"* While Madla left the cove feeling pleased with herself for lightening the load of the fisherman, Krista could feel the weight of her parents' unknown story tugging her deeper as she yearned for answers.

Upon arriving back at the house, Krista found Doma in the bedroom staring at a letter she was writing to Jack, the pen lying next to her on the nightstand.

"Hi, Mom."

Doma looked up from the paper noticing Krista had entered the room. "Hello, Sweetie. Did you and Madla have a good time?"

"Yeah." Krista sat down on the edge of her parents' bed and thought about how to continue. She finally decided just to outright ask Doma what was on her mind.

"Mom, being here in Czech is making me wonder about what life was like for you and Dad here before you moved to America."

Doma glanced back at the paper with a simple, "Hmm."

Krista tried to pry more, "And I was wondering if you could tell me?"

Doma shrugged, "Your dad and I had pretty traditional childhoods."

She reached over and picked up the pen, though she didn't press it to the page. After a moment, she looked up and saw Krista still watching her, waiting for more.

"Your dad and I left for America, Pastor Everson's church sponsored us to come, and we couldn't have contact with people in Czechoslovakia until the borders reopened about five years ago."

"I know all that."

"Then, why are you asking?"

"How did you get across the border if it was closed?"

"There were ways across."

"Dangerous ways?"

Doma's shoulders shuddered as a shiver passed down her spine.

"Mom, it took you almost five years to come back here to visit after the borders reopened, and now that you're here, you spend most of the day like a prisoner in this room. What happened here before you came to America?" Krista's voice began to rise. She had been patient, and now she wanted answers.

Doma's voice remained steady, "Someday, when everyone's ready, Dad and I will tell you."

"I'm ready now!" Krista knew she was acting like a toddler, but she had made up her mind.

"It is a difficult story, Krista."

"I'm not a baby! Why won't you tell me what happened?"

"I wasn't only talking about you; it's a difficult story for me!" Doma finally cracked, her voice heaved. Her shoulders fell, and she shook from sobs that wouldn't release. Krista froze, not knowing how to help the woman she had always seen as strong and unwavering until now. She silently crawled to where her mom sat on the bed and placed her hand gently on Doma's back.

It only took a few moments for Doma to become calm again as Krista imagined her counting to ten in a similar way that she had taught her children to do as small children. Doma let out a final, long breath. She had successfully contained the sobs before any tear spilled from her eyes. Krista realized her mom was like a carbonated drink; you had to coax the cap a little bit at a time.

"I'm sorry, Mom," Krista tried to make amends, "I thought you were keeping something from me to protect me. I didn't think about how it affects you."

"Oh, but Krista, we were protecting you! Your Dad and I had to be careful what we said. We had been told communist spies were living in America who could pass information back to the Soviets in the Eastern-Bloc countries. It could have made it even more dangerous for our families or the people who helped us if there was ever any leaked information. It was for everyone's safety that we couldn't tell you anything more." Krista noticed Doma's hands were shaking as she continued, "But then, we hadn't talked about what happened for so long that your Dad and I couldn't come to terms with everything that had happened. We couldn't change it anyway, so we tried to forget about what we left behind in Czechoslovakia."

"You missed your home here?" Krista guessed.

"I didn't have a home in Czechoslovakia the day I left. The communists had destroyed my home, and I was never able to find a place I could feel at home again."

"But you called yourself 'home;' 'Doma.'"

Doma weakly smiled at Krista, "You've figured that one out, have you? My home in Czechoslovakia no longer existed and America never truly felt like home for me, so instead of searching for home, I let it find me."

Wanting to ask her mom a handful more questions about the home she lost, Krista didn't want to lose the one question she hoped would finally bring answers, "If you and Dad left Czechoslovakia together, what were you trying to forget about that you left behind?"

Like a bandage being pulled off, Doma squeezed her eyes shut and then stammered, "I had a sister." It was as if a bottle of champagne had been opened. There was shock from the cap being released, tears that finally bubbled over the side of the bottle, then pure and painful joy that filled Doma's eyes as she thought about her little sister openly for the first time in twenty years. "I had a sister," she repeated with confidence. Looking at Krista, she whispered, "You had an aunt."

Krista's hand slid off her mom's back. Doma caught Krista's hands in her own, pulling her back into the time of her childhood. She took a deep breath and let the rush of words escape her lips.

"Your dad and I had a great childhood until we didn't. As kids, we didn't realize all the restrictions the government put on us, but as we grew older, we began to understand the control they had. We didn't agree with the rules. There were limitations if a person believed in a religion the leaders did not like. There were many rules about freedom; we couldn't be outside after a certain time at night, and we couldn't leave our country's border without jumping through many hoops. The government controlled all the land. They took the land from the farmers and communalized the harvest. Maybe I would have overlooked all of that if they hadn't flooded my village to make the dam you visit with Madla."

Krista's eyes never left her mom's face. She could see the pain etched in lines around Doma's eyes and watched her bite her bottom lip to prevent it from quivering. She knew she was sitting right next to Doma, but Krista could tell her mom was far away, in memories of her past.

"Your dad and I couldn't live with those limitations, and I had so much hurt from losing my home. We knew whenever we started a family that we wanted to be in a place where our kids could live freely, so we made the plan to escape Czechoslovakia. It was a risky plan. We didn't understand all the ramifications when we set out on the journey. On the night we sneaked out to cross the border, my sister followed us. Your dad and I didn't know she was there, and then suddenly, the guards were chasing after us, and I heard her behind me, calling after me." Doma's eyes closed. She could still hear the final cry and high-pitched wail of her sister. "I turned back to help her, but it was too late. The guards had already caught her wrists and were yanking her to the ground. She was only thirteen years old, but at that moment, she became the bravest person I had ever met. She bore her teeth at the guards. I saw the whites of her teeth from where I stood, like a caged animal ready to attack. How one little girl showed that much courage, I'll never understand. One of the guards slapped her across the face, and at that moment, I also fell to the ground, unable to watch my angelic, baby sister be harmed by those monsters.

She was only a child. Your dad pulled me to my feet and challenged me to run as fast as I could, away from the madness, but he couldn't pull me from the nightmare. I don't know how I made it to the border, but I never looked back."

Catching her breath, Doma continued, "My little sister was always following me. I never realized how much she knew about me because she was always there. At the time, I thought it was annoying to have a little shadow, but now, I would give almost anything to have a moment of that back." Tears rolled over her cheeks and slapped in puddles on her skirt. "She died. Years later, she died. The soldiers brought her to a reformation labor prison. She was required to work with chemicals to dye clothing. Inhaling the toxic chemicals eventually killed her. She never had a chance at a free life all because I was only looking out for myself. I could have saved her, and now I live with the consequence that I could have done more."

Doma's eyelid blinked frantically, unwilling to let more tears drip over her face. Krista's face copied the rivers that ran down her mom's cheeks. For a long moment, the two sat, letting the story hang in the air. Giving a moment of silence for the grieving sister and niece.

Finally, Krista whispered, "How do you know she died? Maybe your sister is still okay."

Doma shook her head, "Zofie and Jakub heard about her fate. People in this area knew about the labor prison and knew my sister was a prisoner there. They said they heard of her death three years after our escape. We had no contact until after the revolution, but when this country was finally freed from the laws of Communism, we were able to contact Zofie and Jakub. They told us what had happened."

Krista rested her head on Doma's shoulder, suddenly understanding why her mom and dad had never shared more than snippets of their childhood before. Like Fisherman Dave's story, this one also wasn't a gentle, bedtime tale. Doma rested her head atop Krista's. They let tears slip from their eyelashes until their breaths matched. A calmness swept over the two as Doma held her daughter. It was Doma who finally broke the silence, "You know, you're named after your aunt."

"She was also called Kristyna?"

"No, your middle name — Marie." She let the name roll from her tongue.

Krista jolted upright, a wave of nausea spilling over her for a moment as she pieced it all together. Peering carefully into the eyes of her mother, she asked, "Niky?"

Doma breathed in sharply. "Where have you heard that name?"

"Fisherman Dave Wessely at the dam told us about his two kids, Niky and Marie."

Doma got a distant look in her eyes. "Dad?" she asked aloud to no one.

Only minutes before, Doma had explained she had taken on her modern nickname to reconcile with the fact that she never found a true home again, but Krista hadn't given a second thought to what her mom had been called before arriving in America. She had assumed her mom would have just been called Dominika, and with sudden realization, Krista uncovered that "Niky" had been the nickname for Dominika all along.

Watching her daughter's thoughts swirl as if they were connected to a motor, Doma added, "I wasn't the only one who took on a new nickname. Upon arriving in America, your dad and I thought it would be best to leave our old selves in Czechoslovakia and begin our new life in America. I knew I could never really feel at home again, and 'Doma' fit so nicely with Dominika anyway, but your dad's name was a little simpler. He decided to go by 'Rick,' short for the end of his name, Patrick, but before leaving Czechoslovakia, everyone called him 'Patty,' but in Czech language, that translates to 'Patja.'" After a short pause, she added, "And it seems that Dad, who had always been called 'Wes' has taken on a new nickname as well."

Doma's eyes stung as she realized all the trips Krista took to the dam she had been talking with her dad. Krista had realized it too.

"Fisherman Dave is my grandfather," Krista's voice stuttered over the sentence.

Doma nodded her confirmation.

Krista quickly piped up, "Let's go see Fisherman Dave now! We have to tell him that you're back; that I'm his granddaughter."

Lovingly, Doma looked at her daughter and then watched the wind play with the corner of the drapes hanging in the window. "I can't go back," she softly uttered. "You don't understand, Krista. Because of me, my parents lived the last twenty years of their life childless. I abandoned them, and

Marie died from my mistake. I can never face my father after that."

Krista recalled the many times her parents telling her that she had never done anything too bad to hide or run away. "Mom," she began, "in all my conversations with Fisherman Dave, never once did he sound bitter. When he told us about Niky and Marie, he said their parents were left with the guilt of losing their children. Fisherman Dave said it was his fault, but he didn't tell us why."

Doma's brow scrunched, and she considered what Krista was saying. "That doesn't make sense at all, Krista. It is because of me that Marie was caught. If she hadn't followed after me, if only I had looked to make sure my Shadow wasn't trailing behind, Marie would have survived."

Krista bit the corner of her lip before saying, "It isn't adding up, Mom. I know I heard Fisherman Dave right. He thinks it's his fault that he lost you and Marie. Maybe there is still a bigger picture. I think it is only fair to all of us to at least try to figure out what exactly happened."

A flicker of curiosity passed over Doma's face. Before Doma could change her mind, she called out into the hall, "Zofie! I need to borrow the car."

Zofie appeared almost instantly in the bedroom doorway as if she had been standing in the hall all along. She tossed the keys to the car onto the bed beside Krista and Doma. "Give my greetings to Ol' Dave Wessely," Zofie winked as her fingers strummed the doorframe.

later on November 4, 1975
still regarding the events of July 19, 1975
— Niky

Patja's forcing me to write, to continue — says it will help me to process and that it will make me feel better. I'm not sure how that is possible — to feel better or worse — since I feel nothing.

I felt my hand hit the trunk of the first tree on the edge of the forest. I hadn't expected to lose. Patja was close at my heels. My best friend's hand never reached the tree but flew past me and grabbed my arm, shouting, "Keep running!" This is what Patja was made for — long distance. I fell into a rhythm behind Patja, weaving around trees, dangling branches whipped at my face, roots pulled at my feet, but all those failed in comparison to my heart breaking inside. The shouts of the soldiers and the growling barks of the dogs grew fainter the further we pushed through the forest. I don't know how long we ran. I can't imagine we ran completely straight. The darkness of night in the forest enveloped us, and we could only hope we were still moving toward the Austrian border. We were finally so far deep into the woods that we could slow down and simply focus on keeping a steady pace as we stumbled forward. Every part of my body wanted to collapse onto the floor of the forest and melt away into the earth, but for Patja, I kept moving. From the research we had done beforehand with Jakub and Zofie, we knew the River Thaya was about an hour away from the border, but it appeared much faster than that. Suddenly, Patja and I were both sliding down the riverbank, and my legs became icicles as the water swirled around my knees. Patja plunged in headfirst.

"Swim, Niky!" Patja called, swallowing and coughing out a mouthful of water.

The current wasn't strong, and the river hardly very wide. I sunk my arms into the water, and small waves lapped at my chest. With strength I didn't know I still had, I felt my arms pull the water behind me and my legs fervently kick. I reached the other side of the river sooner than I expected and would have crashed right into the shoreline if Patja hadn't grabbed my backpack's handle and practically pull me out of the river. I crawled up the bank into the continuation of the forest on the other side, and there, I finally collapsed. I couldn't tell if they were tears or river water dripping from my face, or whether my heaving was the result of sobs or the recovery of exertion. My head rested on the soil, dirt stuck to my cheeks, as I looked over to see Patja lying three feet away.

"Austria," was all Patja could say between tears and gasps of breath.

"Austria," I faintly heard my own voice copy.

Patja fell asleep in the soil like that. I knew we would likely freeze in the cold clothes, but it was nearly dawn, and I hoped the sun would be gracious to warm us in the morning since neither Patja nor I had the energy to keep trekking onward. I knew from the lessons with Zofie and Jakub that it would be about another hour through the forest on this side of the river to the first village. From there, our training ended. Jakub didn't know what was past the border beyond what we could reason for ourselves from a map, though he had heard rumors there were refugee centers for communist escapees who were then sponsored by communities or churches around the world. He assumed Australia, America, and England were the most frequent places for refugees' final destinations if they didn't stay in the Western European states. We all made wishes together that a church in America would sponsor Patja and me as refugees to have a passage and starting block in the United States.

To think that is all we knew months ago, and now we are sitting in the guest bedroom of a young midwestern pastor. His pregnant wife was working on getting the toddler to sleep, while Pastor Everson tried his best in easy English to explain necessary information about the city. No sooner had he left did Patja pull a pad of paper off the desk and held it out to me. "Write it, Niky."

"Write what?"

"All of it, our escape."

"It's in the past."

"It won't be until you write it."

I grumbled and took the pad of paper simply to please Patja. I wrote and wrote. Then, Patja told me to write some more and now, here we are, at the end.

Patja just collapsed onto the bed saying, "America." Each night we were in a different place, Patja has done that: "Austria," "Germany," and, my favorite, "Airplane above the Atlantic Ocean." Hearing Patja whisper "America" tonight, I realized we truly made it. We're here. This is home now. (Even though I doubt it will ever truly feel like home.) There won't be any more nights with different places whispered from Patja's lips. While this should be a joyous moment, a time to celebrate the final nightly-word-whisper, my own heart aches for my own nightly-word-whisper. My voice no longer copies Patja's as it did on the riverbanks that first night in Austria, but now each night, my final word is accompanied by a single tear hitting the pillowcase: "Marie."

still July 26, 1994
— Krista

It was foolish for either Krista or Doma to believe Zofie hadn't known the whole time about Fisherman Dave. As they both stared at her with wide eyes, still red and puffy from crying, she simply placed a hand on her hip and said, "What do you expect? It's a small town, and, of course, I'm still connected with the people in Lazinov. I grew up there too, you know. Ol' Dave Wessely fishes at the dam regularly, and I knew Madla would want to explore along the shoreline with Krista." A flicker of pride sparkled in her eyes, "I was just waiting for the rest of you to figure it out." She aimlessly taped the doorframe. "Sure took you long enough!"

Doma stifled a laugh, "You did this?"

"I only nudged it on. Encouraged Karel to bring the kids to the dam and such. Not enough to be blamed, but I was hoping for this outcome." Zofie looked at the keys still lying on the bed. "Well, what are you gals waiting for? Get going already!"

Curiosity had won the battle Doma was fighting inside. After splashing cold water on her face and combing her hair, Krista pulled Doma to the car before her mom had a chance to change her mind. They made a stop by the dam, but Fisherman Dave had already packed up for the afternoon. As they walked back to the car, Doma knelt by the edge of the water and placed her hand on the surface. The lake reflected Doma's face like glass. Krista had become comfortable next to the water over the past month, but Doma looked over the completed reservoir for the first time with awe. Her heart swelled as she imagined the valley and the village it once held, but the beauty of the lake was undeniable. She could see how her Midwestern daughter had quickly grown attached to the lake.

With her hand still on the surface of the water, Doma spoke, "The water feels the same. Not rushing like the river once was, but the energy is still there."

The two wove their way around the lake on the country road Doma had only traveled on only once before to reach New Lazinov.

"How do you know where to go?" Krista finally asked.

"I was at the house on moving day, though I never came back to unpack. My dad decided to ignore the mess and go camping near the Austrian border, which in return worked out for me and your dad." Doma glanced over to Krista in the passenger seat. "I had come a few times on a makeshift path through the valley to help my dad work on the house. Even though I have only traveled on this road once before, I would imagine traveling back down this street many times over the past twenty years."

Krista knew thoughts were running through Doma's head at rapid speed and decided to simply watch the scenery. Truthfully, she was also worried. She had talked with Fisherman Dave many times before, but this would be the first time she'd talk with the man as her grandfather.

Krista had seen the roof of the little house across the shore of the lake, but at last, she was standing in front of the home on the corner of New Lazinov. She unlatched her seatbelt and reached for the car door handle. Doma breathed in deeply and finally let go of the steering wheel. Facing Krista, she said, "Let's go," though the words were more for herself than her daughter.

They calmly made their way to the door, and Krista gave a firm knock. From behind the door, Doma heard a voice she thought she would only hear again in a dream, "Coming. Be right there!" A shuffle of footsteps and the creaking of twisted locks preceded opening the front door.

"Hi, Dad. I'm home."

It didn't take long before more tears were falling, and an old fisherman and a lost daughter embraced each other after twenty years apart. More hugs were passed between Krista and Fisherman Dave as he quickly realized she was, in fact, his granddaughter.

"I always thought her eyes looked familiar," the old man croaked through sobs. "They're Patja's eyes, aren't they?"

Doma nodded.

The fisherman squeezed Krista's face as he whispered, "My Dominika and Patja. Of course."

He ushered them inside for tea and stumbled around the kitchen, grabbing teacups his late wife had seemed to keep on the shelves for the off-chance that royalty would appear on their doorstep. Somehow, the painted china didn't seem special enough for even this occasion. There was so much to catch up with and no way to start. Krista and Doma sat on the sofa, sipping their hot tea with Fisherman Dave in the rocking chair across from them. A coffee table divided the seating area. Fisherman Dave tried to make small talk. He started with the weather simply because he didn't know how to converse with the daughter he had lost years before.

Finally, the old fisherman cut himself off and looked down into his cup of black tea as he said, "I've thought of this moment every day for years, Dominika, and I practiced over and over what I would say to you if I ever had the chance and how I would start to explain it all to you." Fisherman Dave reached for his handkerchief and wiped his wet cheeks. "I guess all I can ask is, could you ever forgive me, Dominika?"

Doma set her teacup on its matching saucer and replied, "That's what I'm confused about, Dad. I came to ask for your forgiveness."

Dave leaned back in his rocking chair, an action Krista recognized as he was letting himself be brought back to his memories, "But Dominika, it's my fault — all my fault."

Knowing what he was referring to, Doma tried to reason, "How can it be, Dad? I'm the one who Marie followed that night."

"And I'm the one who sent her after you."

If Doma had been holding her teacup, it surely would have shattered at that moment.

"What do you mean?"

"I sent Marie after you that night. You knew that."

"No, I didn't."

"But you had to have known. That's why you haven't come sooner."

"No, Dad, I was afraid you and Mother were angry with me."

The fisherman looked at his daughter and with a burden on his heart. "I could never hold a grudge on my dear Dominika."

Doma's mouth went dry as she let herself go back to the night of Marie's capture. "Dad, I didn't know Marie was following me that night. When I finally noticed her behind me, I tried to go back to help her, but it was too late. Patja pulled me away, but even if I had gone back, there was nothing I could do." A single tear rolled over Doma's cheek and just missed landing into her tea as she leaned over the coffee table. Forcing herself to look up at her father, she choked out the words, "She was brave, Dad. Marie was so brave. I watched her open her mouth and show the guards the whites of her teeth as she defiantly gave all her last energy by demonstrating her courage."

"You mean, you didn't know Marie was following you until after it was already too late?" Dave rubbed his collarbone.

"Yes, Dad. I would have done everything I could have for her if only I had known sooner, believe me."

"I wouldn't doubt it." After a moment's pause, Dave asked, "So, you have thought all these years that it is your fault Marie was caught?"

Doma nodded, another two tears released.

"Oh, my sweet girl, I am so sorry. It was my fault, don't you see? Your mother and I knew you and Patja planned to escape."

Doma's questioning look brought a small smile to the fisherman's face. "Of course we knew. We knew you, Dominika. We are your parents. We could see the way you felt like a caged bird. We knew writing would only do so much, but that is why Mother bought you the journal, to encourage your free-spirit. We knew you were always made to soar. Your mother and I believed you and Patja would make it, but one of the hardest decisions was deciding not to tell Patja's parents. It could have compromised you more if they had known, especially with all the questioning after you left and Marie's capture. It killed us inside to think about losing you and Patja and ultimately giving up our friendship with Patja's parents, but we knew neither of you would be happy here if you stayed. In a way, we were already losing you. The longer you stayed in Czechoslovakia, the more we realized what it was doing to you. When we went on the spontaneous trip to the camping grounds near Austria, Mother and I knew you wouldn't be coming back to Lazinov with us." Fisherman Dave drew finger quotations around "spontaneous trip" as he talked. With each word, the gap in Doma's mouth grew wider.

The fisherman continued, "On the last night at the campground, your mother and I knew you and Patja would try to escape. We talked with Marie before sending her to sleep." Again, the fisherman drew quotes around the word "sleep." "We knew that as much as it killed us to lose you, we knew life without you would be devastating for Marie. We knew the communists would interrogate us, and we'd need to be even more careful and loyal than ever. Your mother and I were willing to do all that knowing you'd be free and happy, but we couldn't ask that of Marie. So, that evening, Mother wrote a note on a clean white paper explaining that we knew you and Patja were leaving, gave you our blessing, and asked as our last wish that you take Marie with you."

Choking on his own words, Fisherman Dave said, "I thought Marie gave you the note. I thought you were so upset after all these years that Mother and I had sent Marie with you. I thought you were angry with me since it was because of us that Marie was caught, and it nearly compromised the escape of you and Patja too."

"You wrote a note?"

Fisherman Dave nodded, his hands vibrating as the elderly man tried to control his emotions.

"Dad, I never got the note from Marie. I didn't even know she was following until too late."

"But if Marie still had the note on her when she was captured, the interrogators would have known your mother and I were a part of the plan to escape. We would have been escorted to prison for aiding an escape."

Fisherman Dave and Doma looked curiously at each other. Sudden understanding cascaded over Doma like a bursting piñata. She spoke to no one and everyone, her eyes searching the room as if applying all the pieces together, "It wasn't Marie's defiant white teeth I saw that night. She ate the note. Marie ate the paper!"

"Marie ate the paper," Fisherman Dave repeated Doma's words in realization. "She saved us," his vocalized thoughts continued.

After twenty years, father and daughter had finally realized the absence of reaching out to each other was a misunderstanding in a note that never made it out of the hands of the currier.

For the first time in twenty years, peace rather than regret came over Doma as she thought about her little sister. "Marie ate the paper — brave, little Marie."

It didn't take long before Fisherman Dave stood up from his rocking chair to retrieve an envelope that lay on the top shelf of the bookcase. If he hadn't known it was there, no one would have seen it. He blew off a small layer of dust that covered the sun-stained envelope and walked back to where Doma sat. She was cradling her teacup between the palms of her hands, still absorbing the realization of essentially how fearless her little sister had actually been. Fisherman Dave held out the letter to Doma. On the envelope was simply written "Niky" in a handwriting Doma didn't recognize.

"What's this?" Doma asked as she set down the teacup and reached for the letter. Krista leaned over to see what was written on the envelope.

"Read it. It's addressed to you. Though I hope you don't mind, I already opened and read it. I didn't know if I'd ever get a chance to give it to you."

Doma waved away the apology, completely understanding her dad was simply looking for clues about what truly happened the night she and Patja had left with Marie trailing behind. Doma pulled the letter out of the already-opened envelope and read the words with Krista glancing over her shoulder.

Dear Niky,

My name is Andrea. I was a political prisoner and condemned to work at a Communist Labor Factory for sharing my faith. The government thought they could keep me quiet by putting me to work in the factory, but I continued telling all the women in the assembly line why I had been placed there to work as a prisoner. It was on one of those routinely unmemorable days when Marie arrived, causing me to remember that day above the rest. I remember how strongly she stood as the guards escorted her in, except for the terror that was impossible to hide from her eyes. I quickly befriended Marie, helping her get accustomed to her new life, all the while shocked that such a young girl could be subjected to this treatment. In one of our first conversations, I remember Marie asked me, "How do you remain so strong?"

I told her, "I'm not strong, but my faith gives me the strength I need."

Marie replied, "My sister was always the strong one, not me."

Over the next years, I heard many stories about Marie's independent, bold sister, Niky. Many of the other prisoners would gather around as Marie told stories about the adventurous risks her sister welcomed. One evening, many of us ladies were all sitting together as we each took turns talking about the homes that were waiting for us when we would finally be released from the labor prison. Most of the women described the layout of their home, the color of the carpet, and which wallpaper they had used to decorate. We all chimed in with the conversation, except for Marie, who was uncharacteristically silent. Eventually, someone asked, "What is your home like, Marie?"

Marie looked across the room at the wall as if looking in a mirror to the past and then said, "I don't remember my house so well. It isn't there anymore anyway." She closed her eyes and continued, "But when I think of home, I see Niky climbing that old tree that overlooked the valley. The way the left side of her overalls notoriously fell off her shoulder and her braided hair unraveled from getting stuck on the branches. I would always find her at that tree, but I'd hide behind the bales of hay Farmer Dvorak had stacked for his goats. I knew it was her special place; that tree was her home after all."

One woman smirked, "Why'd you think of that? It wasn't your home; it seemed to be more of your sister's."

Then, your sister said something I have never forgotten, "Because it didn't matter where I was, I could have been anywhere in the world, but if I was with Niky, I knew I was home." I sat next to Marie in amazement for she understood the essence of "home" better than the women twice her age. While another woman started speaking, I heard Marie whisper into the room, "I hope you found your way home too, Niky."

Marie, though she was the smallest one in the factory, inspired me the most.

Sincerely,

Andrea

Doma folded the letter along the creases and looked up to see her dad smiling at her from across the room. "I always told you Marie was your shadow," he started. "Andrea came a few years ago looking for you. When I explained that I didn't have contact with you, she asked if she could leave the letter with me. By that time, I had been living alone for a few years already. When we heard about Marie's sudden death from the chemical poison in the factory, your mother and I were devastated. Mother began spiraling after that with regret, and she passed away a few years after Marie. I'm so sorry, Dominika."

Doma grabbed her dad's thick hands within her own. "I know Mother died years ago, Dad. Zofie and Jakub wrote to me after it all happened. They said it was rumored that she had died from a broken heart after losing both her daughters. I truly thought you couldn't forgive me for taking Marie and Mother away from you also. It's why I didn't write to you," Doma's words trailed at the end and Fisherman Dave squeezed her hands within his own.

"Before your mother died, she told me to hold onto hope that you would come back. Mother always knew you'd come back even if I didn't believe it myself. I didn't have any hope, but I've stayed each day holding onto your mother's hope and her final wish."

"What final wish?"

"She wanted to give you back your home." Fisherman Dave took Doma's hand in one and Krista's hand in another and rose from the sofa. The girls allowed the fisherman to lead them out the back door, hand-in-hand. The sun was low in the sky as it reflected over the lake. The smell of the water was caught in whiffs of the musty air as Fisherman Dave led the girls across his green lawn to a tree firmly planted on the ridge of the hill before the land sloped to meet the shore.

"Mother wanted to give you back your home," the fisherman repeated, stopping in front of the tree.

Doma reached out her hand to touch the rigid bark. Placing both her hands on the trunk, she covered half the width around the tree. Though what the tree lacked in thickness, it compensated for in height. It reached heavenward as if there were no limits. A low sturdy branch parted from the tree, and Krista reached up and swung her legs as she looked out over the water.

"My tree," Doma whispered.

Fisherman Dave nodded, "Mother had taken one of the seeds from the tree the spring before we knew we had to move. She brought it up here and planted it. You didn't notice it the day we moved in because it was just a little sapling hardly taller than the grass, but your mother and I knew it was there."

Doma reached up and plucked a leaf, rubbing it between her fingers.

"Welcome home, Niky," Fisherman Dave rested his hand on her shoulder. "Welcome home."

August 15, 1994
— Dave

Summer transitioned into autumn with a breeze that brought a sudden crisp of air and a sunset that fell as dinner was being cleared. Being reunited with his daughter, son-in-law, and granddaughter, Dave Wessely hadn't been to his fishing spot on the cove in days. From breakfast until late after the stars became visible, he had been practicing the art of grand-fathering. As the sun rose over Letovice, Dave and Krista walked through the square to feed the ducks that paddled down the river. They returned to Zofie and Jakub's house to play cards until lunch was served. After lunch, Krista entertained Madla and Kai in the garden to give Aunt Zofie a break from the chatter-some duo. During that time, Dave joined Rick and Doma in the sitting room. He would hold a cup of coffee that never failed to be cold before he had the chance to finish it. It seemed that nothing could distract him from the stories that poured from his daughter and son-in-law as they shared all about life in America. Dave was especially partial to stories about Krista and Jack, the grandson he soon hoped to meet.

In the evening, everyone sat around the campfire in the garden, roasting sausages and toasting bread over the flames. Jakub played a tune on his guitar, occasionally passing the instrument to let Krista strum. Dave remembered sitting around campfires many times before when his girls would sit upon his knees. When the flames of the campfire faded into embers, Dave recalled the night he sent Marie after Niky and Patja with the note of explanation. A bitter memory, but one that the patient fisherman has finally forgiven himself for.

Most nights, Rick drove his father-in-law back to his home over the winding roads across the dam. Together, they'd count the deer that lingered in the ditches as the car passed. For days, Dave's routine took on this new structure, and he awoke each morning, wishing the weeks didn't move so quickly. Promises of returning to Czech for Christmas were already made, though it was the months in between that loomed ahead for the retired fisherman.

On this day, the unofficial routine was compromised, and the daily family reunion took place at Dave's house the way it had first started. Madla easily joined in as an additional member of the family; no one recognized that she wasn't related by blood. It was on this final day that Krista slipped the necklace off for the first time in months and clasped it around Madla's neck. She pinched the half-heart explaining to her dear chatter-some friend that both Madla and Ruthie now held half of the heart in her two homes, for Krista had also realized home found her in two places.

As the afternoon pushed forward, Doma and Rick headed out to pick up some last-minute items for the journey back to the states. Although they were in no need of a babysitter, Madla and Krista stayed at the fisherman's home. The three walked down to where the water touched the earth, each girl bookending either side of the greatest storyteller they knew. Dave stopped above the banks of the dam under the leaves of the tree and unfolded his sagging lawn chair. Madla and Krista had grown an attraction to the water over the past couple of months as if their fingertips and the water both possessed magnetic currents. They continued right up to the edge as Dave sank into his chair and scanned the water's surface. The trout mocked the fisherman, making splashes in the lake, but his gaze quickly focused to the foreground as Madla and Krista leaned toward each other, pointing across the dam. Krista's feather-thin hair caught the wind and matched the ripples gliding over the water. Madla's head tilted toward Krista's, finally leveling her lopsided ponytails.

Dave knew it was Madla and Krista sitting with their backs toward him, but his eyes played a trick on the old man as it had many times before. Instead of his granddaughter and her friend, he saw two other little girls sitting on the sloped earth. The smaller one, whose hair matched the color of honey, wore a faded pink ribbon that pulled half of her curls over the back of her head. She held a dust-colored kitten draped over her right shoulder. She scooted closer to her sister, causing the kitten to leap over her back and chase a startled grasshopper. She glanced back toward the cat and then looked up at her sister, whose left overall buckle slipped off her shoulder and braided hair fell out in strands. Her sister looked down at her for only a moment, and then she pointed across the valley to a little home that was nestled in the ridge.

Dave held the memory a moment longer. Remembering that time Niky and Marie sat on this very ridge overlooking the valley after the picnic. A time when the houses and trees once sprinkled the land. A time when there was a river that spliced the valley in two. A time when the road weaved through the valley and the hills rolled like a vacuumed rug. Dave blinked his eyes, and like a shutter of a camera, he held the memory of Lazinov as it had been before. He had long surrendered his dream to return to the home he had always known among those rolling hills, but he never dared to stop dreaming for his Dominika to come back to him. Doma. Even the name his daughter had chosen to call herself now filled the last wish of his aging heart.

Dave Wessely cleared his throat to speak, though the wind whisked his voice and evening air rasped in his throat, he spoke only for the breeze to hear, "It seems there was a time when we were all searching for home before home finally found us."

Epilogue
December 20, 2019

It had been an unreasonably warm winter. Not even a snow flurry or sliver of ice over the lake came to encourage a white Christmas. While mothers made their children leave for school bundled, the jackets were often unzipped and hats pulled off before they reached the school doors. Lost mittens frequented the sidewalk in front of the school as they fell unused from the pockets of children. If the students had been basing the arrival of Holiday Break on the weather, they would have missed Christmas entirely, but the calendar reminded them that school was released and family traditions about to begin. Some took advantage of the warmer winter and spent afternoons meeting up with friends outside, and others began their Holiday Break similar to any other break regardless of the weather — in front of the television.

For first-year university students Tobias, Simon, and Janek, the nice weather on Holiday Break was graciously welcomed. The three grew up attending Letovice's Elementary School together and were inseparable from the start. Teachers often mistook the names of the three, inadvertently swapping them with one another. High school had diverted their paths as each of the three took to a different interest of study, though still all living in Letovice, they had remained tightly knit even throughout high school. It was university that pulled them apart. With each in a different city at a different university, it was only human that they made new friends to socially survive their college classes. Group texts were occasionally sent during that first semester, but with all the changes and workload of freshman classes, chatting wasn't consistent. As Holiday Break approached, the Three Musketeers knew they wanted nothing more than to catch up and enjoy some time together as they had so often done in the past.

Simon met Tobias at the corner where their neighborhood roads intersected. After greeting each other with a sliding high-five followed by a fist bump, Tobias said, "Do you think Janek will be on time?"

"I hope so since he insisted on driving."

Simon sat on the ledge of a garden wall while Tobias shuffled around the corner of the street, aimlessly kicking small rocks off the path; he was never content standing still. Only seven minutes late, Janek pulled up to the street corner in his car. Simon hopped in the front seat and Tobias slid in the back, both greeting Janek and gave him some friendly grief for being late.

"I've got a good excuse, guys!" Janek began his defense.

"You always have an excuse," Simon rolled his eyes.

"I'd like to hear what he comes up with this time," replied Tobias with a chuckle.

"My mom had just pulled those scones out of the oven and wanted to send some for you two," Janek pointed to the container between the two front seats.

"Alright, his excuse is legit," replied Tobias.

"As long as we get scones out of the deal, I'll agree," stated Simon.

It didn't take long before they were at the parking lot in front of the dam's reservoir. It was a path they normally biked together as kids, but driving had become familiar to the young men in recent years. They talked about classes and new friends they had met at school as the three followed the path to the fire-pit near the edge of the water. Janek pulled out a box of matches and started a fire as Tobias gathered a few small, dry branches to burn. Simon was already opening the containers of scones and pulling out a pack of hotdogs from his oversized sweatshirt, "Should we find some sticks and roast these?"

"Oh, man! Great idea!" Janek's mouth watered for the juicy hotdogs.

"It was your idea to have a campfire, and you didn't think to bring something to roast?" Tobias questioned.

Janek shrugged, "I brought Mom's scones, didn't I? Besides, what did you bring?"

Tobias pulled out a small bag of flavored marshmallows he had stuffed in his pocket, "Will these do?" He tossed the bag to Janek on the other side of the fire-pit.

"Alright, so we all brought something to share," smiled Janek.

"Correction — your mom, Tobias, and I brought something to share," laughed Simon.

"Ha-ha. Very funny," Janek's voice was thick with sarcasm.

"Come on, let's look for some sticks to cook the hotdogs and marshmallows," Tobias reasoned.

Tobias and Janek rummaged through the trees that lined the lake, not straying far from the campfire as Simon stoked the flames. In no time, they each had a hotdog sizzling on the end of their sticks, which were quickly devoured and followed by sticky marshmallows.

"I see them do this all the time in American movies, but I don't know what the big deal is," said Simon.

"Maybe their marshmallows taste different," reasoned Tobias.

"One thing is certain, it is definitely a messy snack!" Strands of pink marshmallow fluff dangled from Janek's fingertips as he effortlessly tried to lick the sticky mess away.

"Go wash up in the water, Janek," Simon shook his head like a disappointed mother.

"Alright, alright."

Janek edged his way to the shoreline of the lake, which had receded more this year from the lack of rain and snow. The algae barricaded the rocky shore from the clean water, but Janek's long arms reached over the slimy, green algae to scrub his fingers.

"It's cold!" Janek called back to his buddies.

"You'll live," Simon hollered back.

Janek wasn't sure if he had removed all the clinging marshmallow mess or if his fingertips were just numb from the frigid water. He shook off his hands, dried them on his sweatpants, and began to return to the campfire. When he turned, a mysterious looking rock came into view just a few feet away. Janek walked along the shore to investigate.

"Are you practicing walking along the shore for when you bring a girl home from school?" Simon called down to Janek, but Janek didn't hear the remark for at the same time, he called back, "Hey, guys! Come see this!"

Tobias and Simon dropped their roasting sticks on the ground and joined Janek on the narrow beach. Janek was crouched down over what appeared to be an old, deteriorating grenade.

"Man, how'd that get here?" Simon questioned.

"Washed up on the shore from the low tide," replied Janek.

Simon rolled his eyes. "Well, I get how it got here on the shore, but how did it get in the lake?" Simon rephrased his question.

"I'll call the police. We don't know if it is still active," Tobias pulled out his mobile phone and dialed the number on the touchscreen.

"Probably a dud," reasoned Janek.

"It looks like a World War Two grenade," Simon added.

Tobias was explaining their location on the lake for the police to find them and describing the look of the grenade. He walked down the shore away from the other two as he talked. Simon and Janek waited for Tobias to finish so they could ask him when the police would arrive.

When Tobias finally hung up and walked back to Simon and Janek he said, "They're on their way. Said not to touch it, but that it's probably a dud anyway seeing that it has been in the water and considering it wasn't used back in World War Two."

"We were only guessing it's a grenade from World War Two, but we can't be certain. Why'd you tell them it's a war grenade?" Simon asked.

"I didn't. After I described it, the police dispatcher said, 'Another one?' Apparently, on an annual Clean-The-Lake day back in 2008, a kid found a grenade that was confirmed to be manufactured during the Second World War. The policeman said the description was the same."

"Wow, two grenades from this lake? How could that even happen?" Janek asked.

"The police said they get calls like this more often than we'd expect. Someone is always finding relics of the past washed ashore," explained Tobias.

Simon looked out over the water. The sunset began to set on the horizon and made a golden glow over the glassy ripples. "I wonder what other secrets this lake holds beneath her surface."

There were no flashing lights or sirens when the police car arrived, just the sound of little waves hitting the edge of the shore like thick fingers reaching out for the object now out of the water's reach. Though the lake had lost both mysterious objects that had been drowned years ago when the waters started to rise, the truth of how the grenades came to be in possession of the mighty dam is one secret that forever found a home buried within her waves.

About the Story

*The above picture is Lazinov before and after the flooding of
the dam. The stars are on the same building in both pictures.
The little homes tucked into the hillside on the upper picture
were destroyed in the flooding. Looking closely, there are
rooftops also visible along the hill in the foreground.*

Destroying the homes & the start of flooding in Lazinov (the reflection of the homes is seen in the rising water in the picture).

A couple of homes still partially visible before flooding was complete.

While most of my characters in the story were created from my imagination, there were a handful of people who truly did exist.

Sir Nicholas Winton truly rescued 669 children from Prague and was not recognized for his work until his wife found his scrapbook in the attic of their home in 1988, fifty years after rescuing refugee children from Czechoslovakia. He never considered himself a hero. In the end, only Sweden and England opened their borders to take Czechoslovakian children. Martin Blake called Nicky to come aid Prague's crisis of displaced children. Nicky was followed by spies, rabbis questioned his work, all while he made his office in the cafe of the Sroubek Hotel on Wenceslaus Square. Much of what Nicky said in my novel were based on his own words taken directly from recorded interviews (BBC) and "Nicholas Winton: The Power of Good" by Matej Mináč.

Tomas and Antonin were real children. Tomas Graumann survived the war in Britain due to the efforts of Nicholas Winton and his team. Tomas was one of the last children on the final Children's Refugee Transport Train that left Czechoslovakia. Tomas returned to the Czech Republic years later when the Iron Curtain fell to continue sharing his story. As written in the novel, Tomas's brother, Tony, was sick the day they were scheduled to leave. (Tony stayed at home on the day of the transport due to his illness, though I wrote him in at the platform to bring his story in direct contact with the reader.) Another train was scheduled to leave on the first of September, but on that day, Nazis invaded Poland and all transports were canceled. Tomas never saw Tony or his mother again. They were sent to Terezin, a concentration camp, before being transferred and murdered in Sobibor, a Nazi death camp. Tomas's story is a beautiful description of how saving one life can change the world — a motto Nicky Winton held.

Tomas and Tony with their mother.

I highly recommend reading more about Tomas's life-changing

story in the book, "The Twice-Rescued Child" by Thomas Graumann with Tricia Goyer.

The description of what Wes and Sam saw on March 15, 1939 is how the Nazis entered Prague during the Second World War. Hitler was given control of Sudetenland — the borders of Czechoslovakia which were primarily inhabited by those of German descent. Leaders Hitler (Germany), Mussolini (Italy), Daladier (France), and Chamberlain (United Kingdom) met and determined the fate of Sudetenland without consulting President Beneš (Czechoslovakia). This meeting is known as The Munich Agreement, though it is also referred to as The Munich Betrayal, which some may argue better fits the circumstance. On March 15th, the National Socialist Army marched through a blizzard and arrived at Wenceslaus Square at 10:20 in the morning with tanks, soldiers, horses, motorcycles, and jets overhead. While they were not greeted warmly, there was no official resistance by the Czecho-slovakian countrymen. Records state that the crowds on Wenceslaus Square mourned the arrival of the occupation with tears and joined together in their national anthem as their peaceful protest. As Wes and Sam described, the trains ceased to run on the day of the occupation to eliminate evacuation.

Niky and Patja are fictional characters, though what they lived through was very real. Lazinov was a village, like many others, that was flooded by the communists to prevent flooding along larger rivers. Many amateur divers have found items in the dam over Old Lazinov, and relics have been washed ashore, including two war grenades in 2008 and 2019. It still remains a mystery as to how the grenades ended up in the waters of the dam. Interview accounts state that it felt as if the village was bulldozed overnight and that the completion of the dam was quicker than anyone expected. The high waters on the river in the spring was not an exaggeration, one account records seeing a goose still sitting on her eggs on a bale of hay as it traveled down the river.

Ms. Anna Kobzova truly rang the village bell each day at morning, noon, and evening, and for deaths or to alarm the fire brigade. Niky's account of the population in the first chapter is direct from the census in that year, as are all her comments of the land being traded and the name of Lazinov being recorded inaccurately among the trades between dukes and lords of the ancient world. The stationery store (where Niky's mom buys her journal) was the only little shop in the village. The population of Lazinov significantly dropped the year they moved the village to higher ground — partially due to the many families that moved (as was with Karel and Patja's families) since the mill was no longer offering employment in Lazinov, and there were multiple unexplained deaths of the elderly population in Lazinov (as described by Mr. Halas' death) who had taken the news of the flooding traumatically.

The communist leaders forced their ideology on the Czechoslovakian people through their education system and in "highly encouraged" programs like Pioneers (a Scouts-like program). Pioneers required children to memorize and recite their laws — as Niky does at Jakub and Zofie's home — which promised their loyalty to the Communist Regime. Curfew, required military service, and religious restrictions were only some of the ways the government demanded control.

The borders of communist Czechoslovakia were controlled by soldiers. Those captured were separated from their families, sent to reform prisons and often had to work with hazardous materials. Marie's fate was not abnormal for unsuccessful escapes. Due to the fence being along the border of Czechoslovakia and Austria for so long, it has been confirmed that the deer are still not passing over the border even though the fence has been down for nearly thirty years. There was a great fear that the communist government put in place to keep the citizens of Czechoslovakia from escaping by threatening and interrogating relatives of those who had successfully crossed the border. Churches in America, particularly in the Midwest, offered sponsorship for refugees fleeing communist countries, as was described in the case with Niky and Patja.

Letovice is a city that exists, though it feels as if it is taken from the pages of a fairytale. It is just minutes from the edge of the dam reservoir. There is an old palace on the hill (which, in recent years, has been reconstructed and maintained), a lovely little city square with a river running right down the middle, and a beautiful monastery that has been transformed into a nursing home.

Besides Nicholas "Nicky", Martin, Tomas, Antonin, and Ms. Kobzova, (and briefly mentioned Alphonse Mucha, a famous Czech artist, and Zdeněk Miler, the creator of the Little Mole cartoon) there are three more characters who truly existed in my narrative. All three of them briefly mentioned in the Prologue, as it is how this story fell into my hands. I wrote myself as "Kena." My friend Katie and I went to the screening of the documentary uncovering Nicky's work during Camp of 2012. I tried thanking the Nicholas Winton Foundation Representative for sharing the impactful story with my limited Czech language skills. He later found me, placed a kiss on my cheek, handed me a golden-covered DVD, and whispered it was my task to keep sharing the story.

I've kept my promise.

Acknowledgements

Writing this book started as an impossible idea. I've always been a storyteller and when this story started forming in my head, I approached a friend asking if he knew anyone who could write it. He replied, "Yes, you. I can think of no one better."

Special thanks to my friend, Marecko, and my ever-supportive parents for being my first encouragers and readers of the book. While there were few who knew I was writing, my thanks go to the couple of friends who reassured me, knowing nothing of the book, but knew I was invested in the story. Thanks to my wonderful friends, teachers, and relatives — Kori, Jen, and Angela — for their reviews and feedback.

I'd like to further acknowledge the work of my editor, Vlad, who greatly helped refine the work. A huge thanks also to my brother and sister for their modeling, photography, and editing skills on the cover of the book.

Much of my research came from conversations with friends in Czechia who experienced the changes in their homeland throughout communism and the start of their independent Czech Republic. I thank them for sharing their stories and emotions.

Thank you to Paul, the son of Tomas Graumann, for sharing more of his father's and young uncle's story with me personally.

Lastly, this story would not have been possible without the Nicholas Winton representative who gave me the DVD and impressed on my heart to continue sharing the story. Though I don't know his name, I thank him for gifting me this story to pass on.

Bibliography

BBC News. (2014, April 23). Czech deer still avoid Iron Curtain. https://www.bbc.com/news/world-europe-27129727

Beattie Jr., E. W. (2020). Crowds defiant in Prague as Hitler crosses Czech frontier. UPI. https://www.upi.com/Archives/1939/03/15/Crowds-defiant-in-Prague-as-Hitler-crosses-Czech-frontier/8148408176316/

CAN127 NEWSREEL NAZI INVASION OF CZECHOSLOVAKIA. (2015, July 28). [Video]. YouTube. https://www.youtube.com/watch?v=QV-GguZxgpo&t=215s

Fotogalerie: Kostel ve Starém Svojanové. (1999). IDNES. https://www.idnes.cz/cestovani/na-kole/svojanov-kretinka-cesko-moravske-pomezi.A170601_134129_na-kolo_hig/foto/HIG6badac_svojanov02.jpg

Graumann, T., & Goyer, T. (2019). Twice-Rescued Child: The boy who fled the Nazis ... and found his life's purpose. SPCK Publishing.

Happy 105th Sir Nick! (2014, May 13). Jewish News. https://jewishnews.timesofisrael.com/children-mans-land/

Historie Lazinova. (2020). Historie Lazinova. http://www.lazinov.cz/Historie/Historie-obec_Lazinov.htm

Kulavaiková, D. (2012, November 4). Přehrada Křetínka slaví výročí. Čtyřicet let od zahájení stavby. Deník.Cz. Retrieved 2020 from https://blanensky.denik.cz/zpravy_region/prehrada-kretinka-slavi-vyroci-ctyricet-let-od-zahajeni-stavby-20120411.html

Lazinov - procházka časem 2013. (2013). Lazinov. http://www.lazinov.cz/Historie/Prochazka_casem-2013/content/47-bourani_domu_v_budouci_zatoce-Pr_large.html

McFadden, R. D. (2015, July 3). Nicholas Winton, Rescuer of 669 Children From Holocaust, Dies at 106. https://www.nytimes.com/2015/07/02/world/europe/nicholas-winton-is-dead-at-106-saved-children-from-the-holocaust.html

Mináč, Matej (Director & Producer) & Pašš, Patrik (Producer). (2002). Nicholas Winton: The Power of Good. [Documentary] W.I.P. & Trigon Production.

Nicholas Winton and the Rescue of Children from Czechoslovakia, 1938–1939. (2020). The Holocaust Encyclopedia. https://encyclopedia.ushmm.org/content/en/article/nicholas-winton-and-the-rescue-of-children-from-czechoslovakia-1938-1939

Policejní pyrotechnik v akci. Na břehu Křetínky ležel granát. (2020, January 13). Denik.Cz. https://blanensky.denik.cz/zpravy_region/kretinka-granat-policie-pyrotechnik.html

Říčka Křetínka. (2020, November 2). http://www.lazinov.cz/Historie/Historie-prehrada.htm

Rybníky a přehrady vydávají granáty i mrtvoly. (2008, December 7). Denik.Cz. https://www.denik.cz/z_domova/blanensko_voda20081207.html

Sir Nicholas Winton, November 2014 - BBC HARDtalk. (2016, May 19). [Video]. YouTube. https://www.youtube.com/watch?v=NO63ajFFhDo&t=821s

Tom Graumann (Hochberg) (1931). (2008). Memory of Nations. https://www.memoryofnations.eu/en/graumann-hochberg-tom-1931

Vodenka, P., Stewart, D., & Vodenka-Reed, P. (2010). Journey For Freedom-Defection From Communist Czechoslovakia (First ed.). Journey For Freedom.